This item is no longer property
of Pima County Public Library
Sale of this item benefited the Library

2 ms

Praise for David Stukas and
SOMEONE KILLED HIS BOYFRIEND

A Selection of the InsightOut Book Club!
The *Lambda Book Report* Bestseller!

"This breezy page-turner is laugh-out-loud entertainment.
Irresistible."
—*Booklist*

"A clever combination of mystery and social satire with a
dash of fantasy . . . Those readers who miss Joe Keenan,
both gay and straight, will appreciate this promising and
witty writer."
—*Publishers Weekly*

"While David Stukas' *Someone Killed His Boyfriend* is billed
as a mystery, it is more of a comedy—and, at times, a laugh
out loud one, containing pages of playful, sparkling
dialogue."
—*The Lambda Book Report*

D1054010

SOMEONE KILLED HIS BOYFRIEND

Books by David Stukas

SOMEONE KILLED HIS BOYFRIEND

GOING DOWN FOR THE COUNT

Published Kensington Publishing Corporation

SOMEONE KILLED HIS BOYFRIEND

David Stukas

KENSINGTON BOOKS
http://www.kensingtonbooks.com

KENSINGTON BOOKS are published by

Kensington Publishing Corp.
850 Third Avenue
New York, NY 10022

Copyright © 2001 by David Stukas

All rights reserved. No part of this book may be reproduced in any form or by any means without the prior written consent of the Publisher, excepting brief quotes used in reviews.

All Kensington titles, imprints and distributed lines are available at special quantity discounts for bulk purchases for sales promotion, premiums, fund-raising, educational or institutional use.

Special book excerpts or customized printings can also be created to fit specific needs. For details, write or phone the office of the Kensington Special Sales Manager: Kensington Publishing Corp., 850 Third Avenue, New York, NY, 10022. Attn. Special Sales Department. Phone: 1-800-221-2647.

Kensington and the K logo Reg. U.S. Pat. & TM Off.

ISBN 0-7582-0041-2

First Hardcover Printing: September 2001
First Trade Paperback Printing: July 2002
10 9 8 7 6 5 4 3 2 1

Printed in the United States of America

I

We're Going to the Chapel and We're Gonna Get Married

It was four o'clock in the afternoon and Rupert Everett and I were having a smart cocktail on the terrace of our private house on a small island off the coast of Spain. We were both completely naked, but just as important, we were alone and madly in love with each other. Pedro Almodovar, the gay Spanish film director, had just left in a huff with Karl Lagerfeld after Rupert asked them to leave, or more correctly, threw them out. Pedro, who was still upset over the debacle of his last few films, had been drinking heavily and began making advances toward me, arousing Rupert's possessive nature. Granted, I was gorgeous, muscled, tan, fabulously wealthy, and all things wonderful. But Rupert was Rupert. Well, before you knew it, drinks were flying in people's faces as fast as screams of "putah" and "I'll keeeeeellll you." When it was over, broken bottles and pots of geraniums lay scattered across the patio along with the tattered remnants of Karl's signature fan.

But all was calm now. Rupert, his passions aroused by a good catfight, looked at me with those piercing eyes of his, lust burning brightly as a red-hot coal. As sore as I was from last night's lovemaking (or "banging the box," as Rupert so cutely refers to it), I was ready for more. Rupert rose from his seat and circled my chair like a cat stalking its prey. His muscular, veiny, suntanned hand reached down to pull my chin up so that my lips would reach up to receive his rich, full, pouty lips when . . .

. . . the phone rang.

Catapulted out of my deep sleep, I fumbled for the blasted instrument as I tried to figure out who would be calling at 7 A.M. on a Saturday. Then it hit me. It could only be Michael Stark, one of the most superficial people on earth and a dear, dear, dear friend of mine. It just had to be. Michael was handsome enough to get any man in New York, and it was just like him to steal my sexual ideal—albeit an imaginary one. If he couldn't have my Rupert, no one would.

"Listen, Robert, the most incredible thing just occurred!"

"You figured out who's buried in Grant's tomb?" I replied.

"No."

"You were relieved that they just *call* it toilet water?"

"No."

"You looked on a map and was surprised to see that Washington, D.C. is not next to Oregon?"

"NO! Robert! You're always making fun of my intellectual ability. You know, I did go to one of the most prestigious colleges in Connecticut."

"Michael, get real," I corrected. "The only reason they let you in was because your mother kept adding buildings to their campus. By the time you cheated your way through four—"

"Five," Michael corrected me.

"O.K., five years there, their campus doubled in size."

"So I'm not intellectually gifted like you are. But you've got to admit I'm gorgeous."

Michael had a point. An all-too-true point.

"Anyway," he continued, "I've met the most wonderful man in the world!"

Since you don't know too much about Michael yet, his announcement might seem quite touching. Don't be fooled. Michael loved men, men, men—the more, the better. In fact, the trail of men Michael had picked up and summarily dropped since he came out of the closet at age fourteen would stretch around the island of Manhattan several times. There wasn't a fireman, fitness-training instructor, waiter, or marine within a two-hundred-mile radius who hadn't slept with Michael. Plain and simple, he was a slut. I didn't condemn him, however, since I prided myself on having an open mind. The fact that Michael was the only person I knew in New York who owned a car and had a house on Fire Island—both of which he let me use frequently—had nothing to do with it.

Having asked this question hundreds of times before, I tried to make it seem as fresh as possible. "Tell me all about him."

"He's gorgeous."

"Naturally," I interjected.

"Robert, if you're not going to take me seriously . . ."

"I'm sorry, Michael, tell me more." For a person as shallow as Michael, he was easily offended, but as I had learned over time, it only took an insincere compliment to get him right back on track.

"He sounds wonderful, Michael. Leave it to you to find a guy like this. Does he have all of his teeth?"

"Robert! He's got a body to die for. Huge pecs, biceps so big they have names, thighs that could crack a coconut, and he's hung like a horse. Oh, I didn't tell you the best part."

"I thought the horse thing *was* the best part," I said in confusion.

"No, he's rich, too."

"Money isn't everything, Michael," I chided him, forgetting the fact that Michael was vastly wealthy.

"Money *is* everything, Robert."

"That's not what all the movies and novels say."

"People are so sadly mistaken. Money *can* buy happiness. Poor people just tell themselves that the rich are so unhappy so they don't feel so bad about the fact that they're losers. Now I ask you, if you could be on Nantucket or in the Hamptons playing tennis and eating giant shrimp all summer long, would you be unhappy?"

"No."

"It's just nicer to be dating someone who can pick up the tab once in a while. Anyway, this guy's name is Max and he's just the man my psychic has been telling me I was going to meet."

"Wait a minute, Michael. This isn't Sato the psychic, is it?"

"Yeah, why?"

"I thought you told me he was arrested for grand larceny and mail fraud."

"Robert, Sato was *indicted*. I doubt that they'll be able to prove all those allegations, now that he went back to Japan."

"Fled, Michael. Sato *fled* to Japan to avoid prosecution. At least that's what *The New York Times, People,* and *Newsweek* said, but what do they know?"

"For your information, Robert, he felt called by the spirits of his ancestors. He needed to commune with them and they just happened to be in Japan. Okay, Mister Skeptic? You're getting me off track. Sato said that I would meet a muscular man my age with a Southern accent. And get this: Sato said that this man would have a tattoo on his left bicep and that he'd be wealthy. Need I say more?"

"Michael, that just about describes any guy you bring home. I could've told you the same thing and saved you five hundred dollars."

"One thousand, Robert. I would never see a psychic that charges under a thousand for a psychic *reading*. Anything less and you're operating with a charlatan. The point is, I'm really in love and he's really in love with me."

"I can tell you're in love with him. But how do you know that he's in love with you, Michael?"

"He told me."

"What's so unique about that?" I replied. "I thought all the guys you slept with told you that."

"Not one of them has said anything like that to me. Ever!"

"What do they usually say to you?"

" 'Can you lend me cab fare?' " Michael continued. "Anyway, the reason I called was that the two of us are going to get married!"

It was several seconds before I spoke.

"Robert?!" Michael pleaded into the receiver. "Are you there . . . Robert?"

"Michael, don't you think this is a little bit hasty? I mean, you just met the guy."

"That's where you're wrong. I've been dating him for almost three weeks. That's long enough. Plus, if you get to know someone too much, you'll never get to like them."

With Michael, any relationship that lasted longer than overnight was something to be reckoned with.

"What happened to the last guy you were head over heels about?" I asked.

"Phillip?" Michael offered.

"Is that the guy who models for DKNY?" I asked, trying to clarify things.

"No, that's Zeno. I dropped him last month when he got a bad case of acne. Ruined his face—and his career. Oh, well, beauty is fleeting. You're probably thinking about Marc—Marc with a *c*."

"No, Michael, I know who Marc with a *c* was. Name some of the other guys you've dated lately."

"Richard?"

"No."

"Adam?"

"No."

"Terry?"

"No."

"Warren?"

"No."

"Jaye?"

"No."

"Todd?"

"No."

"Larry?"

"No."

"Harlick?"

"Harlick!?" I shot back.

"Hey, I didn't name him. Anyway, I dropped him."

"Because of the name?"

"Of course! Now where were we?"

"Pete?"

"No."

"James?"

"No."

"Michael, this is within the last year?"

"Oh . . . I thought you said last month," Michael replied with all sincerity.

I was getting lost in the flurry of names and wanted to find my way out. "Michael, what was the name of the guy you were running around telling everyone 'this guy's the one!'?"

"That was probably Trent. No, wait a minute, I dumped him because he had a small dick."

"Michael, a small dick is not a reason to dump someone. Er . . . how small?"

"Vienna sausage," Michael said with disgust. "Hard."

"Okay, you got me there. But of course, anything less than a veiny Goodyear blimp isn't going to blow air up your skirt, Michael."

"Very funny. Maybe you were thinking about Santos?"

"The one you said was following you around all the time?"

"Yeah. A real obsessive type. Always checking on me like he didn't trust me or something."

"Well, I don't blame him. You were fooling around with that Chuck guy at the same time, weren't you?"

"Sure I was," Michael admitted. "But that didn't give

him the right to call me all the time and grill me where I've been. Never wanted to let me out of his sight. Well, I got rid of him because Chuck was so much better."

"If Chuck was so good, then what happened to him?" I inquired.

"Every time he'd come over to my penthouse, I'd notice something would be missing afterwards. Then before I know it, he starts slipping in little questions about my money—and get this—my will. Real creepy! So I gave Chuck the brush-off."

"Where were we?" I said, thoroughly confused.

"Chuck. Then I think I moved on to Mitch . . . the surfer dude from California. Like wow!"

"So how long did he last?"

"About as long as the wax on his surfboard. We did, however, find good uses for the wax."

"I don't want to hear about them, Michael. I'm about to eat breakfast. Are we through?" I asked, hoping that Michael's merry-go-round of men was about to stop and I could get off, figuratively speaking.

Michael attempted to get the conversation back on its wobbly track. "Who cares who I dated before? That's all semen under the bridge. The point is that I'm really in love with this guy. Anyway, it's not like I'm going to be married tomorrow."

"That's good," I added.

"Actually, I was planning three weeks from today, and the wedding doesn't really count—legally, at least. Well, the reason I called was to ask you—will you be best man at my wedding? Oh, and I want you to help me plan the ceremony and reception. It'll be fun! We'll pick out all the flowers and the caterers. We could even have the wedding at St. Patrick's . . . or a nice little church in the Village. A gay church. Do you know of any?"

Not having been near a church since I was old enough to tell my mom that I wasn't going anymore, I confessed that I wasn't much help in that department.

"Michael, why don't you slow down a little? This is awful sudden," I cautioned.

"Robert, I don't want to let his guy get away, so be a good boy and play along with me."

"Fine. Why don't you have an outdoor wedding? Like in Bryant Park for example?" I suggested.

"Oh, Robert, I can't go there. Too many bad memories."

"Bad memories?" I inquired.

"That's where they had that fund-raiser for the homeless. In the middle of the goddamn winter, no less. All the guests sat around open fires, hungry and shivering to death, while the homeless were given down coats and fed till they exploded. The whole thing was supposed to make us feel the plight of the homeless. When it was over, a bunch of us went out and had a five-course meal in an overheated five-star restaurant. Whatever . . . I'll find a church. Now, I've got to start thinking about the reception. How about the Carlyle Hotel? Well, I've got a million things to do. Michael, how about you joining Max—that's his name, Max—and me for dinner tonight at Cafe Dirigible? After all, I want you to meet the man I'm going to marry."

"Sounds fine to me," I responded, knowing full well that since Michael was well-endowed—financially—he would probably pick up the tab. Maybe his lover would pick it up since he was rich. Anyway, my chances were better than good that I would get a free meal out of this. And, being an underpaid advertising copywriter, this possibility was enormously attractive to me.

"See you there, Robert. Dinner at eight," he said.

Michael is settling down, I thought to myself. I hung up the phone wondering whether this was a sign that the world was coming to an end.

As expected, Michael and his new lover were nowhere to be seen at Cafe Dirigible at 8:00, so I parked myself at the bar, staring at the bartender's butt from time to time, then taking in the surroundings. Although the ads for the cafe suggested that it was "an intimate little out-of-the-way place in lower Manhattan," the reality was somewhat different. Suspended from the ceiling was a near-life-size zeppelin that in the words of the cafe's decorator, "evokes a feeling of vulnerability on the part of the diners because of the juxtaposition of human scale to technological immensity." Whatever. In an effort to underscore his theme of vulnerability, the decorator wanted to fill the blimp with hydrogen, but he was forced by the fire department to settle for mere helium, owing to the large smoking section in the cafe. Waiters and waitresses were originally destined to wear oversize inflatable outfits resembling blimps, but after numerous spilled trays, bumped patrons, jokes about the Michelin man, and patrons constantly yelling out "Oh, the humanity," outfits were hastily changed to black stretch pants with black turtlenecks and black loafers. The food, of course, was ghastly. A food critic for *The New York Times*, after skewering the cafe mercilessly throughout his honest but poisonous review, summed up the culinary output of the kitchen by saying that the cafe should be renamed Blimpie's. Despite the deservedly brutal reviews by every major newspaper and magazine in the city, the place was packed.

I felt a hand on my shoulder.

"Been here long?" asked a voice behind my back. Instead of the bartender, (hope, hope) it was Michael, exactly fifty minutes late. As usual, he was right on time. I turned to see Michael standing there with one of the most beautiful men I have ever seen.

"Hi, you must be Robert," the hunk said, extending his manly, veiny, and thoroughly muscular hand for me to shake. I wanted to worship it.

"You must be gorgeous—er, Max," I said. Real smooth, Robert! Why not follow that by asking him what size cockring he wears?

"Glad to meet you, Robert. And thanks for the compliment," Max said with just a hint of a refined Southern accent. Max met my regulation height for a boyfriend: six-foot-one. He had black hair cropped short, deep brown eyes, and a face so precisely chiseled he looked like he belonged on Mount Rushmore. I was in love! I hastily began to plot ways of murdering Michael and taking Max for my own. *I am standing over Michael's lifeless body—another victim of my infamous poisoned martinis. Max takes my hand and confesses his eternal love. We both pack bags, jump into his classic Aston Martin and head for San Tropez, where we will live happily ever after off the money we've stolen from Michael's safe.* Suddenly, Michael's voice broke in on my little daydream.

"Our table is ready." As we followed the maître d' and sat down, Michael tried to make small talk. "Well, Robert, what have you been up to lately?" he asked, trying to break the ice. And my gaze at Max.

"Wha—oh! We'll, I've been assigned to another account," I offered, stifling back a laugh.

"Robert is a copywriter for an ad agency," said Michael, trying to clear up the confusion on Max's face.

"Oh," Max replied.

That accent—oh, heaven! "Get this, Michael. I'm working on a feminine hygiene account!" I spurted as the words slurred into laughter. The wine Michael had been drinking came out his nose as he burst into laughter along with me. Max joined in, more in the spirit of camaraderie than in true appreciation of life's twisting ironies.

"The other day, I'm sitting there in a big meeting with our clients. Ten of the most dried-up fossils you've ever seen. All men, of course, with the exception of one token woman who hadn't had a visit from her 'special friend' in over thirty years. They're looking for names for their new product—carbonated, flavored douches. It seems the carbonation helps make women feel—how do I say it?—fresh."

Gales of laughter.

"I blurted out, 'How about Very Cherry Cola? Or Key Lime Spritzer?' "

More laughter.

"What did they say to that?" asked Michael, brushing aside tears.

"They asked me not to come to any more meetings. Well, enough about me. Tell me about your groom-to-be. Where did you two meet?" I asked, still chortling.

"Well, we met right in front of The Rack," Michael replied wistfully.

"The Rack? How sweet! Did you buy matching tit clamps?"

"Of course not," Michael replied, rolling his eyes innocently heavenward. "I said we met in *front* of it. I wasn't inside buying anything." Although Michael was probably telling the truth this time, he had spent plenty of time over the past ten years in The Rack, buying whips, clamps, and all sorts of sadomasochistic items. Don't get Michael wrong. He wasn't into leather sex exclusively. He was into sex, period. Sex was sex and any was good as far as Michael was concerned.

When I first met Michael years ago, he was heavily into the white party crowd, putting mountains of unknown substances up his nose and dancing the night away. A year later, he had ditched all that and was into S&M (or "SM," as he corrected me). His whole wardrobe went from spandex to knee-high motorcycle boots, leather chaps over jeans, a leather vest, leather jackets, and a leather cap. He pierced his ears, his cock, and his nipples. In fact, he once walked into Tiffany's wearing leather from head to toe—he wanted to see if they would make custom nipple rings. Platinum, dahling. (You know, it's funny, but Michael still gets the royal treatment from the salesmen when he shops there.) Without warning, Michael changed gears again and started wearing nothing but black and shaving his head completely—his "artistic" or "Tribeca" period (lots of art and oversized restaurants, with egos to match). This was followed by his "suburban" period, when he actually rented a house in Connecticut to try and forget his younger, more decadent years and live more wholesomely. He even moved in with a guy named Chad—a Yale man if I ever saw one. Chad wore tweed sport jackets with patches on the elbows and drove a Volvo. Michael went so far as to actually discuss adopting children with Chad. This lasted exactly three days. Since I met Michael some ten years ago, he's gone through more periods than Ann Miller, Katharine Hepburn, and Kitty Carlisle combined.

I don't mean to digress from this riveting story, but by now you're probably asking how someone like myself would ever come in contact with someone like Michael.

Good question. If Michael wasn't regularly appearing in the pages of *Vanity Fair*, he was sleeping with the people photographed in it. So why would he even be seen in my presence?

It all happened a long time ago. I was out at the bars late one Saturday night, looking for Mr. Wrong. As usual, I didn't find him, so I decided to call it a night. I was walking down an almost-deserted street in the meat-packing district of the West Village, only to turn a corner and see a bunch of youths kicking someone on the ground.

"You like it, faggot? I heard you faggots like it this way!" one of the youths shouted, planting a kick in the ribs of his victim.

"Yeah, take this, queer-boy," shouted another.

Being from the Midwest, I have never been especially political, but watching this scene made something in me snap. I felt like a Jack Russell terrier spotting a rat scuttling across an English manor house floor. I went ballistic. I charged at the youths, spraying them with Mace from my handy purse-sized personal protection device (illegal in New York, but so was beating people because of their sexual orientation). Even after they were incapacitated, I continued to spray the little fuckers. Then I took off my coat and put it underneath the man's head. All I remember after that was the sound of my voice screaming for help. The rest was a blur. The police showed up. Then the ambulance. You guessed it. It was Michael Stark.

As if the youths' taunts weren't enough confirmation that their victim was gay, it became clear when he shouted out that there was no way on earth that he was going to Bellevue, even though it had the closest emergency room. No, he wanted to be taken to Sinai Hospital, way up on the Upper East Side; the doctors were better there. Yup, he was gay.

I went to the hospital with Michael, not knowing who he was, but feeling that it was somehow my duty as a homosexual. After it looked as if my "charge" was out of danger, I went home. With the help of a little plastic surgery, Michael recuperated perfectly. Afterward he looked me up through the police report and came to my apartment with the biggest bunch of flowers I have ever seen.

"I owe my life to you. I will never forget it," he said, handing me the flowers.

And to tell you the truth, he never has. Despite the fact that our two lives should never have crossed, I found myself invited to his sprawling apartment in the Village and his house on Fire Island so regularly that he and I eventually became good friends.

But back to the story.

"So you met in front of The Rack?" I asked. "Charming. Absolutely charming."

"Yes," Michael gushed. "He was coming home from the gym and I was running to it. We ran into each other."

"So, Max, tell me about yourself," I said in my *Father Knows Best* tone.

"Well, there's not much to tell. I work for an architectural design firm in midtown," he proclaimed proudly.

What a cliché, I thought.

"I'll tell you all about him, Robert," Michael interrupted.

"He's six-one; his hair's natural; he's originally from Charlottesville, Virginia; his family's lived there for over two hundred years; he graduated from the School of Architecture at Princeton; and he likes snorkeling, wind surfing, sailing, rainy days in October, riding horses bareback, cookouts on the beach, and sex on a bearskin rug in front of a roaring fire. With the right man, of course," Michael said, pointing at himself as if I didn't already get the point.

"He also wears a size ten and a half shoe," Michael added winky-wink style, proud that he had landed a man who measured up in this important physical department. Whereas most men would find this comment ego-boosting, Max apparently found it a little embarrassing, because he blushed a tiny bit. It was adorable.

"Has anyone told you about tonight's specials?" came a voice from behind me. My-name's-Jeff-and-I'll-be-your-waiter-for-the-evening was hovering over us, pen in hand.

"Okay, let's hear it," Michael replied.

"The seafood special is a fillet of salmon rolled in nuts, parsley, nasturtium petals and sautéed in a soy sauce with arugula and chives and served on a bed of wilted prickly pear cactus leaves. The veal, while not politically correct but delicious nonetheless, is sautéed in a Brazilian coriander-butter sauce, then broiled and served with a mixture of fourteen blends of wild rice and poached chicory leaves and dandelion greens. Oh, and we're also offering two fabulous dishes: pork tartar and sundried clams. Just kidding about those last two. Now, can I get anyone a cocktail to start things off?" Our waiter's extra emphasis on the first syllable of "cocktails" was a clue that he was not only on to the three of us, but wanted to join our little band. (Why is it that waiters are always trying to be so friendly with you? Why can't they just serve food and keep their mouths shut?)

"Actually, I think some champagne is in order," Michael volunteered. "A bottle of Dom Perignon, Max?"

"Well," Max replied, picking up the wine list, "I think that the nineteen ninety Bollinger Grande Année is nicer and not so overpriced." Our waiter nodded his head approvingly, then set off for the cavernous kitchen, but not before getting an eyeful of Max as he departed. In a town filled with thousands of gorgeous but painfully jaded homo-sexual men, Max still managed to get stares.

"Isn't he wonderful?" Michael gushed. "His father started teaching him about wine when he turned ten. They have a wine cellar with over thirty-two hundred bottles."

"Oh, it's nothing," Max said, deflecting the comment with an aw-shucks air.

Dinner continued for several hours, and I, for once, re-membered little of it. All too often, I caught myself staring at Max, thinking that he was perhaps the most perfect man I had ever met. I couldn't take my eyes off him. I laughed at all his jokes and flirted shamelessly with him until Michael viciously kicked my shin under the privacy of the tablecloth. I was spellbound by all the stories of the farm Max grew up on. Yes, I was in love with a man who, like most, wouldn't even give me the time of day. When we finally stumbled out onto the street at midnight, Max trotted over to a twenty-four-hour greengrocery, picked out a bunch of yellow roses, paid for them, and came galloping back, holding them be-hind his back in order to surprise Michael, even though his intent was clear. When he reached Michael, he got down on one knee, stared into Michael's face, and asked, "From the bottom of my heart I am asking, will you marry me?"

Michael, welling up with a mixture of pride and tears, threw his arms around Max. "Oh, you bet!" he replied while a single tear trickled down the side of his over-pampered face.

I, too, was overcome by the moment. I was overcome by a need to beat Michael senseless with a two-by-four. With nails in it.

My life is shit. Shit, shit, and more shit. And I hate Michael very much and want him to get hit by a bus. On second thought, I want to poison him, cut him up into small pieces, and throw them into a shark-infested ocean, then make a play for Max, who would naturally fall for me in a big way.

Does God really hate me? The only men I ever got—when I got them—were schmucks. Drunks. Married men. Thieves. I even brought one guy home who insisted on wearing a hockey mask during sex. (I sensibly refused to date him more than three weeks.) What's wrong with me? I'm no GQ model, but not bad, either. I'm 5' 10", have light brown hair, blue eyes, an average build, and a wholesome, Midwestern look (according to the personal ad I once placed—a disaster). In short, painfully average—nothing about me stands out. I'm not muscular or butch, or even feminine. I'm more of the cute and cuddly sort. I would think that my qualities make me a very rare individual: a well-adjusted, caring person who's DESPERATELY looking for someone who I can settle down with. I had it all figured out. Jeremy (that's what his name would be) and I would have a beautiful brownstone in the Village, filled with beautiful furniture. On the first floor, we would have a stupendous front parlor guaranteed to make jaws drop, a gorgeous dining room that would always be filled with witty dinner guests, and a professional kitchen, in which Jeremy and I would spend long hours whipping up fabulous dishes on our Viking (or Garland if I *have* to) professional range while drinking champagne. The second floor, besides housing our fabulous bedroom replete with a huge antique four-poster bed, would have a huge bathroom with twenty-four-karat gold shower heads and onyx walls. The entire third floor would be converted into a gymnasium filled with Nautilus equipment, treadmills, rowing machines, and free weights. On top of the roof would be a deck, complete with hot tub, lap pool, and rooftop garden. We'd have two Cairn terriers named Dorothy and Glenda, a BMW roadster, and a Toyota Landcruiser, both of which we'd use to get to our weekend place in Bucks County, where, of course, we'd have a five-bedroom, two-hundred-year-old Pennsylvania fieldstone house complete with a pool and extensive gardens covering two hundred and fifty acres, reached by a long private drive. Naturally, the property would be patrolled by huge, naked bodybuilders armed with M-16 assault weapons. We'd go to auctions on Saturday, bake breads on Sunday morning, and rake leaves in the fall. We'd have other couples (both gay and straight, but mostly gay) over from neighboring estates for protracted brunches involving scandalous gossip and lots and lots of expensive chardonnays. We'd vacation on Capri or rent a villa in Indonesia or some exotic place, and we'd have so much money that we'd never have to work or enter a 7-Eleven again. Was that too much to ask?

The horrible reality was that I was an underpaid copywriter working on feminine hygiene products who had a lousy apartment on the Upper East Side, no car, no weekend house, no money, and worst of all, no man. I have a theory that nature always compensates for the deficiencies it creates. People like Michael, however shallow and stupid they might be, were compensated by being given good looks. Some people are given incredible wealth. So far, Michael is batting a hundred. Me, zero. But wait; there is justice coming. People like me, who fall into the category of being poor and painfully plain, are compensated by being given above-average minds, which are used primarily for running mental circles around the good-looking. Then there are those who are neither rich, good-looking, nor possessed of great brains. These people get into drugs. Or worse, religion. Their devotion has a purpose, however. It helps them deal with the fact that they really got the short end of the stick. Max, however, seemed to be one of those rare individuals who had it all: the looks, the money, and the intellectual ability. It's my personal belief that these people made up an international, unorganized race of people whose purpose was not to raise all of humanity up out of the mire of our miserable shortcomings. No, these people were put here on Earth to make the rest of us realize how miserably shortchanged the rest of us are.

*   *   *

" 'Gay white male, forty-ish, cuddly, seeks same for long walks in the park on crisp autumn nights, old movies, leather hoods, electro-torture, and intense pain in heavy weekend sessions with possible permanent damage. Sincere.' "

"He doesn't sound like your type, Robert," Monette said, popping another corn curl into her mouth. "You hate Central Park."

I looked up from the gay personals column and gave Monette a look that would let her know that we were not amused.

"I know that look. Number forty-two, isn't it? Bette Davis in *All About Eve*, the scene when she lays into what's-her-name on the stairway during her birthday party."

"Wrong. Doris Day in *Pillow Talk*. The party-line scene with Rock Hudson where she rolls her eyes. Now shut up and listen to this one: 'Gay white male, thirty-eight, a hundred and seventy-five pounds, muscular, but not body-builder. Seeks lifelong companion to share life with. Also must be willing to share emotional and financial support with caring individual like myself.' "

"Big-time moocher. Robert, I don't know why you waste time looking in the classifieds. You never find anyone decent in them."

"I do too," I corrected. "What about that guy Scott? He was okay for a while."

"Robert," Monette reminded me, "Scott pooped in your bed while you were taking a shower."

"He apologized for it. Honestly, Monette! You always forget the details and twist the story around so that all my dates look like losers."

"Speaking of details, did Scott get released yet?"

"Yeah, the mayor's office said they wouldn't press charges if he agreed to stop throwing feces at the mayor's car. Now, can we continue?"

"Yes. Fire away. Sorry, I didn't mean that."

"Okay, one more: 'Mansex. I need plenty of it.' "

"Yes? Continue."

"That's it."

"That's it? Surely there's got to be more."

"No, just a phone number: five five five, nine seven five three. Wait a minute! That's Michael's number!"

"Are you sure?"

"Of course I'm sure. I call it all the time."

"For sex?" Monette was perplexed.

"No, as a friend. Monette, you know that there has never been anything between me and Michael."

She pried further. "Never?"

"NEVER!"

"Oh, c'mon. Michael has slept with everyone. That's why he has so many friends," Monette replied triumphantly.

"Michael has friends because he throws lots of parties and he lends people money."

"And has sex with a lot of men," Monette added, trying to show that she was right.

"Potato po-tah-to. Oh no, Michael has a long-term contract with the personals column and he probably forgot to cancel it now that he's in love with Max. I better call him and tell him to pull the ad before someone calls and Max picks up the phone. Max seems pretty nice."

Monette looked up at me, perplexed. "If he's so nice, then what is he doing with Michael?"

"Heck if I know. Anyway, if he found out that Michael was Megaslut, Max might call the whole wedding off . . . and he . . . could marry someone like me, perhaps."

Monette saw through me immediately. "Robert, what are you up to? Forget it this very instant! Michael deserves *some* happiness. You call him right now. I'm going to stand here and watch you dial."

I picked up the phone and pressed speed dial 2.

"Robert!" There was no fooling Monette. "Michael's speed dial is *one*. You just hit the two, which I happen to know is my number. Three is weather. Now, don't insult my intelligence any further and be a good little boy and push speed dial one."

"You're good. I guess reading all those detective novels paid off."

"Just dial."

"Hello, Michael? Robert dahling here. I was just going through—" Michael abruptly cut me off.

"Oh, Robert. I had the most wonderful evening! Max and I had the best sex ever. Instead of just ramming it into me like most of my dates do, he just long-dicked me slowly for what must've been an hour! I thought my eyeballs would roll completely around in my head. You know, Robert, you really need to get a boyfriend like mine. Oh, Jesus, what am I saying! I mean, look who I'm talking to. I mean, you can't expect to snare a hunk like Max with those miserable, droopy pecs and paunchy waistline. Tell you what, why don't you start going to the gym with me every morning? We'll work that little Pillsbury Doughboy body of yours into something a man can be proud of. Anyway, what were you about to tell me?"

"Nothing. I just wanted to say how happy I was for you."

"Thanks!"

I hung up the phone, muttered some old Lithuanian curses, and got back to Monette, who was now draped across my sofa and staring intently into a book with the most intriguing title: *She-Rah, Queen of the Lesbian Womyn.*

"Jane Austen?" I asked, raising my eyebrows.

"It's a book about lesbian cavewomen who get sick of the way male cavemen are running things, and they start their own tribe and live in peace and harmony with the earth forever and ever."

"Forever?"

"Well, not exactly forever. Things are fine for a while, but then Vesara falls in love with Tonarda, but the evil second high priestess is jealous and makes a play for Narada, who is fawning over the high priestess, Harva. . . . The only thing missing is the prehistoric therapist."

"How can you read that trash?" I asked, holding my stomach.

"There's nothing left to read. I've finished my latest batch of murder mystery novels. I think I've read every one ever written," Monette proclaimed proudly.

This statement couldn't go unchallenged. "Every one?"

"Every single itsy-bitsy one of them."

"*Whose Body* by Dorothy L. Sayers?"

"I cut my baby teeth on that one."

"*Cop Hater* by Ed McBain?"

"That too."

"How about *Murder in the Key of F Sharp?*"

Monette thought for a second, like a supercomputer searching through its massive hard drive, then replied, "That doesn't exist. You made that one up."

"You *are* good."

"Oh, and I saw your posters plastered all over Park Slope."

I decided to play dumb. "Posters? What posters?"

"You know, the ones for Monette Gordonov, the Russian power lifter. One of my friends called me the moment she spotted one."

"Monette, sometimes I just don't know what you're talking about," I replied, feigning innocence.

"The ones where you superimposed my head on the body of Ivan Svetlovsky, the Russian weight lifter."

"Ohhhhh! *Those* posters. Pretty good, weren't they? You know, when you work in an ad agency, getting custom-designed and printed posters is no problem. I had to take the guy who designed it out to lunch for all his trouble, though."

For as long as I had known Monette, we played practical jokes on each other. But not your garden variety snakes-in-the-peanut-brittle-can either. Elaborate ones. Sinister ones. Practical jokes that Tom Clancy probably played on John LeCarré.

Monette probed a little further. "How many did you have printed?"

"Oh, just five hundred or so."

"And let me guess, you put up every one of them?"

"Just about. I mean, there had to be some wastage. The glue was too thick on the first dozen we tried to put up."

"We?" Monette asked.

"Me and a friend who shall remain nameless."

Monette bit her upper lip. "How many boroughs are we talking?"

"Well, not Staten Island or the Bronx, Monette. There'd be no point putting 'em up there—none of your friends would see them. Oh don't worry, they'll probably be covered up in a matter of months."

A great big, evil smile crept across Monette's face. "You realize that I'll have to get you back double for this."

"I can dish it out and I can take it. Take your best shot!"

"Fine, I will."

Whenever I'm depressed, I can always count on my good friend Monette. Over the years, we've created a special bond between us: years commiserating on our common inability to find a lover of the same sex. Mentally stable ones, that is. What can I say about Monette? I met her years ago at a support group for the chronically depressed. We had both joined the group after breaking up with our lovers. Okay, we both got dumped. I can remember that very day. The support group leader, a Navajo woman (or so she said) named Running Deer was lecturing the group on alternative methods of self-esteem building.

"Remember," she had intoned, her turquoise jewelry clattering from every part of her body, "depression is only a state of mind. If we feel depressed, we are depressed." Muffled sobs rose up from certain members of the group. "Depression is, by its very nature, a negative feeling. Science states that when a negative encounters a positive, there is a cancellation of each other, resulting in a neutral charge or state."

I sat there spellbound. Either this woman was incredibly insightful, or the four Valiums I'd washed down with a tumbler of Scotch earlier that evening were starting to take effect.

Running Deer continued. "Now, a neutral state is better than a negative state, but it is neither here nor there. Our goal is to achieve a more positive state."

"How is this achieved, Running Deer?" a group member asked.

"Well, in many Indian cultures, this is achieved with the use of peyote or other hallucinogenic drugs. But it can also be attained by thinking happy thoughts."

Why is it that I never have a gun when I need one? I come here so I can stop having these thoughts of hurling myself out a window and this woman is telling me to put on a happy face. Was I the only person here who thought this?

"Excuse me, but this isn't helping me any," a voice boomed from across the room. Several members of the group gasped at this show of insolence.

"Monette, you must have patience. The road to peace and tranquillity—" She was interrupted.

". . . is a dead end if you're driving," Monette boomed back, her swirling ensemble of flaming red hair and sapphire eyes blazing with anger and frustration. Even the freckles on her face seemed ready to pounce. Monette's jaw, however, summed up her mood best: it jutted so far forward, it seemed to dare Running Deer to take a swipe at it. "My girlfriend of five years calls me up and tells me she's running off with another woman who weighs four hundred pounds and has incurable eczema. Thinking happy thoughts is not going to do it for me, sister! I need an assault rifle with a laser night scope or a bourbon and ginger—no, make that a pitcher of boilermakers, Running Pear!"

"Running Deer," our clueless leader said in an attempt to correct Monette.

"Whatever!" With that, Monette stood up and departed the room—all six feet, four inches of her oversized yet athletic frame exiting as gracefully as a lumberjack with a hemorrhoid problem. I don't know why, but I just got up and followed her. I was so taken in by the brutal honesty of this woman that I followed her out to the street.

"Monette!" I shouted, not quite knowing what to say next. Was it fate or just a lot of Valiums? "I thought you were great in there. I was thinking the same thing."

"Are there any sane people left in this world?" she asked disgustedly.

"Me!" I offered.

Sensing that a meeting of the minds had occurred just then, Monette offered that we go to a nearby bar and talk. My resistance was down, so I agreed. It was the start of a long and beautiful friendship that continues to this very day.

"So, Monette. What do you think about Michael's getting married?"

"Oh, Robert, you know how I feel about what a saddle tramp Michael is. I can't keep up with them all. By this time next week, he'll have dropped what's-his-name and moved on. Today Manhattan, tomorrow, the world."

"I don't know, Monette. I think I saw real love in his eyes that night we went to Cafe Dirigible," I said, sticking up for Michael—I'm not sure why. "Earlier today, I wanted to kill him."

"Whether Michael is in love is one thing. The problem is every guy he brings home can't help but fall in love with Michael. They can't afford not to. He takes them to restaurants, invites them to parties, to his place on Fire Island, and he buys them clothes and watches. But what I think most of his boyfriends fall in love with is his apartment."

Michael's apartment, if you're one of the few who've never been to it, is stupendous. It's surprising that neighbors living below Michael's apartment don't constantly complain of the sound of jaws dropping on the floors above their heads. Located in a prewar building off Eighth Avenue in the Village, the apartment is a penthouse complete with wrap-around terraces—all with sweeping views of the

World Trade Center on one side and midtown Manhattan on the other. There are a total of ten rooms, all fabulously furnished in whatever style an interior designer has connived Michael into believing is the look of the moment. Currently, that meant stainless steel and concrete, with glass block and sandblasted glass. The look is also minimal, which doesn't really work since Michael just throws things down when he's done with them. In fact, Michael has a maid who comes in every day just to pick up his clothes and wash his sex-stained sheets. (I've never seen Ilsa without rubber gloves of the thickness that could pick up plutonium with impunity.)

Let's take a tour, shall we? In the cavernous living room, there are completely impractical but gorgeous stainless steel floors that require constant polishing. The stainless furniture is hideously expensive and unbelievably uncomfortable. From the living room, you can walk out through any of the five sets of French doors onto the terrace that easily holds one hundred people. The terrace is brimming with plants, most of which die each winter and are replaced every spring because Michael can afford to. Now, if you step this way, we'll make a short stop at the two-hundred-thousand-dollar kitchen. Take a look at all the custom-built cabinetry, the three dishwashers, two sinks, wet bar, and over here, the Le Cornue professional stove from France that reportedly cost thirty-five thousand dollars. Not surprisingly, Michael eats out almost all the time, so this kitchen lies vacant—except for the few times Michael makes popcorn in the microwave oven. Okay group, stay together as we move on into the bedroom. It is perpetually dark, lit only by cleverly concealed halogen spotlights that highlight important elements in the decor: the titanium bed, a copper-clad wardrobe containing a TV and Michael's assorted "love" toys, and a genuine Robert Mapplethorpe nude over the bed—not one of Mapplethorpe's beautiful flower photos, but a guy's asshole with a bullwhip handle stuck into it.

There are other assorted bedrooms and a private office which Michael never uses since an accountant handles all of his finances.

I've saved the best for last. The library, besides holding beautifully bound leather book sets dating back hundreds of years that are never even opened by the owner, also contains another object of incredible value. There it is above the fireplace mantel: a genuine Matisse. Michael knows its value but has never really cared much for it. It seems that Michael's grandmother willed it to him when she died. It never fails to amaze me how much money can be made when your family owns a controlling interest in a giant pharmaceutical concern. By the way, the company's biggest moneymaker is a patented ointment for genital herpes. As they say, God moves in mysterious ways.

But back to the story.

"Monette, I really think Michael's in love. I know how he can get obsessed with trivial things, but his obsession doesn't usually last longer than, say, four, five days. Michael's been dating this guy for weeks! And Max is absolutely charming. If Michael weren't so much in love with him, I'd try and steal him away," I said. "But Michael seems really happy for once. I couldn't do that to a friend, could I?"

Monette roared back, "There you go again. That Midwestern goodiness and Catholic guilt that lets people trample all over you. Go ahead. Steal Max away. Michael's stolen more boyfriends from you than I can count," Monette rebuked me. "And I can count pretty high!"

"I can't be the other woman, no matter how hard I try. Besides, this guy, Max, is too perfect. I could never measure up."

"Measure up? I don't know why you guys are so obsessed with *size*. It's not the size of the wand but the magic within it that counts—"

I interrupted her. "No, that's not what I'm saying. And for your information, Monette, it's not length that's important. It's the thickness that counts. Anyway, this guy is perfect."

"Nobody's perfect," Monette responded.

"No, he's legit, all right. Michael's been with Max enough to scope him out. According to Michael, Max comes from an old Virginia family. Very old. And get this—he has a personality!"

"I don't get it. Why in God's name would he be interested in Michael?"

"Monette, you know how he can charm the pants off any . . . okay, bad choice of words. Michael's so good, he could get Pat Robertson into bed with him. Why do you think the towels in his bathroom are embroidered with 'His' and 'Next'? He never has a problem getting some guy to go home with him . . . and they're never ugly. Michael's picky. I guess eventually Michael had to stumble on someone good. After all, even the blind sow finds filth to lay down in now and then. Sorry. My Lithuanian grandmother used to say that."

"I wish I could find someone wonderful," Monette complained. "Right now, I'll take anyone I can get."

"Someone with bubonic plague?" I asked jokingly.

"Is she pretty?"

"Big, ugly boils all over her body! And she just got out of prison for mutilating her last girlfriend. Then she ate her."

"She doesn't snore, does she?"

"No."

"I'll take her. You got her phone number?"

"I've got to get ready to go out, Monette."

"Want me to stay around to zip you up?"

"No, I'm going strapless tonight, but thanks anyway. Oh, and don't forget: the party's on Friday at Michael's. Nine o'clock. Be there."

2

It's My Party and I'll Be Smug If I Want To

Since Michael told everyone to come around nine, I figured that Michael's equally shallow friends would show up around eleven-thirty. Not wanting to be the perennial first-to-show-up guest, I waited until midnight before I entered the building. Just to make sure, I waited in the hall outside Michael's door for ten minutes to make an especially grand and fashionably late entrance. As I knocked, I could hear loud music and the sounds of a blender coming from inside. No one answered. I knocked again. Serves me right for coming so late. Suddenly the door opened. Michael stood in front of me in a bathrobe with a frothy cream spread over his pampered face.

"Oh, Robert, you're early," he said as though it were natural that guests should arrive at least four hours late. "C'mon in and make yourself a drink. No, not that," he shouted, grabbing the blender away from my hand as we neared the bar. "That's my cucumber face cream. People should be getting here soon. Max will be here around one-thirty. He had some emergency design project slipup. Something about a workman being crushed to death at a building Max's firm designed. I just hope this little incident doesn't make him late."

I made a motion to pull a chair out and sit down but thought better since Michael was watching me.

"Oh, you don't have to worry about disturbing the feng shui. I figure people are going to be moving furniture all night. The electromagnetic fields are going to be out of balance anyway, so I'm having a bagua come back in the morning and move everything back to where it's supposed to be. And he's giving me a break since I'm a loyal client of his."

"And what might that be?" I asked, thinking that I should be getting a piece of the action in the way Michael squandered money.

"Five thousand. It's a steal, let me tell you. One of the chi masters I used to deal with charged me seven. Can you believe it? Highway robbery!"

"Michael, don't you think five thousand dollars is a bit much to get someone to rearrange furniture? I mean, you could probably get Laura Ashley back from the dead to do your apartment for less."

"Robert, Robert, Robert. I know that being from Idaho . . ."

"Michigan," I corrected him.

"Wherever." Michael continued, "I know that you don't believe in things like feng shui, but I do, and I've got a lot riding on this. The way my furniture is arranged can have a great effect on my vitality, fortune, and most important of all, my love life."

"So what's that supposed to mean?" I asked.

"If the energy in my apartment is misdirected, I might not be able to sustain a hard-on when Max is porking me," Michael replied with concern in his voice. "Or vice versa. Shit, I've got to get ready. People will be arriving any time now." Michael disappeared down a hallway, humming gaily, leaving me alone.

I took a look around the apartment and saw that Max had already worked his way into Michael's life. There were photographs of Max everywhere in picture frames. This was something completely new with Michael because his former lovers didn't stay long enough even to leave a decent exposure on film. I decided that I would hide in one of Michael's guest bedrooms and watch TV until the party began to fill up. Then I could slip in unnoticed. Over an hour later, guests began to arrive in great waves, so seeing my chance, I slipped down the hall and tried to enter the fray as gracefully as I could. Unfortunately I ran right smack into Sam Tobay, who let out a blood-curdling scream in surprise.

"Oh, Robert! You scared the bejeezus out of me," he continued at the top of his lungs as everyone else stared at the two of us. "Where did you come from? I didn't see you come in, and believe me, I see everyone who comes in that door. Robert . . . don't tell me you were here already. You got here way ahead of everyone else again. Look, everyone!" he shouted while pointing at me. "Robert was the first to arrive again. Twenty lashes with a wet noodle."

I looked at Sam, and to my amusement, he had a four-foot spear protruding out of his back. He tottered for a moment, shot out his tongue, and fell face first to the floor. I stood there for a moment, relishing this vision.

"Excuse me, Sam, but I see Jonathan over there," I said, prying myself from his grasp and heading across the room, leaving him standing there in his fluorescent caftan, alone and dejected. The moment quickly passed as I saw him head off into another gaggle of gay men.

As I caught up to Jonathan, I could see that he was clearly out of his mind. He was going from phone to phone, dialing, saying something inaudible into the receiver, then calmly hanging up. I moved closer as Johnathan proceeded to pick up the receiver of another of Michael's thirteen phones. He dialed, then waited. Emotionless, he spoke into the receiver.

"Separate church and state." He hung up. Feeling that his progress was being monitored, he turned to see me watching him.

"Robert, how're ya doing?" he exclaimed.

"Jonathan, I don't want to seem insensitive, but what the hell are you doing?"

"Oh, the stuff with the phones. Christians Against Sin and Homosexuals—CASH for short. They have a toll-free number and it costs them money every time I call them and hang up on them," he said, proud of his gay guerrilla tactic. "Learned it at the latest In Your Face meeting. And since I dial star six seven before I punch in their number, they can't trace the calls because they're blocked."

Ever since I met Jonathan four years ago at one of Michael's parties, he has always been a member of some gay activist group. He was always popping up on the six o'clock news chaining himself to something or being lead away by police for throwing something at some politician or church figure. His favorite projectile was a condom filled with ketchup. Every cardinal and bishop in the New York area began wearing dark robes to hide the stains better.

"So when does lover boy show up?" he said, sensing the anticipation that seemed almost tangible that night. Michael had done quite a job whipping up a frenzy of interest that night. After all, if Michael was actually going to tie the knot with some guy after pillowing half the good-looking men in the northern hemisphere, this Max character had to be a knockout.

"Michael nonchalantly told me that he'll be here in an hour or so, although I could see that he was about to cream his jeans. He can't wait to show Max off."

"Especially since Michael's slept with most everyone in the room," Jonathan replied. "I think he wants to show people what he's moved on to."

"Michael hasn't slept with me," a voice blasted from behind my back.

"Monette! Glad you could make it," I said, making a faux kiss on her cheek.

"I had to. Michael needed at least one person with balls at the party. Sorry I was late. I spotted Ellen DeGeneres walking down Washington and I followed her so I could get her attention."

"Attention for what?" I asked.

"A date, silly!"

"Well, did you get a chance to ask her?"

"Not really. She walked up to a cop car and told the officers that I was stalking her."

"Oh dear, it's a good thing they didn't arrest you!"

"They couldn't because I ran off. She's nicer than Candice Gingrich."

"Didn't Candice tell you that she had a gun in her purse and that she knew how to use it?"

"She was just joking, Robert. Anyway, am I ever glad to see you here! I was cornered by one of Michael's foofie designer friends who began telling me at great length about a project he just finished for the fabulously wealthy Regina Von Tussel on Fifth Avenue. 'We had just finished putting up acres of raw silk that had been steeped in vats of Earl Grey tea to give it the right color'—Monette mimicked the designer in a voice that resembled a hamster being slowly crushed in a vise—'when Reggie—she lets me call her that; all her close friends get to call her Reggie—comes into the room and says *no, no, no. It's all wrong. I've changed my mind. Please, take it all down.* What class!' " Monette finished.

"Was the guy's name Bertrand?" I asked.

"Yes, how did you know?"

"He did Michael's apartment. Or at least tried to," I said. "It seems that someone told Michael that this guy was good, so Michael hires him to do the annual makeover of his apartment. Anyway, Michael tells this Bertrand that he wants something masculine and bold. Michael decides to go to Milan, do a little shopping, look at a few buildings, and boff some Armani models. When he returns, he's shell-shocked. His whole apartment was done in Louis De Hooey. You know, oversize white ceramic Russian Wolfhounds in the entry, floral chintz in the bedroom, and rococo in the guest rooms. Bertrand even did up Michael's gym room, adding silk tassels and pom-poms to all the

Nautilus equipment Michael never uses. Michael called me on the phone as soon as he saw it and said it looked like the place was done by some drag queen on speed."

"Did someone mention drag queens?" shrieked a voice from my side. I turned to see Bette Davis elbowing her way into our circle of conversation.

"Well, what I meant was . . ." the reply came from my startled lips.

"What you meant to say is that you're boring these unfortunate people to death and that you've lost control of this group and it's time for a pro to take charge," Bette said as she elbowed me aside and took center stage in our little group.

"I haven't lost control of this group," I protested.

"Yes, you have, because I said so," said Bette Davis. "You know, my late husband Gary Merrill was brilliant and engaging when he was onstage or on camera, but get him in a small group of people and he would bore them to death."

"Now wait just a minute; are you trying to insinuate . . ." I said, trying to regain my balance and my dignity.

"I'm not insinuating anything. I'm telling you that you're boring. Boring, boring, boring."

I had just been insulted by the late, great Bette Davis. To all appearances, it was just another drag queen doing the oldest cliché in the world: Bette Davis. But this was no ordinary drag queen. This particular transvestite actually believed that his/her body was possessed by the spirit of the original Bette Davis. Ellis Bachman (his real name) had done uncanny Bette Davis impersonations for years, but in a twist of fate that would affect his life forever, he was onstage in Las Vegas performing a Bette Davis impersonation the day the real Bette Davis died. Ellis, so the story goes, began shaking violently, then collapsed on stage. When he awoke hours later, Ellis swore that he could feel the presence of Bette Davis's spirit in his body. Before long, Ellis began so closely to resemble and act exactly like the late Miss Davis that people began to believe his story. It was spooky. His story got picked up in the sensationalist tabloids, which gave credence to his story among those living in trailers and aluminum-clad houses in many parts of Texas and the Midwest; but the funny thing was, Ellis played the part of Bette so well that it was difficult to imagine that he was making the whole thing up. The final stroke came when Ellis legally changed his name to Bette Davis. As time wore on, Ellis so came to resemble Bette Davis in dress, appearance, and manner of speech that people began truly to believe him. To make a long story short, the two have happily coexisted inside Ellis's body for years, with Bette giving Ellis constant guidance on his routines and Ellis giving Bette a sympathetic place to stay. The trick was to know whom you were speaking to when you were talking to Ellis's body, since Ellis's conversation could unexpectedly lurch from his boyhood tales to Bette telling yet another story about the battles she fought with Jack Warner in Hollywood.

Bette Davis turned to Jonathan, ignoring me. "Jonathan, dear, you're Michael's friend, so I need you to intercede for me and my girls. I'm trying to get Michael to have me as maid of honor and I promised I'd throw all my girls in for free. Picture it. Me in all my glory. Mickey could do Marlene Dietrich, Sammy could dress up as Judy Garland, and Timothy could do JoAnne Worley. Anyway, Jonathan, can you picture me and my girls up there at the altar? An all-star-cast gay wedding! Oh, I can see it now. Me in my Halston with the fifty-foot train, my tiara dazzling the congregation, calla lilies everywhere."

"Bette Davis," Jonathan continued, unsure of whom he was really addressing, "you know that this is a big event for Michael. I think he wants to keep the moment simple and pure," he added, trying to find a way of bringing Bette Davis down to earth without denting a single feather or bead.

"Fine, I'll come as Anne of Green Gables," Bette fired back.

"Miss Davis, you know that Michael respects you a lot. He's constantly telling me how talented you are, but he wants to be the center of attention. He doesn't want too many distractions."

Bette thought for a second. "Okay, we'll go simple. Chic. Something like my navy Valentino suit. Simple pumps. No . . . my Helene Arpel spectators."

Jonathan, sensing that it was useless to discourage Bette Davis from crowning herself maid of honor, decided to go in search of more champagne.

"Bring me another glazz, Jonathan," I said, the words slurring just an eensy bit. Monette, always my guardian, tried to head me off at the pass.

"Oh, Robert, why not have a nice, cold seltzer first?"

"Monette," I volunteered, "you know perfectly well that I can handle my liquor."

"Like the night you peed on Matt Percival's Monopoly board at his party?"

"I didn't want to play anymore. Well, at least I didn't pick up the board and toss it across the room like that one guy."

"That guy *was* you," Monette painfully reminded me.

"Oh," I replied, as humbled as the day Leona Helmsley found herself sharing a jail cell with a woman named Dutch.

"Now watch your drinking."

"Okay."

Just then, a great murmur went through the crowd. Max had arrived. All eyes went from cruising each other to cruising Max. Southern, classy, aw-shucks, unbelievably handsome and well-hung Max. Michael came wading through the crowd like Cleopatra to claim Marc Antony.

"Everybody," he said, quieting his guests down, "this is the man who's managed to get me to the altar!"

"What about all those priests?" came a comment from the crowd. There was a roar of dirty laughter.

"Now, now," Michael continued, "I know that in my time I've sowed some wild oats . . ."

This revelation was followed by the sound of dozens of people choking on caviar, and gallons of gin going down several tracheae.

". . . but I've found the man of my dreams and it's time to settle down."

"On top of whom?" came another catcall.

Michael ignored this and went on.

"As of Saturday, May twenty-seventh, I'll be hanging up my spurs—er, scratch that—and I'll be become a good wife for a change. The invitations have just gone out, and Max and I expect to see all of you there—well, with one exception, and you know who you are. That's all. Enjoy yourself."

With that, Michael plunged into the crowd with Max at his side to receive all the well-wishers, who were gushing with excitement and looking forward to the second biggest gay social event of the season. The title of "Biggest Event" would naturally go to the annual Transvestite Ball and Cotillion, but Michael could still hold his head up high.

All of Michael's friends were here. Or should I say moochers. Over in one corner was Anna, the performance artist whose latest installation required her to sit naked in a tank of Jell-O while reciting bad poetry and farting occasionally to punctuate her readings. Anna was talking to Ohm, a photographer who got his big break taking pictures of his genitals, which he had cleverly dressed up or painted. The whole point, as he described it, was to "dispel the seriousness and importance that our society assigns to sex." Being an artist, he refined his craft and had his first exhibition, entitled See Dick Act. The show—you guessed it—consisted of nothing more than photographs of his penis dressed up to look like Marilyn Monroe, Faye Dunaway, and Cher, among others. Word was out that various editors around town were bidding for a book deal with Ohm. In fact, one critic called him the William Wegman of genitalia.

Against the wall in another corner of the room was Charlie, a hopeless alcoholic who had appointed himself

Michael's art investment advisor. And over there was Shirelle, a tall, lanky woman who dressed in black and had no visible means of financial support. Everyone else there had even more dubious reasons for being there. They had slept with Michael, sold him some worthless piece of trash fobbed off as art, or had simply crashed the party. Monette and I, sensing that we had stumbled into a casting call for *Night of the Living Dead, Part IV,* made a beeline for the drinks table, which was overflowing with champagne. I didn't often get my hands on a good bottle of bubbly, so I drank as much as I could, which loosened my tongue considerably. We were soon joined by Carter and Trevor, both Calvin Klein models and both tremendously stuck on themselves.

"Well, what do you think of Max?" I began. "Is he gorgeous, or what?" I asked the question only because I knew it would irk these two walking Ken dolls.

"Max is okay, I guess. If you like a hayseed," Carter replied tiredly.

Great! I had him going! Fire off another, Robert. Strike a blow for plain-looking people everywhere, even if you have to make things up.

"Well, from what I heard, he's as loaded as Michael. From a Virginia family so old, his great-great-great-great-great-grandfather was good friends with Jefferson."

"Oh, really," remarked Trevor, not wanting to seem overly impressed.

I couldn't stop myself. The blood was in the water. "To tell the truth, I think he said he had blood ties to Washington, too. Maybe that accounts for the strong face and square jaw. In fact, Bruce Weber is putting together a photographic book called Ten, filled with ten of the most gorgeous and hunka-hunka-burnin'-love men on the face of the earth. Naked. And guess who's going to be in it?"

"Drew Carey?" Carter suggested sarcastically.

"Nope. Max himself. Yes siree, without a doubt, Michael certainly caught himself the most gorgeous man in New York. And," I said, lowering my voice to let all present know

Bedroom #2, which was filled with pretty much the same, except that this couple hadn't bothered to turn the lights off. No matter where we went, the story was pretty much the same. Shit. I've got this guy practically in bed with me and I can't find a room. Suddenly, a thought struck me. Michael had a servant's quarters discretely tucked behind the library. I pulled Edward there so fast that he practically tripped the entire way. Luck was in our favor and the room was completely empty. Before I knew it, Edward had my shirt off and I had begun to reciprocate when I could feel the champagne rising to my head like a freight train.

"Woa . . . Edwuuurd," I managed to slur out.

"Am I going too fast?" he asked with a shred of concern.

"No, it's just that I . . . I . . . I . . ." The last thing I could remember before I passed out was the figure of Jonathan walking into the room, ignoring us completely, going over the to the telephone, and picking it up and dialing. A second before the ocean of champagne bid my brain good night, the last words I could hear were Jonathan's:

"Separate church and state."

It wasn't until the next morning that I awoke. I was still in the servant's quarters, but I somehow had managed to crawl into the bed that awaited the manservant that Michael never had. It's not that Michael didn't try to snare one, but they'd always leave once they got wind of Michael's prolific sexual encounters, all-night partying, and the appalling salary he offered.

Edward was nowhere to be seen. Then again, neither was my watch, my wallet, or my jacket. Welcome to my life, folks. I'm so horny I could blow any minute and I don't even get foreplay. On top of that, I get robbed. Just as I was trying to sort everything out in my head, the door burst open and Michael flew in wrapped in an oversized terry cloth robe—monogrammed, of course.

"Good morning, Robert. Or should I say, Mr. Lucky?" he said in tones too loud for my head to bear.

"Not so loud. And for your information, not so lucky. Some guy at your party named Edward took advantage of me last night."

"Congratulations, Robert! I told you that celibacy was no good," Michael replied cheerfully.

"No, no—I meant that I had a little too much to drink last night and when I passed out, the guy made off with my watch and my wallet. My jacket too, I think."

"You said his name was Edward? Never heard of him. Of course, half the people that show up at my parties aren't invited. What did he look like?" Michael asked.

"He had a dueling scar on his left cheek, a hook for his right hand, and a parrot on his shoulder. How should I know, Michael? All I know is that he was good-looking."

"Of course he was good-looking! All my friends are. Come to think of it, I don't know any ugly people. Unless you count that marine I dated a few years back. He did have an incredible set of butt muscles, though. Like a perfect pair of fuzzy melons. He could hold a rifle between those muscles for an hour while standing at attention."

"Michael, beauty is more than skin deep," I triumphed.

"Some scag obviously said that."

"Speaking of ugly, where's Max?"

"I'm glad you brought that up, Robert," Michael said, with a tiny, almost imperceptible squeak of hesitation in his voice.

"What? Look, Michael, I was just kidding. Max's probably one of the most beautiful men I've ever seen. I'm thoroughly jealous and I hate your guts."

"That's the whole thing that bothers me," Michael said, fingering the rim of the coffee cup he was holding. "Doesn't Max strike you as just a bit *too* handsome?"

"Maybe I'm not the only one who's jealous, Michael. I can almost see the green of envy right around your eyes. Don't worry, a little powder will cover that."

"I'm not jealous," Michael complained in a way that made it plain to see that he was clearly jealous. "And it's not just his looks. He's perfect in everything!"

Michael, I'm afraid, had finally met his match. In a way, it was kind of nice to see. For so long, Michael seemed to have it all, like some kind of starlet enjoying her day in the sun. But inevitably, there was always another rising star in the wings waiting to take her place. The story was as old as life itself. Eve probably felt it in the Garden of Eden. The question was whether Michael would go quietly or would only give up the spotlight after a pitiful display of public jealousy. Michael, I suspected, was only in the early stages.

"Yes, Max is hard to believe. He knows about wines, speaks several languages, has traveled the world over, comes from a very wealthy old family, and is handsomer than shit. Sometimes I think he's too good to be true," Michael admitted.

"Maybe he is," I ventured.

Michael left me to nurse my hangover in private while he and Max had "breakfast" in bed (as Michael would say). Since I was a guest in Michael's apartment, I wanted to be grateful, but the constant sound of Michael's cranium banging against the headboard in the next room for what seemed like an hour didn't help my ego or my aching head one bit. Michael has terrific sex. I get robbed. I wish I had a tablet of cyanide.

After I had managed to get some food in my stomach and hold it down, Michael suggested that he and I go shopping for his trousseau. Normally, this would mean hour after giddy hour of going in and out of stores loading up on things I could only dream of buying, so I immediately decided against going, but Michael was persistent. My resistance was down, too—he promised to buy me something.

Our first stop was Portofino, the incredibly snooty men's clothing store on lower Fifth Avenue. Even the mannequins, who looked down at patrons from their lofty stands, had an attitude. Getting cruised by the salespeople was never a problem at Portofino—no one could possibly be good enough for them. Never mind the fact that the bulk of them barely made minimum wage. They were a race apart: arbiters of good taste with an important duty—to claw at the backs of unsuspecting customers through a complex language of raised eyebrows, subtle coughs, and pregnant pauses for the many sartorial transgressions that passed beneath their eyes. They must have had a field day with me. My coat, which looked pretty good to me before I entered the store, inevitably took on a completely different look to these coiffed fashion police. My coat suddenly sported acrylic fur around the hood and a mitten dangling from each sleeve by a piece of yarn. The jeans and L.L. Bean gum boots ("Don't you think it looks like rain, Michael?") provided even more ammo for the deliciously delighted salespeople who stood behind their immaculately arranged tie-and-sock displays licking their lips, tasting the kill. I could feel them tearing me apart, tossing hunks of my flesh back and forth like a gazelle corpse between playful cheetahs.

Thwack! "Look, Sean. Check out the coat. The tour bus from Ohio just got in," I could hear one salesperson mumble to another.

Thwack! "I guess that's what they're wearing in the Midwest this season . . . again," said another.

Thwack! "No, no, honey. K mart is across the river in New Jersey," came another almost-silent jeer.

Michael, immaculately dressed in black jeans, black turtleneck, and $850 alligator penny loafers and sporting a twenty-three-thousand-dollar Rolex watch, oddly enough hadn't encountered a single snipe that I could see. The salespeople had already done a quick mental calculation of the net worth of Michael's wardrobe and decided this bird had big bucks to spend. The salespeople swarmed around

Michael like bimbos around an eighty-year-old tycoon widower.

"May I be of service?" one of the bimbos asked.

"No, we're just looking," Michael said, waving him away. "Look, Robert, this is the tie I bought for Max just last week."

The price on the tie (yes, I had to look at it) was three hundred fifty dollars. I don't even think I had a suit that cost that much. Michael browsed around as if nothing interested him, then hurriedly grabbed five shirts and had the salesclerk ring them up and put them in the famous signature shopping bag of lemon yellow with the name "Portofino" emblazoned on it in big, black letters.

"Let's go up to the fourth floor and look around."

I had only been up to the fourth floor of Portofino once, but I didn't tarry long once I saw the prices. The fourth floor was Mecca to rich homosexual men from around the United States. Even the elevator that we took there was sacred and hushed. When we reached the fourth floor, the door slid reverently open and we were ushered into the holy of the holies.

"Good afternoon, gentlemen. My name is Claude and I'll be your personal attendant."

Without batting an eye, Michael spoke. "I'm getting married in three weeks and I need something wonderful to wear."

"Married?" You could almost see the disbelief on his face. Married? You? I almost expected him to start searching the room for the hidden camera and Alan Funt.

"To another man, of course," Michael added, sensing our personal attendant's confusion.

"Oh, thank God. I'd hate to see someone as handsome as you wasted on a woman."

"I'm still thinking of black tie, but a tuxedo seems too conventional, don't you think? This is a gay wedding, after all."

"Of course. How about something like this from Karl Van Koos?" he suggested as he produced a tuxedo covered from top to bottom with black sequins. It looked like something that Siegfried and Roy wore to funerals.

"Too flashy," Michael replied, as if the hideousness of the thing didn't even register in his mind. Michael was a man on a mission: to outdress everyone at the wedding.

"Now this one is fabulous! It's from Rafael." In a moment, Claude had produced a tuxedo made entirely of black leather with subtle straps added here and there. It looked like formal bondage wear. Just the thing for the little, sniveling, worthless shit of a slave who forgot to clean Daddy's boots. Take that! And that!

"I've got something like that already," Michael replied. Claude's eyebrows arched so high, they almost disappeared off his forehead. Translated, they said, "tell me more."

"Perhaps this number from Christopher Allen would do nicely." Claude produced another tuxedo made of incredibly sumptuous black velvet with satin piping placed discretely in precisely the right places.

"I love it!" Michael said, happy that he had found an outfit that was showy enough but not too vulgar. "What do you think, Robert?"

"I feel that an off-the-shoulder peasant dresses would be a better idea. Slutty, but with a down-home flavor of the Eastern European countryside."

Michael gave me one of those I-can't-take-you-anywhere looks, then burst into laughter.

"I'll have to come back for a fitting on Tuesday. I'll bring my lover too so we can both be fitted. I'll see you then. C'mon, Robert, we have more shopping to do," Michael pleaded as he herded me toward the elevator.

We rode down in total silence because Michael was obviously turning over all kinds of wedding-related thoughts in his head.

"Well, Robert. We've got a lot more to do. Let's keep going," Michael reminded me.

I won't bother you with all the countless details of the umpteen florists we visited, the caterers we talked to, and the deejays we interviewed. After a few hours of this, we decided to have some lunch at Flaubert's Armadillo, a Classic French Tex-Mex restaurant that was currently "hot."

Once we were seated, Michael launched into the details of planning his wedding.

"I've decided to get married at the First Church of Christ, Scientist, Homosexual, on Bedford Street."

"Good choice," I replied. "I went to a lesbian wedding there once. Very tasteful. Very Gothic. I just wish they'd do something about the name, though. How about the reception? Your place?"

"No no no no no no no no! Too small. And besides, I want to have fun. I'm going to rent out Spartacus. It's going to be Sunday and no one goes there on Sunday."

"You're going to rent out Spartacus!?" I said, incredulous.

Michael was obviously very serious because Spartacus was, last time I checked, very hot. Some of the most beautiful men in New York were seen dancing there every Saturday night. "Are you sure you don't want something like Occulus?"

"Absolutely not. They threw me out a few months ago. They caught me making it with one of their bouncers in one of the private cocktail lounges upstairs. The owner caught us and had us both thrown out."

"Bouncer, too?"

"Yeah, he was the owner's boyfriend."

"Oops," I said.

"Oh, no, it was intentional. I was sleeping with the owner a few months back and the shit dumps me for his bouncer, Thor. No kidding, that's his real name. So I got even with him by sleeping with Thor."

"What happened to Thor?" I asked.

"Who cares? I've known amoebas who could outwit him. Okay, so I've got the church, the reception, the florist, caterer, deejay . . . I guess if there's anything else to do, I can take care of it later. Yesterday, I booked our flight to Fiji for the honeymoon. I'm renting a private villa that's attended hand and foot by small Polynesian teenage boys."

"Michael!" I exclaimed.

"Oh, Robert, you know I'm not into little boys. Anyway, I've got my own man now. I just hope that everything goes well. I don't want anything to spoil my wedding. It's just something that a gay man looks forward to all his life."

Michael was too excited about his upcoming betrothal to see to the thousand details needed to carry off the homosexual event of the year. So, after visiting dozens of florists and caterers and the like, Michael blew them all off when he decided there were just too many details to see to. So, like many of the wealthy heterosexuals of New York's socially prominent families, he did the only natural thing: he hired someone else. And not just anybody else, but Oliver Braxxton, a combination interior decorator, florist, caterer, and professional homosexual who agreed to see us by appointment. Since he was obviously too good to come to his clients, he made his rich clients come to his small but tastefully decorated salon off Madison Avenue in the East 60s.

Oliver showed us photo album after photo album of weddings so heinous and horrific that Michael finally put a stop to Oliver's self-love fest, looked him in the eye, and said that he didn't want all those tight-pussy weddings with all the foofy flowers and lace and allusions to virginity long gone. He wanted the wedding to be tasteful, masculine, and hip. Well, Michael might as well have asked Oliver to change the carburetor on his Range Rover, because this direction left Oliver clueless—a mistake that Michael would eventually pay dearly for.

The task of arranging Michael's stag party fell into my lap. Ordinarily, I'd avoid throwing a party for Michael in my own apartment, knowing that Michael's friends would trash the place in no time. But this party would be different. No porn films and gag gifts at this soiree, no siree. This was going to be a black tie affair. I could picture it now. It would look like something out of *Brideshead Revisited*. Some of us would be smoking long, expensive cigars while others played a rousing game of billiards and drank brandy from terrarium-sized snifters. Never mind that I lived in a dumpy one-room apartment with cracked plaster and leaky plumbing. I could dress the place up. Michael would get the best affair that my meager little salary could afford. After all, he was my friend. So I started making calls, getting a caterer to come in and drop off trays of hors d'oeuvres. A florist would do the arrangements. The invitations were to be engraved with fancy script lettering making it clear that this would be an elegant affair. In fact, just as I was putting a stamp on the last invitation, my door intercom buzzed.

"It's Monette, honey. I was just passing through the neighborhood when I remembered that I needed to return your pinking shears. Are you doing anything? Or anyone?"

"No, still unhappily celibate. C'mon up."

I still have no idea what Monette would be doing with pinking shears. I, of course, being a homosexual, had every right to own a pair. Presently, Monette's battering-ram knock broke the silence of my little apartment. I opened the door only to have the shears thrust into my face.

"I didn't want to keep you from finishing your dress for Michael's wedding," Monette quipped. "So what're you up to?"

"Just finishing up the invitations to the bachelor party."

"You mean the stag party," Monette corrected me.

"No, bachelor party. Stag parties are what guys who work in auto factories throw for each other. It gives the groom one last chance to pork the bride's best girlfriend, eventually landing them all in a three-way brawl on the *Jerry Springer Show*."

"Oh, really. And how, pray tell, is yours going to be different?"

"I'm not going to do the old cliche of porn movies and sexual gag gifts. It's going to be rather elegant. I've got a caterer and a florist coming in to do the place," I boasted.

"Am I invited, or are dykes not allowed?"

"Well, to tell you the truth, Monette . . . it's kind of a *guy* thing."

"A *guy* thing?" Monette asked. "You're a homosexual. Homosexuals don't have *guy* things. Just straight men."

"Oh all right, you're invited. Next Saturday, the twenty-third."

"Sorry. I can't come, Robert. I've got a soccer game over in Park Slope. Our encounter group, Lesbians Who Love Too Much, is up against the Leaping Lesbians of Cobble Hill."

"Well, on your way out, could you slip these invitations into the mail? Pretty pleeeease?" I whined.

"Anything to help out a friend. I'll drop them right downstairs."

"Fine."

"You want to see a movie tonight?"

"Maybe. Give me a call."

"See you later," she said and was gone, leaving me to deal with the thousands of details that go with throwing a party of impeccable taste.

The last few weeks seemed to fly by so quickly, what with all the arrangements to be made, trousseaus to be bought, and bitchy florists to be dealt with. But before I knew it, I found myself putting the last finishing touches on my apartment decorations as I prepared for the arrival of Michael's bachelor party guests.

I had planned this one right down to the last detail. Thanks to a gifted (expensive) florist named Christopher, there were flowers everywhere, including two gardenias floating in the toilet bowl. I thought that this little touch was somewhat extravagant, not to mention impractical, but my protests were waived aside and calmed by Christopher's insistence that they were unflushable. Never mind how I would get them out after the party was over—genius couldn't be bothered with those petty little details.

I was just putting some of the hors d'oeuvres onto a silver Tiffany tray that I had borrowed when the door buzzer shattered my concentration.

"Yes?" I asked, pressing the intercom button.

"It's me, Bryan."

"It's the button marked 'penthouse' on the private elevator to your left. Don't use the one on the right—the help uses that one," I said, stepping way up in class.

Although my building was a fifth-floor walk-up without an elevator, I was proud of how everything looked. I ran over to the stereo, put on a Mozart piano concerto CD, and made one last pass through the room to make sure everything was absolutely perfect. It wasn't just the guests that I wanted to impress; I wanted to make sure Michael and Max knew how much I cared for them. Ordinarily, the bride wasn't invited to a bachelor party, but with all the gender confusion generated by two men getting married, and me not really knowing which one was top or bottom, I decided to throw etiquette out the window and invite them both. Even Bryan, who lived in a cubbyhole in the Village, would be impressed.

"Bryan," I said, swinging the door open and bowing with a dramatic sweep of my arm and tuxedo tails.

As Bryan entered, I noticed something a little odd. He wasn't in black tie. In fact, he hardly had any clothes on at all, not unless you count the tiny white shorts that were held up by two tiny spaghetti straps that were, by virtue of the tightness of his shorts, pointless. On his feet, he had a pair of shiny black combat boots with just a hint of white socks peeping out over the top.

"Oh, God. I'm one of the first to arrive! Again! How do you stand it, Robert?" he asked, oblivious to the fact that I was dressed to the nines.

"I've never arrived early in my life," I responded.

Since Bryan could be a little on the wild side, I decided that his outfit was "just the way he was" and decided to ignore the fact that he looked as if he was ready for a white party. No matter how hard you tried to keep things classy, there was always one homosexual who just didn't get it and would wear or do anything he wanted. Of course, these were the types other homosexuals lusted after the most, precisely because these wild types were exciting, fun, and carefree. Unlike me, standing here in tails.

My intercom blared again.

"Yes?" I asked.

"Tommy and Bartholemew," came the reply.

I tried to sound upbeat, but I couldn't help but sound a trifle crestfallen, owing to the fact that Bryan's brazen tackiness had cast a small but noticeable pall on the elegance of my apartment.

"Fifth floor, please. Just leave your hat and gloves with the butler in the front hall."

I pressed the buzzer to open the door, with a sense of relief that Tommy and Bart would make me forget all about Bryan. When I opened the door to usher them in, I was dead wrong.

Tommy's outfit could not have come from anywhere other than Eat My Shorts, an underwear catalog with items so incredibly suggestive, the catalog had to be mailed in a brown paper envelope. Not that I had ever seen this catalog, but it looked like Tommy was wearing The Boomerang. It consisted of nothing more than a length of white spandex cloth the width of a shoestring that "swoops down from behind the neck to offer comfortable support while showing what you've got, then returns to snap behind the neck." The entire thing, folded up, would probably fill a teaspoon. Bart's outfit was a revealing thong that left more to the eye than the imagination. The Bareback, I thought to myself. Not, of course, that I had ever seen this catalog. At the same instant, another horrid thought occurred to me: did these guys walk down the street dressed like this?

"Nice outfit, Robert," Tommy muttered to me as if I were the odd-looking one. He and Bart headed to the hors d'oeuvres without a word. I was stunned. Was I going mad?

"Bryan! I haven't seen you in ages! Where've you been hiding out?" Tommy screamed in that age-old tradition of homosexuals greeting each other.

"I've been living the life of a nun, I tell you! This guy I've been dating doesn't want me running around to all the bars without him. I keep telling him he's a control freak and he calls me a slut!"

"Hors d' oeuvre?" I asked, pushing a tray under Bryan's nose.

"You think that's bad! Bart fixed me up with this guy who wanted me to go to church with him! And the funny thing is, I went! My dear, I'm in line for sainthood!"

All this from a man wearing The Boomerang.

My intercom buzzer interrupted the flow of conversation again.

"I'll get it," Bart yelled as he ran on tiptoes to buzz the downstairs door open. He didn't even bother to ask who it was. He then horrified me further when he opened the door to my apartment and stood in the doorway waiting to greet whoever had buzzed—for all my neighbors to see.

"It's Trent and Olaf."

"Come on up," Bart said excitedly. "Things are really going to get rolling now."

The intercom nagged at us again.

"I'll get that one too, Robert. You just sit down. You look tired."

Bart, never considering the impact that his actions had on others, stood by the door, buzzing in everyone who bothered to ring my apartment. This was New York City, for God's sake!

"Hey, everyone, Michael and Max are on their way up,

too," Bart continued shrilly. "Maybe we should all hide in the dark and shout 'surprise' when they come in!"

"Bart, there wouldn't be much surprise since they know we're all here," I pointed out.

"You're right, Robert," Bart conceded. "You weren't a four-point-oh grade average for nothing!"

I made a mental note to myself. Add to my list of Bartholemew's faults: dumber than a bag of hammers. Good-looking, but stupid.

Presently, the door opened and Michael and Max stepped into the room. Both were dressed in matching studded leather G-strings and black combat boots. That was all. All fourteen men in the room at that moment got moist. I must confess that although Michael had painted a vivid picture of Max's body in all his conversations, his ramblings didn't do Max any justice whatsoever. Max was, without a doubt, the most magnificent man I have ever seen. His pecs and abs were chiseled so deeply, you could almost get lost in them. His butt was so firm and muscular, you could eat breakfast off it. And the thighs! Like two sequoias holding up his muscular frame. Even his G-string was noticeably larger than Michael's. I can't imagine why Bruce Weber or Herb Ritts hadn't discovered Max yet. Beyond the obvious sexual overtones of the two, there was a sight that left me touched. There on Michael's right biceps, was an eagle tattoo identical to the one on Max's biceps. Ah, true love.

Once the initial wave of envy died down, the party returned to normal, sort of. Someone had changed the disk on my stereo from Mozart to Jimmy Sommerville's latest hit—which I didn't even own—and turned the volume up to a deafening level.

"I hope that you don't mind, Robert, but I brought my own CDs because your music sucks," said someone that I didn't recognize.

Two of my potted palms had already been upended, their dirt spilled carelessly on the sisal rug I had slaved so much to pay for. The white linen tablecloth that I had ironed for hours was by now covered with the contents of several over-flowing ashtrays and stumps of asparagus spears left by various guests. One of my leather-upholstered chairs had a cigarette burn already. And lo and behold, there were several decapitated champagne glasses lying on the table, their stems presumably somewhere in my apartment. In all, it was a pretty much normal affair by New York standards.

"Robert, thanks for the party," came Michael's voice over my shoulder. "Everyone's having a wonderful time. Even Max has loosened up a bit."

"A bit!" I replied. "In a minute, the guy's going to be dancing around while our friends stuff dollar bills into his G-string."

I had no sooner said this when my prophecy came true. Charming, debonaire Max was gyrating to the thumping music with an intensity that suggested that he had done this all his life. Guests were approaching him and putting folded dollar bills into the sweaty pouch that seemed to hold them spellbound. Some of the guests started to whoop and cheer as Max danced slowly along the circle that had formed around him, tempting the guests toward the prize with thrusts of his pelvis, pulling back once the money was safely in place.

"Aw, isn't that cute," Michael said. "I guess Max's had a little too much to drink tonight. We started over at my place. . . . I guess we should've had something to eat first."

Leave it to Michael. His husband-to-be in a matter of less than twenty-four hours is dancing around like a go-go boy and Michael thinks it's sweet.

I couldn't think of anything to say, so I said, "Well, he certainly is good at it!"

Michael smiled back. "Yes, I'm very proud. Usually he's so quiet and reserved. He never has been able to hold his alcohol," he added in explanation.

My door intercom buzzer sounded the arrival of yet another guest. As I watched Max dancing around my living room, I crossed the room to open the door to the latest guest. As I opened it, a man with enormous, rippling abs and rock-hard pecs and clad only in a red fireman's hat, danced into my apartment.

"My name's Harry and this is my firehose," he said, pointing to his you-know-what. "I'm here to put out your fire. Now which one of you is Michael?"

I can't remember how many pairs of hands went up at that point.

"Well, wherever you are, Michael," he shouted, "this dance is for you."

Harry entered the ring of spectators and joined Max. No sooner than he began to grind his hips, something extraordinary happened. Harry's gaze met Max's. Max's met Harry's. Max froze momentarily in shock, then lost his balance, and tumbled into the crowd, knocking down several guests in the front row. Michael rushed to comfort his fallen gladiator. Never mind the rest.

"Are you all right, Max?" Michael asked with true concern for another human on his face—a first for Michael.

"I'm fine, Michael. I guess I had a little too much to drink tonight. I'm sorry. I just caught my foot on the rug . . . and over I fell."

"There, there," Michael cooed. "The bigger they are, the harder they fall. Maybe I should get you home. We've got a big day tomorrow. Remember?"

Max screwed up his face in mock ignorance while scratching his head. "Something about you and I getting married?"

"Yes. And you better be there," Michael reminded him.

The guests, while concerned for Max's health, were mildly revolted at Michael's puppy-love antics. Michael was never one to kowtow to anyone, because he had never found anyone he thought superior to him. The bride and groom rose, bade a fond farewell, and left. The party, shaken by the departure of the happy couple, departed *en masse*, planning their next stop for the evening.

As Bryan passed me on the way out, he patted me on the shoulder and thanked me for the great time.

"What great time?" I asked in disbelief. "I plan an elegant evening and it turns into an orgy. The only thing missing was the leather sling."

"Robert, if you planned for an elegant evening, why didn't your invitation say so?"

I couldn't quite grasp what he was talking about. "It did!"

"Well, then why did you put 'You're invited to a slut party for Michael and Max. Appropriate attire required. The cheaper and sleazier, the better.' Huh?"

I was incredulous. "My invitations didn't say that!"

"Did too!" Bryan countered. He went over to a table and picked up an invitation someone had left.

He was absolutely right. The invitation was on the same cream-colored paper that I had originally chosen. The lettering was the same. But the words were totally different from what I had engraved on them.

"I don't believe this. These can't be the invitations I sent out! Maybe I'm going crazy," I added in disbelief.

"Robert, I think you've carried this celibacy thing too far. Catholic priests have better sex lives than you. Go out and get laid. Even if you have to pay for it. You'll feel a lot better."

"Thank you, Doctor Freud. I'll take that into consideration," I said to Bryan as I saw him out.

Maybe Bryan was right. Going years without sex very well could drive a person to insanity. How else could you explain Nancy Reagan?

"**I** wish I was there to see the look on your face when Harry came in," Monette roared into the phone.

"I had a feeling it was you," I replied.

Monette continued, "I had to get you back for the posters."

"I admit I was a little surprised when Harry arrived."

"Are you complaining?"

"No, not really. He's as close as I'll ever get to having a man that gorgeous and naked at the same time in my apartment. I did proposition him wildly. It couldn't hurt."

"Did he respond?" Monette asked.

"No. But you should've seen the look on Michael's face. He looked like a kid with an American Express Gold Card at a candy store. Here was this stud who was being dangled right in front of his face, and he couldn't bite. I wonder if Michael had second thoughts about getting married."

"I'll bet the only thing he was thinking about was whether he could cheat on Max and get away with it. You know how Michael can't resist adding another notch in his headboard. Harry wasn't sleazy, was he?"

"Sleazy?" I remarked, wondering how a person who made a living prancing around naked in front of complete strangers could be thought of in any other way. "So I'll see you at the wedding?"

"I'll be there. This is something I just have to see. Michael settling down."

"I think it's a clear sign that the end of the world is near. So have you decided what you're going to wear to the wedding?"

"Either my red Galanos or my black Fortuny," Monette began with just an ever so slight sense of sarcasm. I could almost feel the sledgehammer hitting me in the head. "No, I think I'll wear my best flannel shirt, a clean pair of Levi's, and my construction boots. See you there," she said as she hung up.

3

Get Me to the Church on Time

"**W**hat da fuck is this?" my cab driver blurted out the moment we pulled up to the church where Michael was to be married. "It looks like somethin' outta dat movie, *Mrs. Doubtfibble.*"

"Doubtfire," I corrected him. "Perhaps you're thinking of *Tootsie?*"

"Hey, don't take this personal or nuttin, but are you one of them cross-dressers?"

"I am not; now on your way," I said, discounting his tip and slamming the door to his cab.

Not satisfied, he stared at me, squinting his eyes, as if trying to imagine what I would look like in a red dress and sling back shoes. Finally, he shook his head and sped off, laughing hysterically.

I knew that today would not be a normal one. In fact, I was sure that sixty years from now, when I would be in a convalescent home drooling on myself, this day would still haunt me. It was only after I ascended the steps of the church and entered the vestibule that I was convinced that this was a day from some wacky parallel universe. Gaggles of impeccably clad gay men, lesbians, and numerous drag queens chattered ceaselessly to each other about the impending event. It all seemed so silly, really. Since the State of New York didn't officially recognize same-sex marriages, the day's ceremonies and festivities were largely symbolic. Nevertheless, Michael, in his giddiness, had seen to it that the wedding had every trapping of heterosexual marriages, albeit much more tasteful and expensive ones. Of course, Michael couldn't have done it without his trusty decorator, Oliver. Oliver, for the past few weeks, had been running up a tremendous tab at Michael's expense. He had ordered enough exotic flowers to strip the entire countryside of a South American nation. Mountains of food had been ordered, oceans of champagne—why, you almost got the impression that Oliver was on a percentage, which he was.

The vestibule of the church was also crammed to the fake eyelashes with drag queens in matching light blue taffeta gowns with forty-foot trains that snaked across the floor in a tangled confusion of rustling silk. Never mind that Michael told Bette Davis that he didn't want drag queen maids of honor. Michael was used to snubbing people, and Bette Davis was no different. Michael was ready to accept the fact that for the next several months, he faced the very distinct possibility that the tires on his car would be repeatedly slashed, he'd receive an avalanche of unordered magazine subscriptions, and he'd be totally disbarred from any drag show in New York City. It was *his* wedding and he was going to have it his way. Obviously, Bette Davis and her handmaidens had decided to dress appropriately for the role they would not play, if only to show Michael that they were not pleased. And dress they did. Several of Bette Davis's maidens of honor were running to and fro, shooing guests away from the expensive trains on their dresses. Bette Davis was different. Wedding or no wedding, she wore what she wanted. She whispered to me that it was a stitch-for-stitch copy of the famous red dress Bette Davis wore in *Jezebel*. I had to admit, it made a statement. So did her cigarette, which was lit. The reverend, who stood nearby, asked Bette Davis to put it out, which she reluctantly did, grinding the butt deeply into the carpet.

As much as Michael wanted to have a traditional wedding—as if that were possible—he did relinquish control of the big day to Oliver to handle, and was therefore at the mercy of his judgment. This was a mistake of the magnitude of Neville Chamberlain trusting Hitler. The inside of the church, when I eventually saw it, was a riot of fabrics, ribbons, and bows everywhere. Since I was to be best man, I went in search of Michael to make sure everything was perfect for what was supposed to be the happiest day of his life. I found him downstairs, excited as a homosexual in a warehouse full of fine English antiques.

"Robert!" he yelled suddenly as if he hadn't seen me for years. "I'm so jumpy. Did you see the inside of the church? I didn't have time to look."

"Yes, Michael. It's tasteful, masculine, dead butch," I said, crossing my fingers, hoping not to be struck dead for lying in church.

"You don't think the flowers are too much?"

"No, Michael."

"Is everyone here yet?"

"Michael, you invited over fifteen-hundred homosexuals to your wedding. You'd be lucky to get a hundred here on time. But to answer your question, yes, most of them are here."

"I know it's bad luck, but Max stayed at my place last night. In fact, I left him there. I wanted to look over the church to make sure everything was perfect. I mean, it has to be. *Out* magazine is out there, for God's sake. Anyway, Max called to say he'll be here in a few minutes since it's only a few blocks. Punctuality is his nature, not mine."

I looked at Michael, rolling my eyes. "You can say that again."

"Gad, look at the time. I've got to get upstairs. C'mon, best man!"

I followed Michael upstairs. I did have to hand it to him. He looked stunning. Handsome. Michael and I made our way up through the crowd in the vestibule, evoking oohs and ahhs from onlookers. Michael paced nervously back and forth, waiting for Max to come flying heroically into the church. Most of the attendees sensed that the event was about to begin and began trying to muscle their way into the front pews, closer to the action. Michael made a last-minute check to make sure everything was ready to go. As I was helping him primp himself for his trip down the aisle, one of the church elders approached Michael.

"Mr. Stark?" he asked timidly.

"Yes?"

The elder continued, "I just got a call from Max, and he said to go ahead and start the wedding. He'll meet you down at the altar. He says he's got a romantic surprise planned and doesn't want to tell you. You'll see, he said."

All trace of nervousness faded from Michael's face and was replaced by a look that was a mixture of excitement and pride. "You see, Robert, this is too good to be true. I just can't believe this is happening to me!" he said, laughing nervously.

"You're a lucky man. Now, more than ever, you've got it all," I said, revealing more than I cared to.

"Thank you, Robert," he added, and gave me a hug. "Okay," he said, turning to the elder, "let's start the music. Are you ready, Robert?"

"As ready as I'll ever be. I'll meet you down at the altar."

Since it was a homosexual wedding, Michael and I decided that for me to walk down the aisle while the music was playing was a bit much. I would go down to the altar before the music started and Michael began his procession. If it weren't for the seriousness of the occasion, I would have burst out laughing from all the tangled wedding etiquette. As I took my place in the front of the church, the absurdity of the moment was amplified by the sight of the gaggle of drag maids seated in the front row next to Bette Davis, who was again smoking. My eyes began to drift around the rest of the pews, taking in the menagerie of guests: fashion de-

signers, artists, publishers, and wait . . . a face that seemed
familiar. What was his name? Ned! No. Edward! Yes, that's
it! Edward. The son of a bitch who stole my wallet, coat,
and watch the night of Michael's party. Just as I was about to
go over and stomp the hell out of the little hustler, chords of
organ music thundered throughout the church. The ceremony had begun. All heads turned to see Michael walk
down the aisle to Handel's "Hallelujah" chorus from the
Messiah (my little touch). Michael was positively beaming.
Several of Bette Davis's contingent began crying even
though they barely knew Michael. Michael floated up to the
altar on a cloud of the congregation's admiration and sheer
jealousy. When he reached the front, he took his place and
turned to watch Max come down the aisle.

But Max didn't appear.

The music thundered on, but no Max. The music reached
a tremendous crescendo and came to a tumultuous finale.

Still no Max.

There was a moment of awkward silence; then the music
started up from the middle of the piece. It soared to an even
mightier conclusion, shaking the buttresses of the church
and causing several flower arrangements to fall from their
perches. This was followed by a horrible, deafening silence.
Murmurs began to ripple through the church, with heads
turning this way and that, trying to surmise what was going
on. Michael, standing at the altar looking so proud and
handsome, regained his composure temporarily, hoping
that some unforeseen circumstance was preventing Max
from arriving. He stood up straight for a moment, then
seemed to deflate before my very eyes. Because I was so
close, I could see him physically trembling. He turned directly toward me and opened his mouth to say something,
but only two raspy words came out:

"Something's wrong." He then turned and leaped down
the aisle in long, athletic bounds and disappeared down the
steps of the church.

*   *   *

For the next week, I, like hundreds of other homosexuals in New York, tried to get in touch with Michael, but to no avail. He stopped answering the phone, refused all visitors, and was scarcely seen around town. According to the reports, Michael was spotted by several friends, roaming the streets still dressed in the tuxedo he was jilted in. His hair was unwashed and uncombed, people said. The look on his face was blank, but then again, when wasn't it? One person said he had seen him at the army recruiting station in Times Square. Sensing that Michael wasn't getting over this very well, I decided to pay him a visit and I wouldn't take no for an answer. After being the dumper for years, Michael had suddenly become the dumpee. It was more than he could handle.

After calling up to his apartment, the doorman waved me on. I could barely imagine what he must look like now, one week later. From what I had heard, it wasn't pretty. Letting his looks go was totally unheard of with Michael. Every year, he spent more money adorning himself than most third-world countries spent on food. He had weekly manicures and leg and arm waxings, worked out daily, had his hair cut every week, tanned every four days, and got massages every Tuesday. To picture Michael as anything but perfect was a frightening turn of events. I fully expected to find him, upon entering his dark apartment, curled up in a fetal position and sporting twenty-inch toenails. As I ascended in the elevator, walked to his door, and knocked, I assumed the worst.

"Hi!" Michael said perkily, flinging the door open spryly. "C'mon in, Robert. How ya doin'?"

"You're not whacked out on Valiums, are you, Michael?" I asked gently.

"No. Why? Should I be?"

This is too weird, I thought to myself. "Are you okay, Michael?"

"Yes, perfectly." And he wasn't kidding. His hair was

freshly cut and combed. His clothes were clean. And the blank look on his face . . . well . . . two out of three ain't bad. Even his apartment was immaculate. As I scanned around his place, nothing seemed out of the ordinary, unless you counted the painting by Matisse that was noticeably missing from its place of honor over the fireplace. And the fact that every picture in the apartment of Michael and Max together had one eensy-weensy peculiarity: Max's head had been cut out. Sensing that the pin might be out of the grenade, I decided to handle Michael very gently.

"So . . . you're lookin' good, Michael." I thought a compliment would be just the thing to break the ice.

"Of course I am. I've got a reputation to uphold, you know."

Good. Keep him talking. Steady, now.

"So, Michael," I asked hesitatingly. "Weird weather we've been having lately, isn't it? House on Fire Island opened yet?"

"Yeah. I thought I might go out this weekend," Michael said as he rose from a sofa and headed off to a closet down the hall. "They say it's supposed to be much cooler than normal this summer. El Banjo or something."

"Niño. El Niño. It's over," I added gently, realizing that I shouldn't contradict or correct him.

"Whatever."

His voice grew louder as he returned, package in hand. Without breaking stride in the conversation, Michael tore open the package to reveal a particularly nasty-looking rifle topped by enough high-tech gadgetry to make the Pentagon drool with envy. Michael was making progress in confronting his hostility toward Max: he was obviously going to kill him. I decided to remain cagey about the whole matter.

"Michael?" I asked politely.

"Yes, Robert?"

"What's that?"

"This? It's a rifle."

"I can see that. It looks like a *nice* rifle."

"It *is* a nice rifle, Robert. A real beaut. Cost me a pretty penny. Bought it from some Lebanese guy over in Astoria. It's a British-made L85 rifle with a laser-guided targeting device and a night vision scope. Makes it easier to find your prey in the dark. Why, Robert?"

"Oh, just asking." Michael never failed to amaze me. Because of his wealth and endless sexual connections, he could produce anything from stolen works of art to embarrassing photographs of celebrities if he wanted. If I were to walk into Michael's apartment and see the Mona Lisa hanging on a wall, I wouldn't be surprised.

"I can see right through you, Robert. You think I bought this gun so I could hunt Max down and kill him in cold blood."

"Well, didn't you?"

"Of course I did, but I just wanted you to know how completely transparent you are. Yes, I am going to find that son of a bitch and make him pay for what he did to me. He made me the laughingstock of all of New York. I've spent a lifetime carefully cultivating an image of a sophisticated, urbane gay male who is arguably the most gorgeous man in New York, with, mind you, an unbroken record of sexual conquests that run the gamut from the most depraved to the sublime. Then, in less than a month's time, the bastard breaks my balls in front of a thousand—"

"Fifteen hundred," I corrected. "That's what Oliver's billing you for."

"Fine, breaks my balls in front of fifteen hundred of my most intimate friends, comes back here, ransacks my apartment, and to top it off, helps himself to my beloved Picasso."

"Matisse."

"Whatever."

"Michael, you never cared a fig for that picture," I pointed out.

"I cared that it was worth a fortune! That picture gave

me financial security. My mother or my trust officer could never take it away from me because my grandmother left it to me in her will. If my mother ever decided to cut me off, I could always sell it."

"You said it was insured," I countered.

"It is. But do you know how long I have to wait to get reimbursed? Months! Years, maybe! The insurance company has to be sure that the thing won't turn up later after they've given me the money."

"Because a person like you would've spent the money by then, wouldn't you?"

"Of course. That's why I've got to put up with a police detective coming over here asking me a lot of stupid questions. The insurance company needs an official report."

Michael's doorman buzzed the intercom, alerting him that there was someone in the lobby who wanted to come up. "That's probably him now."

I looked deep into Michael's eyes and, in my best school marm voice, warned him, "Listen, Michael. Since there will soon be a member of the New York Police Department—"

"Special Investigative Services," Michael added.

"Whatever." I continued, "Now, as much as the idea of having a real cop in your apartment should send your libido erupting with testosterone like a horny Mount St. Helens—"

"Don't be silly, Robert. This guy is a special investigator. He's not going to be hot. The really hot ones are the ones on motorcycles or horseback."

"Okay, but the point is, Mr. Policeman probably wouldn't look too kindly on illegal, terrorist-class firearms in the hands of ordinary citizens. Maybe you should put the gun away in a safe hiding place until the police are gone. Then we can talk about you blowing holes in Max in a calm, rational manner."

"If you insist," Michael replied, trying to give as little ground as possible. "I guess I don't have time to show you the grenade launcher I bought?"

There's nothing worse than an only child. Let me modify that last remark. There's nothing worse than an only child when he also happens to be gay, spoiled, and rich.

Soon there was a knock at the door. In Michael's absence, I answered it.

"Sergeant Peter Rickels, Special Investigative Department. Mr. Michael Stark?"

"No, I'm just a friend, but come on in. Michael's just seeing to a little problem. He'll be back in a second. Care for a drink?" I offered.

"No, thanks. I'm on duty."

"Oh, of course. How silly of me! I wonder what's keeping Michael? MICHAEL! IF YOU'RE THROUGH PUTTING YOUR PACKAGE AWAY, THE SERGEANT IS HERE FROM THE POLICE DEPARTMENT!"

As I sat across from our man in blue, he seemed more typical than I had imagined. Despite his "civilian" dress, he looked every bit the cop. Big, clunky black police oxfords on his feet, black nylon socks, a cheap navy blue suit, white dress shirt (short-sleeved, no doubt), topped off with a textured polyester tie. I could see the tie in question being sold on a Home Shopping Channel TV program. As it rotated on the royal blue velvet stand, I could almost hear the announcer intoning that the tie was not only washable, but had a half-life of fourteen million years. The only thing I found unexpected about the inspector was his age. He seemed to be relatively young: maybe thirty-five, thirty-six.

"I'm Michael Stark and I'm gay. Hopelessly so," Michael trumpeted as he entered the room.

"Fine," the sergeant replied, not knowing what to say. The sergeant opened a small spiral-bound notepad and began scribbling with a well-chewed pencil.

"I just wanted to get that out of the way, because it was bound to come up," Michael said as he continued his breakneck conversation. "You see, I was going to get married to this guy and he jilts me at the altar, comes back here and steals my painting, then takes off for parts unknown. Screwed me real good. In more ways than one. And he had the nerve to do it the morning of the wedding. I'm still having trouble walking."

Sensing that the sergeant was in way over his head, I intervened.

"Michael, I think that Sergeant Rickels wants to get your story from the beginning. You're getting a little ahead of yourself," I said through gritted teeth.

"Right. That makes sense. Well, I met this guy a month ago in front of The Rack."

"The Rack?" Sergeant Rickels seemed mystified.

"It's a leather bar on Christopher Street. It's a bar where investment bankers from Wall Street hang out so that burly men with scary tattoos and big mustaches can pick them up and take them home and tie them up and drop hot wax on their genitals."

"I see, Mr. Stark. Please continue."

"I wasn't inside The Rack, I was just in *front* of it. But I go there all the time. So after I bring this guy home and we screw each other, I start to fall in love with him—Max. Max Crawford. I mean, he seemed so nice and caring. Well, we start dating, which is a real change for me since I normally love 'em and leave 'em."

Michael was making enough social gaffes to make Miss Manners throw up.

"Did this Max have an apartment here in the city?" the sergeant asked.

"Yeah, but I've never seen it. Max preferred to spend the night here since it's bigger and more comfortable. He said his place was small, roach-infested, and overpriced. Naturally, who'd want to spend time there? Don't bother calling. The number's been disconnected."

"Where did this Max work, Mr. Stark?" asked the sergeant.

"Please, call me Michael. Everyone else does."

"I thought everyone else called you 'slut,' Michael," I added.

"Okay . . . Michael." The sergeant was clearly as uncomfortable as Gloria Vanderbilt at a monster truck pull.

"Please continue . . . Michael."

"Max told me he worked at a Dewey & Cheetham, on Fifty-first Street and Third Avenue. Don't bother writing it down. It doesn't exist."

"It wasn't Dewy, Cheetham & Howe, was it?"

"Did Max tell you that too?" Michael asked in earnest.

"Michael! Oh for God's sake. Dewey, Cheetham & Howe! That one's so old . . ." I broke off, incredulous. I said it before and I'll say it again: it's a good thing Michael is buff and rich.

Sergeant Rickels scribbled furiously. The look of perplexity on both his face and mine was apparent.

Michael continued. "I called right after I got back here from the church. The number's disconnected there too. Just like the one Max gave me for his apartment. Maybe I ought to buy some swampland in Florida while I'm on a roll."

"Don't be too hard on yourself, Mr . . . Michael. This guy Max is a real professional. Could I have Max's office and home numbers?" the sergeant asked.

Michael went over to a Rolodex sitting on a desktop, took out a card, and handed it to the sergeant. "You might as well keep it. It's not going to do me any good."

"I can trace these numbers and find out where the calls came from. I'll go visit the apartments or offices where the calls originated, then look for evidence there. That's a real good start. Is there anything else you can tell me about Max? Did he ever talk about where he might've grown up, where he went to school?"

Michael looked up toward heaven as if looking for an answer. "He told me a whole crock of shit about him being from an old Virginia family, the plantation, going to Princeton, all that stuff. About as genuine as Cher's face."

"Sometimes even the smallest piece of evidence can turn

out to be a gold mine." The sergeant stared at his notepad. "Mr. Stark, you said that this Max worked out a lot. Was he overly muscular?"

Michael snorted with ironic laughter. "He was built like a brick shithouse. Ask anyone who was at Robert's apartment the night of my stag party. He was dancing around like a professional stripper, the no-good whore. Why do you want to know?"

"Well, that means that he probably belonged to a gym. You don't get a great physique using home gym equipment."

"You should tell that to Robert here. That Abdominizer of his hasn't done him one bit of good. Oh, well. Changing gears here, Mr. Rickels, I know it's hard to know such things, but do you have any idea how long it might take for you to find that bottom feeder and the painting he stole? Just a ballpark."

"Mr. Stark, I don't want to promise you anything only to let you down if the investigation takes longer than expected. I need to act on these clues and see where they lead. Is there anything else about Max that struck you as different?"

"You mean like the tattoo on his arm?"

"No, not exactly like that, Mr. Stark. Anything that struck you as odd about him?"

"Now that you mention it . . ." Michael started.

"Good, good. Things like this can be important," Sergeant Rickels said, his eyes widening with anticipation.

"Max never had a hardon in the morning. Never! Now that's odd, according to my experience."

I was about to break into raucous laughter, but I noticed that Michael wasn't laughing. He actually thought that this might be a piece of important evidence. This was so Michael. He could talk for hours making common sense; then suddenly, without warning, some synapse in his brain would go dead, leaving his thought to struggle its way through some other unrelated portion of his memory, picking up useless bits of information on the trip. I decided that it would be a good idea to send Mr. Rickels on his way before he abandoned all hope. The look on his face was beginning to betray the idea that this case was clearly a police department booby prize and he, the unlucky recipient.

"All I can say is that when I get my hands on that little scumbag, I'm going to kill him. I swear it," Michael said with all seriousness.

The detective wrote this comment down. "Maybe, Mr. Stark, we shouldn't say things we don't mean."

"Oh, I mean it, all right," came Michael's reply.

I decided to change the course of conversation. "Well, Mr. Rickels, I think Michael has said all he can for now. And more. If we think of anything else, we'll call you at the number you've left us."

With that, I ushered the sergeant out the door, hinting that Michael's unorthodox responses were a result of the extreme stress he was undergoing.

Michael looked at me from across the room as I returned. "Well, I am certainly not going to wait around until doomsday for that bumbling idiot to retrieve my painting. I'm going to go find it myself."

The scary thing was, I believed Michael was telling the truth.

I had just settled down for a comfortable evening reading about feminine deodorant sprays when the buzzer blared from my kitchen wall. By the time I had reached it, the obnoxious person at the other end had buzzed me no less than fifteen times.

"Yes, who is it?" I asked.

"It's me, Michael! I've found Max! You've got to come with me!" Michael screamed breathlessly into my ear. "Get your butt down here now so I can show you."

Since my heart wasn't really into the required reading for my job, I jumped—no, leaped—on the chance to avoid something I did not know, and would never care to know about. Plus, I felt a little rush of adrenaline from the idea of playing detective in solving an art heist.

When I reached my decrepit lobby, Michael was panting like an octogenarian after a hundred-meter dash.

"I've found that son of a bitch! C'mon, I'll show you."

Not wanting to stand in Michael's way when he was on a mission, I let him throw me into a waiting cab.

"Where are we going?" I asked as delicately as possible.

"Just wait. You won't believe it. *I* didn't believe it when I saw it," he exclaimed, and then he fell silent until the cab reached what must have been the seediest part of Times Square. Michael paid the fare and dragged me out of the cab by the arm toward the box office of the Hercules all-male porn theater. There on the marquee, shouting in what seemed to be ten-foot letters, was tonight's double-header cinematic attraction: *Pork Sausages* and *Mellonballer*. "C'mon. I'll pay for you."

I must admit, with all prudishness, that I have never been inside a male porn theater. Sure, I've rented my share of porn videotapes, but that's different. Very different. As we sat down inside the darkened theater, I began to shyly scan the audience to spot Max before Michael pointed him out. While I looked around, I managed to ascertain the kind of people who frequented a place like this. Lots of raincoats although it wasn't raining outside. Men with greasy hair slicked back. I even thought I spotted a hook on the end on one patron's arm. The only thing missing was a dueling scar on his cheek. I unfortunately established eye contact with one patron, causing him to get up out of his seat and move directly behind Michael and me. He gazed greedily at the two of us. I decided not to look around anymore, figuring Max wasn't in the theater yet but would arrive soon.

"When do you think Max'll get here?" I whispered.

"In just a few minutes," Michael spoke back.

I decided to watch the movie. The plot, thinner than a slice of fine prosciutto, revolved around a butcher shop. The only patrons who visited this shop were, of course, young boys in very tight workout shorts, mostly without shirts. Some of the hungry young boys would come into the shop and announce to the butcher's assistant that they wanted a good cut of meat. Top-grade sirloin. Another pleaded that he couldn't afford to pay for the tab he'd run up in the past few weeks—at least not in money. Whatever the predicament, the solution was always the same. The assistant promptly pulled the shades down and went at it with the young boys one by one on the meat chopping block.

Michael was intent on watching the action, no doubt making mental notes to visit a butcher real soon.

As the movie ground on (literally), a sudden break in the action happened. The shop owner suddenly emerged from the refrigerated meat locker catching his assistant and a patron *en flagrante*. He decided to join the action, stripping naked in a matter of moments.

I couldn't believe my eyes! The butcher was none other than Max. I tried to hide my shock but received another jolt when I discovered that all that Michael had said about the size of Max's member was true. Like the movie poster in the lobby said, "This guy has plenty of meat." I won't go into all the sordid details of the movie, only to say that the action then shifted into the meat locker and involved several sides of beef, a foot-long knife-sharpening steel, and the creative use of a meat hook. I decided then and there to become a vegetarian for life.

"Well, there you are. I almost married a porn star. And a bad porn star at that! In a crummy movie. Think of what that could've done to our good family name!" Michael exclaimed, forgetting that he himself had probably put more tarnish on his hallowed namesake in one month than Max could do in thirteen generations.

I found myself unable to take my eyes from the screen. "Whaaa?" I babbled.

"Robert! Stop drooling and listen to me! I'm going to nail that guy's balls to the wall when I get ahold of him!" Michael foamed at the mouth.

"Well, where do we go from here?" I asked naively.

"We're going to stay and watch the end of this. I need to see the credits."

"To see if Edith Head did the costumes?"

"No, to find out who produced the film," Michael shot back.

"I don't think anyone produced this film. I think they just started the cameras rolling and made it up as they went along."

Michael seemed especially annoyed. "Whatever! If I can find out who was responsible for this film, I can probably locate the boys who played in it."

Half an hour later, the credits began to roll, and Michael began jotting down information into a small black book.

"Good, I think we should give these people a call in the morning," Michael triumphantly reported. "Did you want to stay for the next show?"

I looked at Michael in horror. "I don't think so. Are you going to tell Inspector Rickels about this? This could really blow the whole thing open."

"Absolutely not!" Michael retorted. "I'm not here to do this guy's job for him. Plus, what satisfaction am I going to get if I solve this thing, then let the police take care of Max? He'll get off on a technicality or something and I'll be left in the lurch. No way. I'm going to get to him first and hurt him real bad."

"But why bring the police into this at all?" I asked.

Michael looked at me incredulously. "I told you, the insurance company is making me do this. I'm going to give Sergeant Rickels just enough information to keep him busy. I'm the one who's going to serve justice on Max."

"Michael, just what are you planning to do to Max if you find him?"

"Well, at first I was thinking of something crude like castrating him with rusty garden shears. Then I thought of shooting off his pecker, just a little at a time with a shotgun filled with rock salt. Then I thought, no, I'm being too hasty. I want to give this a little thought."

I turned to Michael. "It looks like you have already."

Michael placed a call the next day to Los Angeles as I listened in on one of his extensions.

"Good morning, Star Quality Male Models. How can I help you?" came the voice on the other end of the line.

"Yeees. I am a film deerector and I am looking for a man to use in my next film, *Beachballs*," Michael intoned in a not-altogether-convincing accent of no particular country. "I have seen one of your models in *Pork Sauseeges*, yes?"

"Which model would that be, Mr. . . ."

"Mr. Fr . . . er . . . Fritzenmeijer." Quick thinking was not one of Michael's best traits. "I vas interested in Max Crawford."

You could hear the secretary on the other end tapping the name into a computer.

"Max Crawford. Let's see. Here he is. Right now, he's vacationing on Cape Cod. His schedule says he'll be there through August twenty-fourth. I can give him a ring and see if he's interested. . . ."

"No, dat vill be fine. He ist available. Good! I vill call you back when I decide on a few things. Goodbye." Michael hurriedly hung up the phone.

"Provincetown!" I screamed like a gay Nancy Drew. "Oh, this is going to be too easy, Michael. All you have to do is go up there and nab him."

Michael looked me straight in the face. "What you do you mean, me? You're going, too."

"Oh, no, Michael. I don't want to get wrapped up in this whole thing. Besides, he was your lover. And it's your painting." From the stare he was giving me, I knew getting out of this one was going to be impossible. "How am I going to be able to get out of work?" I pleaded.

"You have vacation coming, don't you?" Michael probed.

"Yes."

"Your workload can be handled by someone else, can't it?"

"Yes."

"You're penniless as usual, aren't you?"

"Yes."

"And that means you'll probably spend your entire vacation at home with your folks in Michigan unless someone like me asks you to go somewhere better, doesn't it?"

"When do we leave?" I asked.

4

Have I Got a Girl for You!

Michael offered to pay for the whole trip and all my expenses, so naturally I protested strenuously, but not too strenuously.

His travel agent found a house for rent in the peak season of summer. Apparently, the house had been rented to three RPQs (Rich Powerful Queens) from Washington who ran a successful interior decorating business in Georgetown. The three partners had recently had a falling out due to a squabble over a young apprentice and consequently had decided not to take the house after all. The house, by the way, was in the quiet west end of town where the tonier (if there was such a term in Provincetown) guest houses were located.

Under normal circumstances, we would have flown to Provincetown, but that was out of the question. Michael had been involved in so many heated arguments with airline personnel over the weight of his luggage and the number of allowable carry-on pieces that no airline or private charter worth its salt would have anything to do with Michael Stark. The topper was when he opened an emergency exit in a plane sitting at the gate so that he could get out and talk to a particularly hunky baggage handler. Michael swears to this very day that the exit door was loose anyway and that his antic only saved the lives of everyone on board.

Downplaying his being banned, Michael announced that it would be better to take his Range Rover because it was more comfortable and would allow both of us to bring anything we wanted. He took this last statement quite literally. I came with a single suitcase and an L.L. Bean carry-on bag, whereas Michael had bag after bag of clothing—even several suiters. Why was he bringing a suit? I found all of this perplexing since Michael wore nothing but T-shirts, indecently short shorts, and tall, black work boots. When he went dancing at the bars, he wore even less: Calvin Klein underwear, socks, and boots. A shirt was usually optional.

"What's with all the suits? You planning on attending church?" I asked, pointing to the numerous garment bags he loaded into the back of his Rover.

"Suits? These are my police outfits. Those first three bags are all leather, and the rest are various uniforms from cities around the U.S. Look at my pride and joy here," he said, reverently unzipping one bag to show me its contents. "Vintage California Highway Patrol, circa nineteen seventy-five. In mint condition. You couldn't buy one of these babies for love or money," Michael said proudly. "I can get ten dates the instant I walk into a room with this one on."

And to think that I was worried that one of the tank tops I brought was too sleazy because it showed a hint of tit.

Michael also justified driving, since it would allow him to stop in Newport to see his mother. This desire struck me as odd, since he always tried to avoid Newport as much as he could. In contrast, Newport seemed like a wonderful stop to me, with images of Michael and me playing croquet on carefully manicured lawns while servants served Campari and sodas to the parched players.

For most people, the trip from Manhattan to Newport would take about three and a half hours. But since speed limits were made for other people, the trip would be reduced to two and a half. For a while, Michael and I amused ourselves commenting on the various bumper stickers we saw along the way, either being just plain bitchy about them or interpreting their real meanings.

" 'Practice random kindness and senseless acts of beauty,'" I read on one bumper sticker on a car sporting Connecticut license plates. "Translated, I'm a lesbian but I live in a homophobic part of Connecticut, meaning the entire state, and I want to let other lesbians know I'm here but a gay flag would be just too much. What would the neighbors say?"

"Pretty good," Michael commented. "Okay, I've spotted one over there. 'Mean people suck.' "

"HOMOSEXUAL!" we both yelled at the same time.

"Oh, look at that one over there, Robert." "Rejected on earth. Accepted in heaven," it proclaimed. "Loser," was all that Michael had to say.

We drove for a few more miles before I saw one that caught my eye: " 'Nice people swallow.' That one has your name printed all over it, Michael. I'm surprised that you don't have it yet."

"Now there's my favorite," Michael said.

"Where?" I asked.

"Over there. The Saturn. They've got a four-inch gay flag that's barely noticeable because it's elongated to a slit of the rainbow colors."

Michael was absolutely right, I thought. Why hide anymore? This version was so subtle, why even bother putting it on your car? It defeats the whole purpose of showing that gays aren't going to hide anymore. Take Michael for instance. He had no intention of hiding. His Rover had two gay flags on the far left and right sides of the bumpers, but just in case you hadn't gotten the message, the one in the middle said it all so plainly, it embarrassed even me. "BOYS WILL *DO* BOYS," it pronounced. The *do* was in italics. Even Pat Robertson's mother would get it.

I looked over at Michael singing along with one of his

house music CDs blaring over the umpteen speakers in the Rover. He looked so dashing at the wheel: tanned, handsome, impeccably well-dressed, even though he wore as little as he could. How different his life was from mine. A life of shallow pleasures and privileged existence. What went through his mind all the time? Did he have the same fears, the same hopes, the same ambitions as someone like me? What effect did financial independence have on what he thought about?

"I thought woodchucks only came out at night," Michael exclaimed after a particularly loud thump was heard underneath the car. "That's the nice thing about this vehicle. Nothing hurts it."

For such a shallow person, he was such an enigma to me. An even bigger enigma, however, was how I thought about him. I was always wondering what it was like to be him. My feelings toward Michael were a mixture of curiosity, pity, and insane jealousy. Michael was, quite simply, a gay playboy. He could go wherever he wanted and he usually did. He would fly off to Los Angeles on a moment's notice. He'd phone me from Brazil, gushing about how beautiful the men there were. Michael's life was one big fantasy. A string of sexual conquests only briefly interrupted by bouts of shopping trips, expensive lunches, all-night parties with some of the richest and most powerful homosexuals in Manhattan, summers on Fire Island—you name it. But above all, it was sex that powered Michael's engines.

"Michael, I know that you really like sex, but do you find it all that fulfilling?" I finally ventured.

Without his eyes even leaving the road for a second, Michael replied most matter-of-factly, "If you have to ask a question like that, you wouldn't understand if I explained it to you. You know what I think your problem is, Robert?"

"No, what? Not enough hide-the-salami?"

"No. You analyze things too much. You consider every angle to a situation before you act. You stop yourself from enjoying a lot of things in life because you're afraid to take a

leap once in a while. I mean, your idea of living life dangerously is drinking milk after the expiration date."

"I'm a cautious person. Why stick your head in a lion's
mouth if there's a chance of having it bitten off?"

"If you don't stick it in," Michael said as he whipped the
car around a rusty Buick sporting a Christian Coalition
bumper sticker, cutting it off, "you'll never experience the
thrill, either."

"Touché, Michael." Michael's last few words continued
to echo in my head for some time. Years, in fact. I let the
subject drop and was quiet a minute before I spoke again.

"Michael, slow down; there's a cop on the side of the
road," I warned, sounding a little too much like my mother.
Michael, instead of hitting the brakes in a vain attempt to
get down to the legal speed limit, punched the accelerator,
causing the Rover to rocket forward. I turned to look out
the back window only to see the trooper's car turn on its red
and blue lights and tear off from the road's shoulder in a
cloud of dust and smoke. In no time at all, the trooper's car
was on our tail, sirens wailing away.

"I think he wants you to pull off to the side of the road,
Michael."

He slowed down and pulled over, followed closely by the
trooper. Michael made no attempt to find his license or vehicle registration as the trooper approached his window.
The trooper was grinning from ear to ear. I could tell we
were in for one of those you're-in-a-heap-of-trouble-boy
speeches. While I sat there cowering in fear, Michael was
absolutely spellbound by the square-jawed, mirrored-Rayban-
wearing figure of authority standing at his window.

"Could I see your license?" the trooper boomed at Michael.

Michael fumbled for his wallet and pulled out something
and handed it to the trooper, stopping just short of the window in order to make the trooper reach inside to retrieve it.

"This is a condom, sir. I need to see your license."

"Whoops! Now how did that get in there?" Michael puzzled, rolling his eyes innocently heavenward. "Heeeeerrre's my license," Michael said, handing it to the trooper. "You can keep the condom, sir. For later."

Needless to say, the trooper returned the unused condom to Michael.

"If you'll just wait here while I run a check . . ." the trooper instructed him.

As soon as Mr. State Police was out of earshot, Michael exploded with excitement that made him physically tremble. "He is so hot, I could just burn through the floor of this car right now! That dark brown crewcut. That tight outfit!" Michael practically screamed, "Oh, God, I could just feel his gloved hands probing all around my naked body. I can just see it now. He pulls me over for speeding, just like what's happening now. Then he finds out that my license is expired, so he has to take me in for questioning. He strips me naked . . ."

"Michael," I said, trying to re-establish contact.

". . . then he handcuffs me to the bars of the cell."

"Michael."

"He thinks I might be carrying something illegal, so he tells me he has to check every orifice of my body, so he pulls out his nightstick, lubes it up . . ."

"Michael, wake up."

". . . and looks me straight in the eye with those mirrored sunglasses and says that this is really going to hurt, but I'll get used to it. In fact, in time, I will grow to love the pain."

"MICHAEL!" I bellowed. "Snap out of it," I said, shaking him lightly. Michael, bleary-eyed, shook his head like a small child waking from an afternoon nap.

"Where was I? God, It's getting hot in here. . . . Maybe I should turn up the AC!"

I was shocked and appalled. "Michael, I think I'm learning more about you than I care to know."

The trooper returned.

"Here's your license, Mr. Stark."

"Michael, please."

The trooper ignored Michael's comment.

"You were going ninety-five in a fifty-five mile-an-hour zone. Here's your ticket."

"Yes, sir!" Michael barked.

The trooper looked intently at Michael, then spoke. "Didn't I pull you over just last month on this same stretch of road?"

"Yes, sir!"

"And a few months back before that? What is this thing you have going with me?"

"I'm not sure, sir!"

The trooper absorbed this last comment, then began to smile. He let out a chuckle and turned to head back to his patrol car, shaking his head. Michael again waited until the trooper was back in his car when he let out a tremendous whoop.

"Yes! Yes! Yes! I'm breaking him down. I'll have him in bed in no time. Did you see the size of his hands—even through the gloves I can tell he's huge! And that butt! Mama mia!"

As Michael pulled back onto the roadway, I was once again reminded of the fact that he was a true master in the art of seduction. He handed me the ticket and asked me to put it in the glove compartment, which, by the way, was crammed with dozens of yellowed parking and traffic tickets.

"Don't worry. I'll have Mom fix that one. My mom contributes heavily to both political parties in Rhode Island."

We rode on down the freeway to the cranked-up dance hits that played on Michael's CD jukebox. Since he never talked about his mother, and his father had died years ago, I decided to get the inside story to avoid embarrassing faux pas during our brief stay.

"What's your mother like?"

"My mother is a typical mother," Michael reported matter-of-factly.

Now came the real question. "How does she feel about the gay thing?"

"Neither of my parents took it real well when they found out. But it didn't happen under the best of circumstances, either. They caught me and the pool boy in the cabana. I was fourteen."

"Wow," I replied. "That beats the teacher from Tampa who stole my cherry."

"Mother still hasn't totally faced up to it. She tries to act like she's accepted it, but deep down, you can tell she never will. But she's really quite nice. I think the two of you will get along quite well."

Michael turned onto Bellevue Avenue. I had never been to Newport before, so I was amazed by the monstrous size of the houses that lined this famed street. Houses hidden behind imposing gates and strategically placed hedges slipped by my window. It finally dawned on me how much money Michael's family really had. I had some vague definition planted in my head of Michael's family wealth, what umpteen million looked like when translated into houses, apartments, cars, and boats. I was way off. We were talking bazillions. This thought was confirmed as Michael slowed the car and pulled into the driveway of a truly gargantuan stone building guarded by massive black iron gates sporting signs that said "PRIVATE PROPERTY" and "SILENT ALARMS." Michael casually slipped a plastic card into an electronic card-reading device, and the imposing gates swung magically open. As he eased the car up toward the house, I was completely aghast. The house, while not one of the absolutely largest on Bellevue, could still hold its own against its more outlandish neighbors. Clad entirely in limestone, the building had a central entry portico flanked on both sides by two equally impressive wings that disappeared into the distance. A fountain splashed in a central courtyard. The building sported urns and mythical figures hurling thunderbolts and large, heavy objects down on those approaching the house—just the sort of welcome mat you would have expected on the Stark doorstep. Nonetheless, I decided right then and there that I was never going back to my shabby apartment again.

Michael brought me back to reality.

"Robert?"

"Yes, Michael, dear? Just have the servants take care of it, whatever it is. I don't want to be bothered."

"Robert, be serious. I don't want you to say anything about my missing painting."

"I'll be the soul of discretion."

"Good! If Mother found out that it was missing, I'd get a huge lecture on the importance of responsibility and crap like that."

"Well, Michael, you did let a common hustler, correction, a porn star, rip you off for a painting that's worth millions," I intoned.

"Oh, Robert! A little lapse in judgment on my part. We'll be off for P-Town tomorrow, so just forget about the painting for just twenty-four hours, please! We've got all summer to catch and castrate Max. The painting's too hot now for him to try and sell it, so he's going to sit on it for a while. Plus, Max has no idea that we're on to him. It was just coincidence that I saw him in that movie. Mum's the word, now."

There was something I had to know. "Michael, just one question."

"Yes?"

"What were you doing at the porn theater that night?"

"None of your business," he replied and let the matter drop.

No sooner had Michael turned off the ignition, than one of the two immense doors that graced the front of the house opened, and a wrinkled old man in an ill-fitting butler's uniform hurried down the steps to greet us near the tailgate of the Rover.

"So glad to have you with us again, Master Stark."

I thought that they didn't make butlers like this anymore. This guy was straight out of a P. G. Wodehouse novel.

"And this must be your friend, Master Willsop. Welcome to End House."

"Wilcox, you can call him Robert," Michael added.

"Master Robert," Wilcox replied defiantly.

"Robert. Just plain Rob—whatever." Michael's face brightened. "Actually, we also call him Roberta," Michael added, remembering that night we all dressed in drag and went out on the town.

This bit went right over poor old Wilcox's head. "*Roberta*, sir?"

"Never mind. 'Robert' will do." Michael made no attempt to carry anything and even slapped my hand when I went to reach for my bag. "Let Wilcox do it. It keeps him going."

My heart went out to poor old Wilcox, who would no doubt suffer a heart attack from carrying anything heavier than an envelope, but I had to remind myself that I was staying with the Starks. Caring for another human being was out of the question. Michael put his arm through mine and led me toward the front entrance. As we climbed the stairs, Michael's mother emerged, noted our arms locked, scowled for a nanosecond, regained her composure, and then held out her arms so that Michael would be forced to unlink his arm from mine. All of this went unnoticed by Michael, but then again, Michael rarely noticed anything.

His mother was exactly as I had pictured her. Her white hair was cut in a neat but unimaginative style that she had probably been wearing ever since she went to Vassar back in the Stone Age. Her overall appearance was in keeping with her economic status. She had that desiccated, skeletal, tanned look that resembled beef jerky. Her clothes were most likely unimaginably expensive, yet they looked as if they'd come from the Junior League secondhand shop. But most telling of all was the look on her face. Like every overpriviledged Republican woman in America, she sported that unmistakable, permanent grimace-cum-smile. Monette and I called it the "I-smell-poop" look.

"You must be Robert. Michael's told me so much about you." Mrs. Stark strode toward me, extending a bejeweled and liver-spotted hand to shake.

"Glad to meet you, Mrs. Stark." As we politely shook hands, I felt my lower arm turn to ice. The feeling traveled quickly up my arm like a mixture of Benzedrine and Novocain, prompting me to pull my hand away prematurely.

"Julia, please. Sorry . . . I have the coldest hands. Poor circulation, you know. Let's go into the house. Wilcox will take your things."

Mrs. Stark—er, Julia led the way. As we passed up the front steps and into the house, I was transported into a world that I only knew through the pages of home design magazines. Everything in the house was massive. Hall tables were overblown to ridiculous lengths. Chandeliers made futile attempts to look proportional for the rooms to which they had been assigned. The furniture, whether decades or centuries old, was exquisite. And the house, despite its size, was immaculate.

"Why don't you two boys go up to your rooms and freshen up a bit, then maybe we can go down to the pool for some lunch," Julia offered. "Michael, I'm putting Robert in the Chinese Room. Did you want to show him the way? Wilcox will bring your bags up in a few minutes."

"Sure, Mother. This way, Robert."

"Michael, you never told me the place was this big. I should've brought my Roller Blades."

We ascended a massive stairway and proceeded down a hallway that was equally ridiculous.

"This is the room I grew up in . . . and where I lost my virginity to our high school tennis coach, Mr. Anderson," Michael reported longingly as he tossed open the door to his room.

"Michael, I thought you told me that you lost it to the pool boy."

"No, we jerked each other off, but I didn't let him *do* me. No, I saved myself up for a *real* man. Mr. Anderson. Oh, it was magical that first time. No, wait a minute. My swimming instructor was my first—Mr. Clement. No . . . it was Mr. Bruin, the captain of our sailboat. Yeah, that's right, Mr. Bruin."

"Michael, I'm going to need a shot of penicillin before I listen to any more of this story. Where's my room?"

"That one, right across the hall. Get unpacked and I'll come by in about, say, thirty minutes to get you for lunch. I've got to take a hot shower. Ta-ta," Michael said as his door swung shut with a massive clank.

I tried the doorknob, expecting to find the land of Oz on the other side. I wasn't disappointed. The room probably measured seventy by ninety feet with fifteen-foot ceilings. The bed was on a raised platform, giving the appearance that only VIPs slept here. The lamps suggested Chinese. The fabrics suggested Chinese. Even the carpets suggested Chinese. But of course, nothing was real Chinese, God forbid. Over the bed was a huge painting of what must have been one of the family ancestors. The bathroom was old and antiquated, with fixtures dating back to the Victorian era. The tub was perhaps the strangest of all because it had not one but two faucets. One admitted plain tap water while the other one was reserved for seawater, heated to a pleasant ninety-six degrees, Michael told me later. I was getting drunk on all this luxury when a small but sour note was soon sounded. When I went to use a towel to dry my face, I discovered a dirty family secret. Embroidered on the back of the towel in plain lettering were the words "HOLIDAY INN." The soap in the soap dish had obviously been swiped from the same hotel. The water from the sink faucet came out brown and full of crud. Yes, dear friends, the rich really are different from you and me—they're cheap. I heard a light knock on the door and in walked Wilcox, huffing and puffing with my overnight bag. I didn't know whether to tip him or not, never having been in this situation before. When in Rome, do as the Romans do, so I asked myself, *What would Mrs. Stark do?* Then I gave Wilcox a hearty thanks and nothing in the way of money.

The moment I opened my bag, something seemed amiss. I knew that I had put my polo shirts right on top, because I thought that I would wear them while in Newport. But there they were, halfway down the pile inside my bag. My shaving kit was unzipped and the contents arranged differently from the way I had packed them in New York. Worse, two of my best pairs of Calvin Klein underwear were missing. Did Wilcox take them? Even if he did, I couldn't really say anything about it. It was just too weird. I decided to put all of this out of my mind and changed for lunch. I did, however, lock my suitcase this time and took the key with me. Presently, there was a knock on the door. I crossed the vast expanse of the room and opened the door.

"Ready for a little lunch?" Michael beamed. "Mother can't wait to get to know you better."

"Devour me, you mean. Michael, I don't think your mom likes me very much."

"Nonsense. She's very warm and caring when you get to know her." Michael hesitated for an instant before continuing, "It's just that some people in this town spread rumors about Mother because they're jealous of her wealth."

My ears shot up. "Rumors? What rumors?"

"Now, Robert. I don't want to dredge up all that stuff about the chauffeur being impaled by Mother. That all happened a long time ago."

I was horrified. "Your mother impaled someone!?"

"Not with her bare hands, Robert. She's not that strong."

"Michael, what do you mean *impaled?*"

"Well, since you must know—and Robert, you must promise not to bring this up again or let this color your judgment of my mother—it happened when I was about fifteen. Mother had the chauffeur drive her downtown to

Harry's Restaurant to have dinner with a friend. When they returned, it was late and raining. The chauffeur went to open the gate—the gate didn't have an automatic opener at the time—and a huge gust of wind caught the gate and slammed it shut. Unfortunately, the chauffeur was standing in the way and the gate sort of hit him."

"But Michael, you said the chauffeur was impaled."

"Okay, so it didn't just hit him. A projecting spike on the gate went right through him."

"Through him?"

"All fifteen inches. There. Are you happy with yourself? The police chief officially reported it as an accident."

"The wind did it, huh?"

"Yes! And why not? Tornadoes have been known to blow cows miles away. Anyway, a witness testified that he saw Mother quarreling with the chauffeur just before the accident, and before you know it, the townspeople jumped to conclusions and said that my mother intentionally killed Markham. Er, Markham was the chauffeur's name. Then, when my mother refused to cancel a party she had scheduled for the very next day, well, the final nail of condemnation was in the coffin, so to speak. People couldn't understand why my mother didn't go into mourning."

"Oh?" I couldn't think of anything to say.

"Robert, my mother doesn't mourn. When my father died in a yachting accident, she actually laughed a lot. So why should she mourn for a mere chauffeur? It wasn't like he was family. Anyway, from that day on, people were looking for any instance where there was even the slightest bit of irregularity involving my mother. So naturally, when Markham's replacement chauffeur fell off Cliff Walk behind our house, fingers were pointed."

"Fell off Cliff Walk?"

"It's a public walk that runs between the big houses and the ocean."

"Is it that treacherous?"

Michael rolled his eyes heavenward. "It is at night."

"And that's when chauffeur number two went for a walk? In the middle of the night?" I asked.

"I forgot to mention that it was in the middle of a storm, too."

Michael just didn't have a clue. "Oh, well, that explains it. Michael, your mother wasn't anywhere near the walk that night, was she?"

"Well, she did run out to find out what had happened to Burroughs. Burroughs was the name of chauffeur number two. Weird, huh?" Michael replied without a hint of suspicion. "Well, there were still a few people who refused to cast the first stone at my mother's innocence, but when Winchell was accidentally electrocuted . . ."

"Michael, let me guess. The replacement for the replacement chauffeur?"

"Correct."

"Okay, let me guess. Winchell was taking a bath when the electric radio he was listening to fell into the bathtub."

"Actually, it was an electric fan. To make a long story short, accusations flew right and left. It's taken years for this dark cloud to pass over, but some people still haven't forgotten the past. Now, Robert, not another word about this. Ever. You promise?"

"Michael, answer this one last question and I'll drop the whole thing."

"Oh, all right, what is it?" Michael asked, the exasperation showing in his voice.

"Were you ever romantically linked with any of the chauffeurs?"

"Romantically? Absolutely not!" Michael answered curtly.

"Let me rephrase that last question. Did you sleep with any of them?"

"Oh, yeah. They were all pretty hot. Plus, Mother used to make them wear those outfits with the jodhpurs and tall black boots. How could I resist? Why? What's that got to do with anything?"

"Oh, nothing. Let's eat."

"Fine. I'm famished." Obviously, Michael believed in his mother's innocence, but I cast a skeptical eye.

As we headed down to the pool for lunch, I wondered if I was dressed properly for a poolside lunch in Newport. Especially at End House. Would a bullet-proof vest go with khaki shorts?

"This is a very beautiful place you have here, Mrs. Stark," I said, fumbling for some way to start the conversation rolling.

"We like it here. So peaceful. So quiet . . . now that the von Bulows moved out."

"Mother," Michael responded. "They didn't exactly move out."

"Okay, got wheeled out on a stretcher. At least Sunny did. Oh, it was completely dreadful. Ambulances screaming up and down their driveway. Reporters dogging me and Mr. Stark all over town, trying to get us to say something terrible about the von Bulows. People climbing over our walls to get a better picture of the von Bulow house. A great big inconvenience, if you ask me. At least Sunny was in a coma. But I had to put up with all this!"

"Mother!" Michael pleaded. "You're giving Robert the wrong idea about us." Michael then turned to me, trying to paint a more saintly picture of the runner-up for the Lucrezia Borgia humanitarian award. "Mother donates a lot of her time to the local charities. She's head of the gardening committee, the historic restoration club, the fundraising committee for historic preservation, and the move to save Cliff Walk. . . ."

Julia began to glow as Michael continued to rattle off her list of accomplishments, ignoring completely the fact that none of the "charities" Michael mentioned were really charities in the humanitarian sense. I didn't hear any mention of the homeless, battered women, or orphaned children. I figured that Julia strenuously avoided any charity where you had to meet the recipients. Plus, joining such ethnically tainted charities would be an admission that such conditions existed in Newport.

"Michael, stop," Julia said giddily. "You're embarrassing me. I just think of all my efforts as something that I owe society. And my Maker. The way I see it, we all have to contribute something to this earth."

Julia babbled hypocritically for some time, but eventually she broke the train of conversation.

"Michael, I'm inviting a few people over for cocktails tonight. I'd be so happy if you and Robert would attend. Does that sound good to you, Robert?"

I noticed that Julia didn't even bother to ask Michael, fearing that he didn't bear the guilt that I did as a guest at End House. What choice did I have? "Why, that would be lovely, Mrs. Stark."

"Julia, please."

"Forgive me. Julia."

"Well, I'll go tell Wilcox to expect you two as well." She rose from the table and began to walk toward the house when Michael interrupted her.

"Mother, who's coming tonight?"

"Just Binky and Margot. They just got back from Russia. You should see the things they picked up for practically nothing. Icons, gold Russian crucifixes . . . They need the hard currency there so badly. I guess one person's loss is another one's gain. Oh, and Roger Marteen said he'd try and make it. Now, why don't you two boys go for a swim or, better, yet, Michael, why don't you take Robert for a tour of the town. Have you ever been to Newport before, Robert?"

"No, this is my first time."

"Well, see! Michael, take Robert around and show him the sights."

After Julia was out of earshot, Michael appeared to be lost in thought, which I have to admit was a new look for him.

"What's the matter, Mikey?"

"Oh, nothing. I was just wondering. Anyway, why don't we finish our lunch, then head out for a little sight-seeing. All I have to do is drop my name and we'll be able to go into any place in town."

We finished our lunches, helping ourselves to a second bottle of French Chablis before we headed out on the town. Michael and I played tourists and drifted from one historic mansion to another until I was numb from the extravagant display of wealth. Knowing that I was an antique buff, Michael suggested that we head downtown and poke in some of the shops there. We went from store to store, bumping into scads of men Michael had tricked with when he lived in town. As we left one particularly snooty store, I noticed one particularly odd-looking man who seemed to be following us. When I mentioned this to Michael, he merely replied that this guy was obviously trying to cruise him.

"What makes you think he's cruising you, Michael? Who am I? Walter Matthau?"

"Robert, I caught him looking right at me. So there."

I decided to let this one go, especially since this guy was a pretty sad specimen of a gay man living in the new millenium. Everything seemed to be wrong about him—at least for a gay man. In all candor, I'd be the first to agree that the biggest myth in homosexuality is that all gay men look terrific and know how to wear clothes. But this guy seemed all wrong from the word go. His clothes didn't have the carefully put-together look of a gay man. His shoes were cheap. And his hair was obviously cut by a straight man. A barber, no doubt. Michael could have him. But before I had time to write up any more fashion citations in my mind, our pursuer had tired of the chase and disappeared down the narrow streets of old Newport. Oh well, no matter. There were more important things to think about. Like dinner.

Cocktails were called for at eight, so I left my room at the appointed hour only to meet Michael coming out of his

SOMEONE KILLED HIS BOYFRIEND 97

room at exactly the same time. Punctuality was never one of Michael's strong points, but it became one when he was on his mother's turf. Julia, who was nowhere to be seen a moment ago, suddenly appeared at my shoulder, unusually happy, mumbling something about having the cook prepare Michael's favorite food for tonight's dinner. We all had just begun to descend the imposing stairs, with Michael at my side, when I felt the ground slipping out from under me. Like a slow-motion scene from some murder mystery movie, I tumbled head over heels down the marble steps. When I came to a stop at the bottom, I looked up to see Michael bounding toward me.

"Are you all right, Robert!? I told Mother not to have the steps waxed when guests are coming."

"Yeah, I'm okay. A little shaken, but intact. Clumsiness, I guess. Think nothing of it."

Mrs. Stark, who stood immobile at the top of the stairs, finally descended, made a feeble gesture of helping me up, and suggested that we all go into the music room for cocktails, then dinner. Perhaps my mind was playing tricks on me, considering the unreal nature of this house, but as we passed into the dining room, I had the most curious feeling that I'd been pushed.

I must admit that one of the most egregious losses to modern living is the passing of the cocktail hour. As we sat there, all dressed up, I was truly struck by how pleasant some of these older customs really were. At the same time, another thought struck me: cocktails must have been invented by a homosexual.

"So Michael tells me that you're a writer," Julia asked, feigning interest in me.

"No, a copywriter for an advertising agency in New York. I think up ads and commercials." This comment was greeted with a blank stare. "It's not worth talking about. Pretty boring stuff. You know, femin—never mind." I shut up.

Julia took this lull in the conversation to plan her attack.

"Michael, Mr. Reeves from the foundation called to tell me that you didn't attend the last board meeting. He said that you declined for personal reasons."

"Mom, it *was* something personal," Michael whined. Probably some trick he had picked up and didn't want to kick out . . . right away.

"Well, in that case, you're forgiven. Just don't miss any more meetings," Julia replied, waving her little finger reproachfully at Michael. "After all, this is supposed to be your job. You need some kind of work to give you a center in your life, Michael."

"Dad never did," Michael countered. "I never saw him work."

"Your father did lots of work when he was alive!" Julia said, returning Michael's serve. "Do you think those barnacles just magically disappeared off our yacht? No siree."

"Dad didn't scrape them off personally, Mother," Michael protested.

"No, but he gave the orders, didn't he? And followed up on them too! If he wasn't sitting there with a Manhattan in hand watching the workmen, they'd complain all day about their bloody knuckles and there would still be spots on the hull they missed. It's like dear old Ronnie Reagan always said, you can't let people get away with shoddy service. Anyway, the point is, Michael, I want you to work a little bit for your money. You know, to earn a living."

To give your salary some justification, I thought. Poor Julia must have felt that she just couldn't give Michael money. She obviously concocted a sham position at the Stark Foundation to keep Michael under some sort of control. But it worked. When you had Michael by the finances, his heart and mind would follow.

As Michael and his mother continued their symbiotic conversation, I began to realize that no matter how much she seemed to disapprove of Michael's lifestyle, he could do no wrong. In reality, he could do anything and she would approve of his behavior. *Practically* anything.

"*Michael, Mr. Templeton at the foundation tells me that last week you shot a man just to watch him die.*"

"*That's right, Mother. Killed him in cold blood. Can I have another drink?*"

"*Oh, you mischievous little scamp. Good for you. I was beginning to think you had none of the spunk we Starks are known for. And I guess that the story about you driving your Rover up on the sidewalk on Fifth Avenue and mowing down a whole crowd of nuns was true as well? Hmmmm?*"

"*Oh, Mom. You know how I hate to wait for stoplights.*"

"*Now really, Michael, just because I told you that only the little people obey stoplights, I didn't expect you to take me literally.*"

"*For God's sake, Mother, it's not like they were Episcopalians or something.*"

"*You're quite right. I don't want you to get overly worried about the loss of people from lower socioeconomic levels of society.*"

I was suddenly shaken out of my fantasy when Wilcox appeared in my face asking if I wanted another stuffed quail's egg.

When it came down to it, my fantasy wasn't far from the truth. For as long as I had known Michael, he had pretty much acted exactly like in the scene I had just imagined. He ran red lights, treated salespeople and servants abominably, left every lamp and appliance on in his apartment, never recycled, heated the pool at his Fire Island home practically year-round yet rarely swam in it, and threw out mountains of uneaten food. Like mother, like son, I thought.

Wilcox, who had disappeared for a while, reappeared, announcing to Julia that tonight's guest had arrived for dinner. Michael, who had been relatively docile throughout the entire cocktail hour, suddenly was flushed with a mixture of anger and frustration.

He spun around to face his mother. "Mother, you said Binky and his wife were coming to dinner. Roger, too."

"They couldn't make it. So I had to make a last-minute appeal to someone else," she replied with the evasiveness of G. Gordon Liddy at a Watergate hearing.

"It wouldn't happen to be Lauren Mitherton, would it, Mother?"

"Honestly, Michael. She's a nice girl. I'm sure that if you'd give her half a chance—"

"Oh for God's sake, Mother," Michael fired back. "I'm not sure this is a good idea. . . ."

Julia headed Michael off. "Michael, just give Lauren a chance. Let's not discuss this right now. She's waiting and I don't want you to be anything less than gracious. Remember, you're a Stark." Julia hurried out the doorway to greet her guest, but not so quickly that she didn't have time to fire a this-is-all-your-fault look at me out the side of her eyes. Michael, who was justifiably angry, also knew what side his bread was buttered on, and he merely shook his head, resigned to the embarrassing fact that Mommie Dearest was the only person on God's green earth who could yank his chain.

Michael, seeing the need to explain what was to come, pulled me aside to give me the dirt on Lauren. She was once one of Newport's most eligible debutantes and a complete nymphomaniac. The fact that she was talked about behind her back seemed not to bother her one bit. Lauren had but one mission that she wanted to accomplish: to marry someone as filthy rich as Michael. She, like most of Newport, knew that Michael was so gay, you could spot him from a plane. This didn't matter to Lauren, because Seacrest, the Bellevue Avenue mansion she had inherited from her parents, was crumbling about her ears due to her late parents' parsimony. Money was all that mattered. Despite her appearing to be a thoroughly modern woman, she clung to the old idea that she would live out all her days throwing the sort of glamorous balls that, frankly, had disappeared with mink stoles.

Julia, for her part, was only too happy to tap into Lauren's desire. She knew in her heart that her Michael was gay. So did Lauren. But Julia found in Lauren that overwhelming desire to convert her gay son into a respectable married man, albeit a gay one. Also, Julia had discovered that Lauren could be ruthless when it came to getting what she wanted, so there was a common personal characteristic. And anyway, even if Lauren would function as no more than just a cover marriage, with Michael being periodically discovered sucking dick in the locker room at the country club, so be it. Lauren would spend the rest of her life in Newport and not go gallivanting off to vulgar cities like Los Angeles, Paris, or Milan. No siree. Born in Newport, die in Newport, Julia liked to say.

From afar, I could hear Julia's excited voice mingled with what was obviously Lauren's. Presently, Julia burst into the room leading Lauren by the hand like some prized possession for all to see. I half expected to hear a blare of trumpets.

"Michael, you remember Lauren," Julia said as she practically threw Lauren in Michael's face.

Michael, who initially looked at Lauren as if she were a spitting cobra, suddenly lit up, then put his arm around her as if she were an old pal, leading her toward the drinks tray. "How nice to see you again, Lauren."

Lauren was taken aback by Michael's friendliness. "Michael, it's been years! Why, look at you—so handsome and all grown up now!"

"Lauren, why don't I take you over here and make you a drink?" Michael said as he led her off to the liquor. They talked briefly in low, hushed tones, then returned, saving me from the uncomfortable silence that ensued whenever I was left alone with Julia.

Julia seemed abnormally pleased until she noticed Lauren's empty hand. "Wilcox!" she called out. "A drink for Lauren. And Michael, you look like you could use another. Now where is Wilcox?"

Never mind that Michael had barely touched his glass.

Before he could utter a word of protest, Julia had swept the glass out of his hand and set it carelessly on a priceless piece of furniture. She disappeared for a minute, then returned with two drinks in hand. Lauren took hers, then finished off the contents faster than Ray Milland in *Lost Weekend*. Michael took a small sip, then choked loudly.

"Mother!" Michael exclaimed. "You should never make drinks. You make them far too strong."

Julia brushed this comment aside. "Why don't we start making our way in to dinner? It's eight-thirty already." She herded us all into an adjacent room that would have done the Vanderbilts proud. The table was so lavishly set and decorated with flowers, Evelyn Waugh would have cried. The dining table must have been eighty feet long if it was an inch. It was set for dinner on one end in a lost attempt to make the setting more intimate. Julia directed everyone to sit where the little name cards indicated. As everyone made their way to their seats, I searched in vain for mine. I finally found it: I was seated behind a huge floral display that completely blocked my view of practically everyone else at the table. I was about to protest, but apparently everyone else was happily seated, so I decided not to make a big deal about it.

Course after course of bland, overcooked food on silver trays appeared at our table, carried by Wilcox and two other butlers. Conversation was equally dull, with Julia going on and on about Wimbledon, yacht races, and fundraising efforts to preserve the mansions of Newport. Throughout all this, Michael was paying an unusual amount of attention to Lauren, who, not surprisingly, was returning his advances.

"So much has happened in my life lately. I feel like I've changed a lot since I was last here," Michael suddenly piped up, interrupting Julia's conversation.

"What? Last month?" Julia replied, not quite getting what Michael was trying to convey.

"Well, it hit me the other day how much I'm wasting my life. It's party, party, party in New York, but I don't feel sat-

isfied. Down deep, that is. I feel that I need someone to share my life with. To give it some meaning. Now, where am I going to find a person who could give me that?"

Julia, who had been egging Lauren on to join Michael in conversation throughout the night, was utterly dumbfounded. She couldn't believe her ears, but she truly wanted to more than anything else in the world. "Well, Michael, sometimes it's easier than you think. Sometimes the answer is *right* in front of you."

Michael looked across the table, saw Lauren, and smiled. He giggled.

This was getting too weird. Michael just wasn't himself tonight. But a mother like Julia could make even Oscar Wilde straight. As long as Michael held court in New York, he never did what anyone asked of him. But here on Julia's turf, Michael was spaghetti in his mother's hands. What strange power did she have over him? Money, money, and money, in that order. He would do anything to get his hands on it. He would lie like crazy just to get the money that fueled his lifestyle—a lifestyle that only got seven miles to the gallon. And now the big question: Would he sleep with Lauren just to get it?

Julia's face was lit up like a Park Avenue matron's at a Sotheby's red tag sale. "Flexibility is the key to happiness in life, you know, Michael."

Michael seemed to accept this advice from Julia. Even though conversation then drifted back toward local events, the four of us became extremely watchful of anything happening around our table. Julia would steal quick glances at Michael; then Lauren stole glances at Michael, then at me and so on. It was like being in an Agatha Christie mystery: all of us possessing hidden agendas and unsuspected poisons.

The conversation droned on for some time, but the real center of attention was Michael and Lauren, who were still looking at each other almost without pause. It was Michael who broke the tedium.

"Well, it looks like I'm going to bed now. I just want to talk over a few things with Lauren, so if you don't mind excusing us . . ."

"Not at all," Julia replied happily, blood dripping from her lips. "Robert and I were just going into the sitting room," she added, grabbing my hand in her liver-spotted vise grip and leading me to an uncomfortable antique sofa, where she sat close beside me.

"A good night to all, and to all a good night," Michael bellowed as he led Lauren out of the room and upstairs. "Mother?" Michael called as he disappeared.

"What is it, Michael?"

"You're the greatest mother."

"Thank you, Michael. And you're the greatest son."

I had just passed through the looking glass with Alice. Michael was showing signs of converting to heterosexuality and had just gone off—willingly—with Newport's version of Cruella De Vil. I tried to explain it all away, that people do act differently in front of their parents. Julia was plainly satisfied that she'd thrown her son into the clutches of Lauren. I could just see her rationalizing that it's better to have her gay son sire a child than waste his sperm in a condom up the butts of thousands of men. Was I the only sane person left in this house?

"Well, Robert, that leaves you and me. Now . . . what shall we talk about?"

"If you don't mind, Mrs. Stark . . ."

"Julia."

"Oh, yes, Julia. I think I better go check on Michael to see if he's all right. He's had a lot to drink and he doesn't seem to be himself."

"And that's bad?" Julia interjected.

"Well, I'm his best friend, and I'd feel terrible if something happened to him. I'll just run up real quick—"

I started to get up from the couch where I had been sitting, but Julia's hand darted out like a cobra and caught me by the arm, forcing me back down into my seat.

"Robert, Michael's just fine, so why don't you sit here and keep me company? Or . . . tell you what . . . why don't we go out on the grounds for a walk?"

Visions of Julia pushing me off a cliff went through my head. "The grounds, you say? That sounds lovely, but I kinda like it right here. So warm and well lit." So full of witnesses, I thought, eyeing the servants nearby.

"So you're Michael's best friend. So what do you two do together in New York? I'll bet you go to a lot of bars."

"Oh, not too many. Although Michael and I go out a fair amount, I don't tag alongside him all the time. Michael's lifestyle allows him a little more freedom in his schedule. I, unfortunately, have to work."

"That's too bad," Julia said, sounding truly sorry for my predicament.

Despite the fact that my impatience was about to explode, Julia and I continued our inane conversation for over an hour, while I let out a series of overly obvious yawns. Julia, sensing that I could no longer thwart her plans, allowed me to go upstairs. She didn't trust me completely, because she chaperoned me up the stairs, one arm around my shoulder. When we came to my door, she released me.

"I just thought you'd need some help finding your room. It's easy to forget where it is in a house this size." As she casually strolled down the hall in the direction of her lair, I started to creep across the hall to Michael's room, when Julia turned suddenly and called out, "We usually have breakfast served to each room in the morning. Wilcox will leave it outside your door. Coffee, eggs, toast, orange juice. Does that sound okay, Robert?"

I wiped the guilty look off my face and replied, "Oh, that would be fine."

"Good. See you in the morning, Robert. Sleep tight," she said as she disappeared around the corner and headed for her web.

I distinctly thought I heard her quietly snicker as she disappeared.

I waited a moment, then tiptoed across the hall to Michael's room. Not a single sound came from the other side of the door, so I decided that the situation called for me to let things lie and try to pick up the pieces in the morning. What's done is done. I went back to my room and closed the door, turning the key and locking it securely. The hour was late, but since this was my only night in such luxurious surroundings, I decided to fill the tub with sea water and just soak for a while.

I had to run the sea-water taps for almost ten minutes before the water ran clear, but eventually my patience paid off and I was rewarded with a tubfull of hot salt water. I poured a glass of sherry from the decanter that was thoughtfully left in my room and climbed into the tub, wondering what the poor people were doing tonight. Minutes passed like hours. I was just about to doze off completely when there was a tremendous crash in the other room. I couldn't see anything from where I was soaking, but the crash was loud enough to wake the dead. I got up carefully, put on my robe, and crept timidly into the room, expecting to find a burglar, but what I found was no less startling. The huge painting of some Stark family member had fallen off the wall and landed directly on my bed. If I had been in bed sleeping, the heavy carved frame would have done serious damage to my skull. I tried to convince myself that it was just another coincidental accident until I looked at the title on the painting, affixed on a metal plate at the bottom of the frame: "Julia Stark, 1936" it said.

Rather than end up as another of Julia's long line of victims, I decided to listen to my thoughts of self-preservation and take matters in my own hands. I crawled under a very heavy table and spent the night there, fruitlessly trying to sleep. I must have finally dozed off in the wee hours of the morning, but was awakened at 8:30 by a knock on my door.

"Yes? Who is it?" I asked, hoping it wasn't Julia brandishing a kitchen knife.

No answer.

I tried again. "Is somebody there?"

Still no answer. I decided to get it over with once and for all. I unlatched the door and threw it open suddenly, only to find that it had been Wilcox leaving the morning's breakfast trays in front of each door. There was an identical tray across the hall in front of Michael's. I stooped down and retrieved the small card that had been left next to the Spode (I checked) coddled egg container. The card was printed on a very florid, very expensive paper, and contained just five words: *Hope you slept well, Julia.*

Julia had poisoned my eggs. I just knew it. Call me paranoid, but there was no way I was going to eat that breakfast. Without a second thought, I grabbed my tray and hurried across the hall to Michael's door, where I quickly switched my tray with his. If there was nothing wrong with the food, no one would be the wiser. If the food was poisoned, well . . . tough.

Seconds after I had switched the tray and was picking up Michael's, the door opened, with Michael looking as chipper as ever.

"Robert, so thoughtful of you to bring me my breakfast," he said, grabbing his tray back from my treacherous hands. "And I see that you brought yours too! Why don't you grab yours and come on in and we'll have breakfast together."

I bent over and picked up my tray as if it were a rattlesnake. Michael led me over to a balcony and pointed to a table, where he commanded me to sit. He placed his tray down and proceeded to eat heartily. The only thing that looked "safe" was the toast, so I nibbled on that.

"Could I have some of your jelly, Michael?" I pleaded.

"You've got some right there on your tray, see?"

"Oh, but yours looks so much nicer. All full of great big strawberries."

"Whatever. Here."

"Thank you ever so much."

"You're welcome, Robert. Now, we can pack after breakfast and head off for—"

"Michael?"

"What, Robert?"

"Can I have some of your coffee?"

"Fine, Robert. Now, as I was saying—"

"Michael?"

"Robert, what now?! You're starting to annoy the shit out of me."

"Your eggs. Can I have a spoonful?"

"Yes, anything. Just let me finish one sentence without you interrupting me. Let's finish breakfast, pack, and get on the road."

"Michael?"

"YES?!!! OKAY, ROBERT, YOU CAN HAVE MY WHOLE GODDAMNED BREAKFAST! HERE! HAVE MY EGGS. EAT MY TOAST. DRINK MY COFFEE. ARE YOU SATISFIED?"

"Actually, Michael, I was going to ask you about what happened last night."

He quieted down instantly. "I don't want to talk about it."

My universe suddenly made no sense. Michael, the most confirmed homosexual ever to have walked this planet besides Liberace, had slept with a woman.

"Michael, I can't believe what I'm hearing."

He fixed me with his two brown eyes and clenched his teeth so tightly, I thought they would shatter in my face. "I don't want to talk about it, Robert. Do you UNDERSTAND THAT?!"

I didn't know what to say, except, "Fine, Michael. I won't breathe a word of it."

He relaxed a bit. "Thank you. Now, can you finish my breakfast so we can get going?"

"I'm not hungry anymore."

"Okay, let's start packing. I'll tell Mother we're leaving."

Michael got up from the table and went into the bathroom. Taking this as my cue, I grabbed another spoonful of eggs and headed back to my room to shower and pack. We were leaving Hell—I mean End House, and I had survived.

I met Michael downstairs, where we unloaded everything on Wilcox to carry out to the car. Julia came down to see us off. She was looking unusually happy this morning.

"Michael, I'm so glad you stopped by to see your devoted mother. I'm so glad to see you again. Oh, and Lauren called this morning to tell me to thank you for you-know-what—whatever that means," Julia reported, as innocently as Hitler pretending he had no idea what his troops were doing in Poland.

Michael was especially affectionate in front of his mother. No one was acting normal this morning.

"Bye, Mother. It was a visit I'll never forget. I feel like a new man."

Julia was so happy, she was visibly shaking. "Oh, Michael, you don't know how happy I am to hear that."

"Well, Mother, thanks for everything. Robert, we're ready to go."

Michael and I climbed into his Range Rover, waved to Julia and Wilcox, and drove through the gates to freedom.

We drove in silence for some time, then Michael broke the ice.

"Robert, I'm sorry that I was so short with you during breakfast. I had my reasons."

"I understand. I imagine how confused you must feel."

"Confused!?" Michael blurted out, then he started laughing. "I knew exactly what I was doing."

Now I was the one who was confused. "You willingly slept with Lauren?"

Michael burst out in a fit of laughing so loud, I thought he was going to drive off the road. "You thought Lauren and I..." Another round of laughter. "Oh, my God, Robert. You really *are* from the Midwest. I didn't sleep with Lauren. She was in on the whole thing."

"Noooooooo," I said like an incredulous schoolgirl learning that the prom queen had given blowjobs to the entire football team. And then the band.

"Yes! You see, I knew what Mom was up to the minute Lauren came to the house. Lauren's a smart girl. Ruthless and smart. She knows I'm gay, so I figure she knows she's not going to get into my pants. She knew that before she arrived."

I still didn't get it. "So what made you think she would go along with you in the first place?"

"M-O-N-E-Y. Lauren will do anything to get her hands on it. So when I took her over to the table to make her a drink, I spilled the deal for her. I'd give her thirty-five grand if she would play along, make google eyes, go up to my room, and stay the night. We sat up all night laughing and drinking champagne. I even had her sneak out of my room in the morning at precisely the right time so that Mother would see her leaving."

"Thirty-five thousand dollars!" I screamed. "Isn't that a bit steep for a little acting?"

Michael smiled at me with his Cheshire cat grin as he handed me a folded piece of paper.

"Not when it means getting four-hundred thousand," Michael said calmly.

The piece of paper was a check from his mother, made out for—you guessed it.

"Your mother gives you a check for four-hundred thousand dollars just because she thinks you boffed Lauren. I don't get it."

"More than anything in the world, she wants to think that I can be converted. And as long as she goes on thinking this, I'll go on pretending. Actually, I must be the only gay man in America who doesn't want his mother to accept him for what he is. I can't imagine myself poor."

"Neither can I," I replied, lovingly stroking the full-grain leather seat beneath me.

As we sped off down the road, our attentions were focused only on what lay ahead of us.

5

Beach Blanket Himbos

As usual, Michael babbled all the rest of the way to Province-town. He talked about the men at his gym, parties he had attended lately, and the fact that no matter how hard they tried, the men of Provincetown just couldn't hold a candle to the men of Fire Island. That, of course, wouldn't stop him from sampling all that he could get his hands on.

"So how long do you think it'll take to corner Max?" I said, trying to get us back on track and to put the bad memories of Newport behind us.

"Probably a few days. Four. Five at most," Michael replied.

Michael's confidence stemmed from the fact that although P-Town is mobbed by thousands of gay men and women each summer, there are a limited number of dance bars. With so few places for dancing, spotting Max would be no problem.

As we pulled into town, we drove past hundreds of scantily-clad men and women heading to or from the beach in a never-ending parade of the hunky, the ridiculous, the outra-geous, and the pathetic. We stopped momentarily at a cot-tage on the East End to pick up keys for the house we were staying at and then went on. When the car pulled up to the house Michael had rented, my heart stopped. We'd be staying at the Plover, a house perched on the harbor side of Commercial Street with its own private beach.

When I came to Provincetown, I usually stayed at The Crustacean Guest House, a pit of a bed-and-breakfast decorated with rejects from local flea markets. The breakfasts sucked, it was hot as hell, and your lamps and fans all ran off a single electric extension cord that was woefully overloaded. But it was affordable.

The Plover was another story. For years, I had walked by in total envy of those who owned or rented the house. The interior, which was plainly visible through the always-open blinds, was painted white and filled with plump, overstuffed furniture. Beautifully (and expensively) woven rattan furniture dyed in natural earth tones was scattered about the main room, which overlooked the deck that overlooked the harbor. There always seemed to be a party in progress on the deck. I would have given anything merely to be among those witty and beautifully tanned, muscled boys who laughed and drank till dawn. Now I was going to be one of them at last.

"Robert, would you wake up and help me with these bags?" Michael begged annoyingly. "Once again, I've brought too much."

Michael never traveled anywhere without all the entrapments of his life in New York. If the clothes weren't overkill, he also brought numerous bags of personal items: special soaps that cost an entire paycheck, special shampoos, special creams, special lubes, and special medications of the herbal, legitimate, and black market kind.

"Let me get your bag and you carry this one of mine," Michael offered.

"Why do you want to carry mine?" I asked.

"Because it's lighter than mine."

Michael carried my shabby American Tourister suitcase (in blue-gray) that was patched at the corner with silver duct tape. I picked up several of Michael's beautifully crafted bags, whose exquisite craftsmanship was lost on people like

Michael. Anyway, it didn't matter. I was staying, all expenses paid, at the Plover. As Michael inserted the key in the lock and disarmed the security system, I could feel the breeze off the harbor whoosh past us and into the street. The breeze was scented with gardenias and oleander that bloomed in profusion in oversized pots on the deck. The furniture was absolutely the latest in exotic woods, and rattan was everywhere. I never wanted to leave and began to entertain thoughts of slowing down Michael's hunt just a wee bit so we could extend our stay. Michael, of course, took the best room and let me have my pick of what was left. Then, oblivious of his surroundings, he decided that we should get down to work immediately.

"Why don't you freshen up a bit and we'll have a drink on the deck and make our plan of attack."

"Sounds fine to me, Michael."

I walked down the hall, peering into one bedroom after another, finally deciding on one with sweeping views of the harbor. I don't mean to constantly dwell on the details of this house, but if you lived in a crappy, overpriced rental on the Upper East Side of Manhattan, you'd know how wonderful it was seeing and experiencing how the other half lives on vacation. It was depressing. Even though Michael had taken the best room, I couldn't complain about mine one bit. Everything about it, from the sisal on the floor to the fabric on the chairs and the bedcovers, was off-white bordering on light sand. I was afraid to sit down. In fact, every time I entered the bedroom with a glass of red wine, I would leave the glass on the ledge of the sink in the bathroom for fear of spilling it.

I unpacked, showered, and put on my official homosexual beach outfit: denim shorts, blue pocket T-shirt with the sleeves rolled up, white push-down socks and high-top Keds in black. Then I went on the deck to meet Michael, who, I discovered, had already beaten me there. Obviously, modesty was going to take a backseat during our stay in Provincetown. He was wearing a swimsuit so small, it was indecent. He had his Armani sunglasses on, a drink in one hand, and he was leaning on the edge of the deck, gazing out to the harbor, knowing full well that dozens of eyes were on him. Sometimes I just hated Michael.

He formulated our attack plan. "I thought we would go out to the beach to see if we could spot Max, but it's too late," he lamented.

"Michael, it's one-thirty. It's peak melanoma time."

"Robert, Robert, Robert. How many times do I have to tell you, you can't stay at the beach past two o'clock."

"Why?"

Michael rolled his eyes. "So you can shower, go to the gym to get a pump, then hit the tea dance before dinner. So why don't we get ready to go to the gym? You did bring your workout clothes, didn't you?"

"Of course I did, Michael."

"They are decent, aren't they, Robert?"

I heaved a sigh of aggravation. "Why, is there a strict dress code at this gym?"

"No, I just didn't want to be seen with you if you were going to wear those gym shorts with your college logo on them."

"I haven't worn those since that first time you took me to the Chelsea Gym," I said defensively. "Hey, I was just out of college."

Michael was unforgiving. "Yes, but you're gay. You should know better."

"Sorry. I promise I won't let it happen again."

"Okay. Let's drink up, change, and get going."

The gym was packed, but no Max. There was, however, one cute guy who had that summer's requisite stubble hair-cut and a fairly decent set of muscles. Like all the other boys there, he would've paid no attention to me had it not been for the fact that I walked in with Michael. Suddenly I was someone. Despite the fact that some of the guys there were pretty well pumped up and a few of them were pretty cute, Michael stood out completely. I hate to admit it, but

Michael was in a class by himself. If there was a fabulous one hundred gay men of New York, Michael would have been among them, right near the top. His workout outfit looked expensive. His haircut was expensive-looking. The watch he wore was obscenely expensive. Best of all, Michael carried it off perfectly. Guys who usually had no competition in this town were humbled by Michael. Guys just couldn't take their eyes off him. Normally, I would have hated all this, but some of the admiration toward Michael rubbed off on me, like a remora feeding on bits of food dropped from a shark's mouth.

We worked out for over two hours, did one last check of the gym, but Max was nowhere to be seen. So we went back to the Plover and changed for the tea dance.

For those of you who live in Montana and don't know what a tea dance is, I'll let you in on the secret. Tea dance—at least in Provincetown—is where you go to a bar with an outside patio and pool, stand around in your trashiest outfit (well, next-to-trashiest outfit—the trashiest, of course, you're saving for the evening), and drink five-dollar domestic beers while looking around at all the other boys who are doing exactly the same thing. I felt it was all pretty mindless. Pointless. And right up Michael's alley.

I was waiting on the deck for Michael to finish changing when he joined me. He was wearing a black suede loincloth and black construction boots with white socks. Nothing else. I guess I was lucky. On Fire Island, he wore even less.

We went to tea and Michael wormed his way into a few gaggles of homosexuals, chatting away as if he had known them for years. I tried to make the rounds to see if I could spot Max, but the crush of bodies made it impossible to see everyone. Every once in a while, I saw some guy who looked a little like Max, but once I got closer, I would be disappointed. The only concession was that Max wouldn't be hard to spot since he was so striking. Roughly two hours later, tea dance disbanded. Max didn't show. It began to run through my head that maybe he just wasn't in town. Maybe he had to dash out of town to make an emergency appearance in a porno film to replace Johnny Footlong, who had been injured in a scene involving a runaway vacuum cleaner. Naw. Max was here. His agency said so. Even better, he had no idea that we were here.

Michael took me out to dinner and paid for it. I protested *vigorously*, but there was no swaying Michael. After dinner we poked into several of the shops that lined Commercial Street, looking for Max. I kept my eyes peeled. As I was fingering an overpriced T-shirt in one store, I asked Michael if he had seen any clues that might lead us to our quarry. Did he remember any little shred of evidence, any snippet of conversation that he might have thought unimportant at the time?

The look on Michael's face suggested that he had just come out of the many mental fogs in which he spent most of his life. "Oh, God. I've been so busy looking at all the men here, I forgot to look for Max."

"Michael! We came here for a reason. We're going to find Max, and you are going to get your painting back, then personally nail his balls to the wall."

"Right," Michael barked.

We went into a few more stores. Crystals here. "Gay Pride" T-shirts and flags in another. Then a shoe store, followed by another clothing store. I could never understand why there were so many clothing stores in a town were people wore so little clothing.

After fruitlessly hitting a few more stores, we went home, changed, and went out to the bars. We hit the dancing bars, drag bars, leather bars, piano bars. Nothing. So we went back to the Plover, but not alone. Or at least, Michael didn't go home alone.

Thanks to Michael's unquenchable libido, we had a guest for the night. His name was Kirk and he was a lifeguard in Miami Beach. Gorgeous. Blond. Crewcut. Fabulous. I only had my right hand to console me that night. It didn't help matters much that I had to hear the gasps and moans of Michael and Mr. Lifeguard drifting down the hall for much of the night. As I sat there in my room watching the moonrise over the harbor and feeling the breeze gently blowing through my window, a single, serene wish repeated itself in my head over and over, hour after hour: I wished that Michael would get the crabs.

Besides the quick call I put into Monette to keep her up to date the next day, our routine was more of the same. A gay man's dream life. Get up. Beach. Work out. Tea dance. Dinner. Bars. Home. Sleep. The day after that was the same, too. The only deviation was that Michael added a man each night to his personal bed guest list, bringing two men home the second night and three home the third. Michael's king-size bed was overflowing with men and I couldn't even get one guy to go home with me. It wasn't as if I hadn't tried. I asked plenty, only to be rejected. Then I tried to play hard to get. It didn't work, because no one knew they were supposed to get me.

The next morning, I was having breakfast on the deck overlooking the harbor as Michael drifted out to join me, ensconced in a huge terry cloth robe.

"Oh, what a gorgeous day!" Michael exclaimed. "I just love vacations. Such a wonderful break."

"From what, Michael? You don't work. And don't mention the foundation. You haven't been there in some time."

"I entertain. I throw parties all the time. You try working with bitchy caterers and tight-assed florists and find out how much work it is. Entertaining looks like a lot of fun, but it's harder work than most people think."

"Speaking of entertaining, has last night's audience left yet?"

"Yeah, they're gone."

"All three of them?"

"Yeah. Two of them were brothers."

I looked at Michael with a mixture of disgust and amazement. "Brothers?!"

"*Twin* brothers," Michael said proudly.

"Ohhhhhhhh. Twins. Well, that makes it perfectly okay. Michael, that's disgusting! Illegal too, isn't it?"

"Why? They were legal age."

"Michael, they're brothers!"

"Gay brothers," he reminded me. "And besides, they hardly even touched each other."

"Could we change the subject?"

"To what?"

"Well, maybe the little and inconsequential fact that we've been here a few days now and we haven't gotten any leads. No Max, no painting. Zilch."

"No, but we've had some great fun, you've got to admit. Okay, oh, dull one. What do you propose we do?"

"I think we've got to go downtown more and scan the streets."

"Right now?" Michael whined. "Robert?"

"Yes?"

"You see that big round yellow object in the sky? It's called the sun. And you see that blue, wet stuff out there? That's called water. And that brown stuff out there is called sand. You lie on it and look at other men. You put all three together and you get fun. That's part of what I came here for. Part fun, part find Max. So why don't you put on that thing you call a swimsuit and let's go to the beach. We'll search for Max tonight."

So we went out to the beach for a few hours, then came back, showered, and headed off for the gym. Michael rationalized our going to the gym by saying that Max would need to keep up his physique, so the gym was a natural place for him to go. So we went. That was followed by tea dance. And dinner. At night we went to the bars. No sign of Max, but then fate finally smiled down upon us.

Our last bar stop for the night was the Trap. Short, of

course, for Lobster Trap. It was tackily decorated with buoys and all sorts of marine paraphernalia. Go-go boys danced in oversized lobster traps hanging from the high ceiling. The music was loud, the smoke impenetrable, and the crowd was elbow-to-elbow. Michael had been on the dance floor for over a half hour with what he hoped would be tonight's trick. I was standing against a wall off to the side when I saw him: Max. I had almost given up hope of ever spotting him anywhere in P-Town. So when I saw him, I wasn't sure that it was him. I moved a little closer to get a better look, but not so close that he might see me. I didn't want to tip him off and send him scurrying. This had to be done with the care and dexterity of a surgeon's scalpel. Yup, it was Max all right. There on his upper bicep was the eagle tattoo he got when he was dating Michael. I moved cautiously across the bar and headed for the dance floor to alert Michael. I could hardly hear my own voice as I screamed the good news into his ear.

"MICHAEL, I SAW MAX!"

"YOU'VE GOT GAS?! WHY DIDN'T YOU TELL ME BEFORE WE CAME IN HERE?!" Michael screamed back.

"NO, YOU DIDN'T HEAR WHAT I SAID. I JUST SAW MAX!"

"WHAT?"

"MAX. I'VE FOUND HIM!"

Michael looked as if someone had told him he was completely bankrupt. "WHERE?"

"OVER NEAR THE BACK BAR! NOW TAKE IT EASY, MICHAEL. WE CAN'T LET HIM KNOW WE'RE HERE. WE'VE GOT TO SNEAK UP ON HIM SO . . ."

If Michael had been a cartoon character right then, his face would have turned beet red and smoke would have poured out of his ears in great big puffs. His head rolled back and he shouted so loudly that he was easily heard above the roar of the thumping music.

"PAYBACK TIME, MAX!!!!!"

Michael tore off across the dance floor like a cat on crack, swimming through the crowd toward Max. Every coiffed head in the place turned to watch Michael, and unfortunately, that included Max's. Max saw Michael coming toward him and bolted toward the door with Michael snapping at his heels. Before the two of them went flying out the door and into the street, Michael had managed to grab hold of Max's T-shirt and rip it clean from his body. As soon as the two disappeared from the bar, everyone went back to whatever they were doing as if nothing had happened.

I made my way toward the door, knowing that I wouldn't be able to keep up with either Max or Michael. I vainly searched a few of the surrounding streets but decided that it would be best to head back to the house and meet Michael there. Sure enough, he returned, covered in dirt, his shorts looking as if they had been put through a giant leaf shredder. But he was smiling from ear to ear.

"Are you all right, Michael? Here, sit down and I'll get some peroxide for your legs."

"Never mind. Whew! I didn't get him, but I scared the shit out of him. I mean, I was right behind him for blocks. Chased him all the way to the East End of town. I actually tackled him at one point, but he fought me back, then threw an enormous flower pot at me and knocked me down. He took off and I lost him."

Michael looked over his wounds, then went to the refrigerator for a glass of champagne. "Let's celebrate. How's about it?"

"Celebrate what?"

"Finding Max. At least we know he's here. We're not on a wild goose chase. Oh, and to our minds. Let's salute our minds. We got this far all by ourselves."

"Well, I hate to throw cold water on our little celebration, but I don't think Max will hang around here much longer now that he knows we're here."

"I have the feeling that he'll be around here for a few more days. I have a hunch. Homosexual's intuition. Anyway, we can't do anything tonight . . . except celebrate."

"Sounds fine with me."

We opened the first of several bottles of champagne and celebrated. It's unfortunate that our celebration was perhaps a bit premature.

I awoke the next morning to find a naked man in my bed. Normally, I would have enjoyed a situation like this, but the hangover that banged my brain against my skull as I lifted my head made me unable to appreciate the good luck I supposed I had just experienced.

I tried not to move for fear of waking him up. Unbelievable. I had just had sex with a man with a killer body and I didn't remember a thing. I pinched myself to see if I was awake. Yes siree. I wasn't dreaming. I raised my head slowly to see if there were clues in the bedroom that might tell me what this humpy young guy was doing there. A quick look around my bedroom told me that there were two other naked men there. They were all breathing, so I obviously hadn't brought them home in the middle of the night and killed them. One was laying next to me on his stomach. One was lying at the foot of the bed. The last one was draped over an upholstered chair as if I had had my way with him, then disposed of him like a broken plaything. My bedroom was littered with several empty champagne bottles and the empty remnants of dozens of foil condom wrappers. Well, at least we had safe sex. I just wished I had some memory of it.

Just then, the man lying next to me stirred a bit, putting his arm lovingly across my chest.

Naked Man #1 spoke in a sleepy voice. "You were great, man . . . total, fucking great. My asshole will never be the same."

Naked Man #2, who heard Naked Man #1, awoke and

rolled over on his back. "You were quite the machine last night, Robert."

I must have had sex, because these guys knew my name. I didn't know what to say, but figured I had to say something. "Oh" was all I could manage.

Naked Man #3 felt it was his turn to join us, so he tried to get up from the chair, but he had some difficulty since his hands were handcuffed in front of him. He struggled to stand up, falling a little to the right, then to the left. Finally, he managed to get on his feet.

Naked Man #3 spoke. "Oh man, who shoved the telephone pole up my ass last night?"

Naked Men #1 and #2 pointed accusingly at me.

"That's some rod you got there. Jeeeesus. You make Jeff Stryker look like a peanut—shelled."

Naked Man #1 piped up. "How's about another round, boys? We've got a couple of hours before we should head out to the beach. Just take it a little easier this time, Robert. The penis can be an instrument of pleasure, not just pain."

Now I knew what it felt like to go crazy. You seem to make sense, but the rest of the world doesn't.

Just then, Michael tapped lightly on the door, and before I could tell him to go away, he opened it and walked into the room. He was nude, of course. His face lit up when he saw the men in my room.

"Well, well. Three at once! And I suppose you're going to tell me that these gentlemen are all Jehovah's Witnesses who've lost their way."

"This is not what it looks like, Michael," I pleaded.

"Tell me, then, what this is all about. This ought to be good."

Michael stood across the room, arms crossed, looking for an answer. Suddenly, he roared with laughter, only to be joined by hoots from Naked Men #1, #2, and #3.

"Oh God, we really had you going there!" Michael said, wiping tears from his eyes.

Someone could have told me the word *gullible* wasn't in the dictionary right now and I'd probably believe them. Even though I was annoyed at being outwitted by someone with Michael's limited intellectual capacity, I decided to play along good-naturedly. After all, if I couldn't laugh at myself, then I was a sorry person indeed. Plus, I needed time to plot my revenge on Michael.

"My God, Robert, you should've guessed right from the beginning. I mean, you couldn't attract gorgeous guys like this. Er, what I mean is, you're cute and precious in your own little way, but these men require a different kind of man."

"Now, wait a minute, Michael. If I weren't such a thick-skinned New Yorker, I'd be offended. I suppose these are your guys from last night?"

"Of course. After you passed out last night, I decided I needed a little noogie. So I was just looking out the window facing the street to see what the weather was like when I saw these three guys walking by. I invited them in."

Sure, Michael. Rub it in. He doesn't even have to leave the house and he picks up not one, not two, but three gorgeous men.

"Okay, guys. Time to head back to my room. We still have some time left before you have to go."

The three guys got up and began to march single file out of my room and out into the hall. As they were leaving, Naked Man #3 stopped in front of Michael and raised his cuffed hands.

"I think we'll leave those on you for just a little while longer."

Naked Man #3 smiled.

"See you in a few hours, Robert," Michael whispered to me.

"Michael?"

"Yes, Robert?"

"Could you let me have just one of them? Pleeease?"

Michael looked at me incredulously. "No! I found them

first. And I'm keeping them . . . at least for another three hours."

With that, Michael followed his playthings down the hall to his bedroom and shut the door. It was clear that whatever I did to get back at Michael for his little joke had to be more than good. It had to involve shrapnel.

I threw on some clothes, then had breakfast on the deck. It was still early and the harbor beach was almost completely deserted. After I finished breakfast, I decided to go for a walk through town while things were still quiet. As I was leaving and shutting the door behind me, my eye caught sight of a note taped to the glass. It was addressed simply, "Michael."

I figured it was probably important, so I pulled it off the door, opened it, and read it.

Dear Michael,

I'm sorry for all the trouble I've caused you and I want to make amends. Please meet me tonight at exactly 9 P.M. on the beach behind the Shiver Me Timbers bar. Seeing you again has made me realize what I've lost, and if I can't get you back, I at least want to return your painting and beg your forgiveness.

Love,
Max

My heart began to race. This was too good to be true. Okay, maybe it was. Was it a trap? Or was Max feeling that he had gotten in over his head and was trying to get Michael to forget the whole thing? I had to tell Michael right away. I had no sooner run down the hall and burst into Michael's room without knocking than it dawned on me that Michael was still "entertaining" friends. Naked Men #3 and #2 were hog-tied together, stomach to stomach on the bed and gagged with wool socks. Naked Man #1 was wearing an elaborate mask made of dark bird feathers and was busy, as they say, polishing Michael's German helmet. I was so shocked that I just stood there speechless.

"This isn't what it looks like, Robert," Michael interjected. "It's actually much worse. Care to join us?"

I shut the door and went for a walk.

When I returned, Michael was sitting on the deck overlooking the harbor, innocently having breakfast.

"Good morning, Michael," I offered.

"Good morning, Robert." That was all.

"Well?"

"Well, *what*, Robert?"

"Aren't you going to explain what was going on in your
room this morning?"

Michael looked at me with an expression of "poor, pitiful, celibate Robert." He then looked out toward the harbor
and spoke without even looking at me. "Listen, Robert, you
know darn well that sex is something I get a kick out of. And
when you do it as much as I do, you not only have to find
new ways of making it interesting, but you deal with all
kinds of men who have different tastes."

"So everything that I saw was their idea?"

"No, it was mine."

"You know, Michael, I'm surprised that you aren't held
on bail more often. Anyway, take a look at this!"

I took Max's note and threw it on the table in front of
Michael. He read it, then tossed it back to me.

A smile played across his face. "So the bastard wants to
make amends, does he?"

Michael was already relishing the idea of getting his
painting back, but I wasn't so sure and I felt it was my duty
to say so. "This is really odd, but it's possible; maybe he's
tired of running."

"I wouldn't worry, Robert. Even if Max has other plans,
we could always yell for the police. Plus, the beach isn't too
far from Commercial Street. It's not like we'll be miles away
from everyone."

"Right."

We looked at each other with a cloud of uncertainty over our faces. Needless to say, we couldn't wait for the appointed hour to arrive, but it was only morning, so we went to the beach.

Being homosexuals, it was imperative that we arrive early so that we didn't have to park amongst the heterosexuals and their recreational vehicles on the unfashionable north end of Herring Cove Beach. Many people rode bikes to Herring Cove Beach or walked though the dunes in the hope of getting a peek at the sexual encounters that were rumored to take place in the sandy byways. Some rollerbladed. Michael, being Michael, proudly drove his Range Rover and managed to find a parking spot close to the sand so we wouldn't have as long a way to drag all the trappings that he insisted on bringing.

Whereas most people find solace in the roaring of the surf and a good book, Michael brought every convenience of civilization along with him. Besides very expensive and cleverly constructed sand chairs capable of 4,358 positions, Michael brought a mini-CD player with umpteen CDs, the latest *Vanity Fair*, more sunblock than was used during the entire Gulf War (wrinkles, you know), binoculars, an extremely light lunch for two, and several liter bottles of Evian water—not just to drink, but to splash on his body. Michael's clever little rifle was nowhere to be seen. I didn't ask. As we walked down the beach, I could see out of the corner of my eye the heads that turned ever so slightly (and just plain blatantly) at Michael and me. Or rather, at Michael. Why shouldn't they? Michael was wearing an almost-nothing swimsuit, with every muscle perfectly toned. I, on the other hand, looked like a heterosexual who had stepped fresh from the pages of a Land's End catalog. My boxer-style trunks in nautical blue and green stripes only garnered looks from men reading *Scientific American* or the latest title from Steven Hawking. I tried to suck in my stomach a little but gave up on the futile idea. I wasn't fat by any means. I was just—how do you say it?—lacking definition in any part of my body. A scrawny sack of potatoes. Sensing that I didn't want to parade in front of these people any longer, I suggested to Michael that, my, this looked like a beautiful spot to claim.

"Robert, this isn't far enough. Everyone still has their suits on around here," Michael replied so calmly and nonchalantly that I thought he was kidding. "We need to go far enough so we don't get hassled by the park rangers."

"For what, Michael? Feeding Yogi and Booboo?"

"No. So they don't try to make us put our swimsuits back on, silly."

"Why? Are they coming off?" I asked, knowing full well what Michael had in mind.

"Oh, Robert, don't be so prude! I don't want too strong of a tan line, so we have to go down the beach a little further where I can take my suit off. I need to get an even tan on my dick and balls. Plus, that's just the part of the beach where Max would be."

"Michael, we know he's in town. What would you do if you found him here at the beach? He's going to apologize to us tonight."

"Oh, Robert, we can't count on him showing tonight. I want to catch him ASAP. Plus, I want to see some hot men!"

I had heard about the nude section many times before. In fact, I had walked past it many, many, times before on the pretense of being out for a summer stroll. I would turn my head toward the ocean while snatching glances, from behind my dark glasses, of the men lying naked on their towels. I tried to keep an air of being open-minded, but I couldn't help feeling . . . Midwestern. Seeing Michael nude was no surprise. Because he had such a drop-dead body, he was never ashamed to show it. He walked around his apartment completely nude for hours after taking a shower. He thought nothing about answering the door nude if that suited him. Mailmen, maids, repairmen all had the honor of seeing Michael in the buff. Forget Fire Island. He would strut around the outdoor deck of his fabulous house nude, knowing that half the men in the Pines section of Fire Island would have stiff necks the next morning.

Now me, that's another story. I was born in the Midwest. And raised Catholic. Nudity was an option only when showering. The penis, however, was an instrument of the devil. A horrid pustule of fetid man-odors that stunk of the sin of sex and always would. At least that's what Sister Margaret taught us in third-grade Sunday school. Plus, my body was not the type that needed exposing. In fact, no amount of clothing was ever enough for me.

Michael dragged me farther down the beach until we reached the nude section. It wasn't especially crowded, but there were plenty of men there to see.

"Okay, this looks like a good spot," Michael said as he peeled off the nylon shoestring that he passed off as a bathing suit. I sat down on my towel, shyly pushed my suit down, then turned over on my stomach in a pointless attempt at modesty. Michael, however, remained standing and actually stretched lazily to show the whole world what he had to offer. I saw one man far off in the dunes raise a camera with a long lens the length of a cannon and fire off a round of photographs of Michael. Closer by, a group of three men turned their gazes our way. One of them, a handsome bald man with pierced nipples and cock (not that I was looking *there*, but you couldn't miss it), got up from the man he was lying on top of and came in our direction, lowering his sunglasses to get a better look at Michael.

"Michael! Michael Stark! I thought that was yooouuuu!" the bald man exclaimed.

"Mitchell!" Michael said as he matched a crotch to a name. "God, what are you doing here? I thought you never came to P-Town."

"I rarely do, but I'm up here on . . . business with a friend," Mitchell replied. Mitch's eyes ran up and down my body, trying, no doubt, to figure out why Michael would even be seen in the presence of my company. Seeing no

clue, he turned back to Michael and continued in his Darth
Vader baritone.

"Oh, Michael, I saw the spread in *Domicile* about the
makeover on your house on Fire Island. When are you
going to have your next party?"

"I already had a big one last fall. I sent you an invitation
for the housewarming, but you declined if my memory
serves me right."

Mitchell was completely animated. "I was out in La-la
Land, Michael. The orgy of the century! Actors, high-ranking
studio execs, producers, directors, all gay and all ready to
go. In a house so fabulous I couldn't begin to describe it.
And out so far on a private point, no one would hear the
screams." Mitchell was practically salivating.

Mitchell was one of those people I would lump into the
category of "dangerous." You know the type. Sleaziness
covered with a thin veneer of civilized behavior. As he
talked, I could almost picture his tongue as a snake, waving
to and fro, loaded with deadly poison.

Mitchell slurped up a small bit of saliva that began escap-
ing from the corner of his mouth.

"It was great—leather, rubber, electricity, raw sewage,
Saran wrap, breath control, frozen tomatoes. You name it;
they had it. It was totally wild. Look . . . they're having another orgy at the end of the summer. Care to join ussssss?"
Mitchell said, hissing the last part.

"Sounds interesting. Give me a call when I get back to
the city in a few weeks. I'll write it down on my calendar."

I could just see Michael's calendar. August 21, visit den-
tist. August 22, attend orgy in L.A.

"Look, the guy I'm staying with here in town is having a
party at his house tomorrow night. I know that he'd love to
have you there because you're our type of people. I just
know you'll have a good time. Should I tell him you'll
come?"

Michael relented. "Okay. Robert and I will be there."

Mitchell covered his mouth and feigned embarrassment. "Oh, I'm being rude, aren't I? Yes, of course, Robert . . . you're invited too."

"So, Mitchell, who's the guy you're staying with?"

"Well, he's this art dealer from New York. Nathan Cavendish. He's up here for the summer. Fabulous house off Commercial Street. You know, the one with the Dobermans and the high hedges."

"Oh, that one. Robert noticed it right away. How's it inside?" Michael probed.

"Fabulous! Paintings from just about every major artist."

Michael looked perplexed. "I didn't know you knew him."

Mitchell leaned forward with a just-between-you-and-me look. "He's one of my clients. I work with him all the time in the city, and he wants to keep things up now that he's off for the summer. So he lets me stay there free."

"Are you staying long, Mitchell?" Michael asked.

"Until the end of July. I don't want to keep you from your sun too long. And don't forget the party tomorrow night, ten o'clock." With that, Mitchell sauntered back to his gaggle of friends.

Michael looked at me as if thunderstruck. "Did you hear what Mitchell said, Robert?"

"Absolutely. What the hell were they doing with frozen tomatoes?"

"Robert! You weren't even listening."

"What?"

"Mitchell is staying with an art dealer, Robert. *Art.* The man collects and sells major artists. Max has a painting of mine that was painted by a major artist. And he came to P-Town to hock a painting because things aren't as hot as it would be in New York. Well, duh!"

"Do you really think there's a connection? It could be just coincidence."

"Yeah, and Oswald just happened to be in Dallas that day. We've got to find Max before he sells the painting.

We've got to step up our search, starting now. Well . . . after we get a few hours of sun."

"I guess that was pretty lucky that Mitchell spotted you. By the way, Michael, what does Mitchell do?" I asked.

"You don't want to know."

"I don't? C'mon, tell me."

"He's a model."

I snorted at the thought of Mitchell walking up and down a catwalk.

Michael must have read my mind. "Not the kind of model you think. He has to call himself a model so he doesn't get arrested."

"What?"

"He's a paid bondage expert and sadist. Men come to him and he ties them up and disciplines them."

"That's disgusting, Michael."

"You wouldn't say that if you made over a hundred thousand dollars a year doing it."

"I gotta change careers."

"Forget it, Robert. You'd hit some guy with a whip and you'd go apologize."

Michael reached into his extremely expensive backpack, pulled out his personal CD player, and plugged the earphones into his ears, preparing to tune me out for the next few hours.

"Michael, tell me just one more thing."

"Yes?"

"What were they doing with those frozen tomatoes?"

The night had finally made it here. We were going to find out if Max was going to forgive us or ambush us, or . . . ?

I called Monette around six to give her an update on the latest developments in the Max saga. But as we talked about what possible actions Max could take, the ambush part didn't seem to make much sense.

"Relax Robert," Monette said, sensing the anxiety in my

voice. "There's really no point in ambushing you two," her voice boomed over the phone wire. "After all, Max has the painting. Getting rid of the two of you wouldn't stop the search for the painting. The insurance company wants to find it. The police would like it. No, I think Max may be ready to give up. It's not like he's done this sort of thing before. He could be feeling that he's gotten in way over his head."

"Yeah, but he did go through this whole elaborate setup to get the painting from Michael. That took some sort of criminal mind to pull something like that off," I shot back.

"Robert, you know nothing of the criminal mind. What Max did was so simple, a child could've pulled it off. Max reads about Michael's wealth and possessions in the paper, he noses around town, and within minutes, he runs into the first of many who've been pillowed by him—and bingo! Max knows that he has the right bait to snare Michael. Max follows Michael around and purposely runs into him, dates him, puts the suggestion for the wedding into Michael's mind, and Michael falls for it like a ton of bricks. Max takes off for P-Town with Michael's painting, gets scared, sees Michael, panics, then gets penitent all of a sudden. After all, he doesn't want to be a pretty boy in prison. He writes a note, close curtain. The end."

I was amazed. It all sounded so simple. "So Max is not going to pull a Luger with a silencer and rub us out on the beach?"

"I doubt that. He could be scared."

"Not as much as I am. Michael's a little suspicious, but you know that the only thing on his mind is getting revenge on Max."

"Well, whatever you two do tonight, be careful. And remember to bring a flashlight in case there's an emergency. Call me back in the morning to fill me in. See you tomorrow. Good luck."

"Yeah, Monette. I have this feeling that we're going to need it." In fact, the last thing that I did before Michael and

I went out was to leave Max's note on the hall table. Just in case the two of us didn't come back.

The time was 8:55 and we were standing on the darkened beach, waiting for Max. While the location for our rendezvous wasn't totally isolated, I could see why Max chose it. Although the harbor was ringed by houses, restaurants, and stores, the vast majority of these buildings had their backs turned to the water, making it darker than one would imagine it to be at night. Despite the fact that most of the action in P-Town was happening a hundred yards away on Commercial Street, the beach was relatively quiet.

We waited patiently for Max until it was 9:05.

Michael broke the silence so suddenly, I practically jumped out of my skin.

"The note said to be on time. Now, if Max wanted us to be here exactly at nine P.M., you'd think he'd have some reason and show up on time."

"Are you sure this is the exact spot, Michael?"

"Yes, Robert. I looked for the big red X on the beach and there it is," Michael said irritably, flashing the flashlight beam at nothing in particular in the sand.

"Michael, you're not supposed to use the flashlight unless we need it. It might scare Max off! Maybe he's down the beach a little farther. Why don't we walk just a little bit?"

"Okay, but not too far," Michael agreed as we both started out. "He said behind the Shiver Me Timbers. And this be ye place, arrg!" I grunted, trying to put a little pirate humor into the evening.

No sooner had Michael uttered those last words, than he went down onto the sand like a sack of potatoes. I was so uptight, I was sure that Max had thrown a knife from some unseen location, hitting Michael squarely in the back. I screamed. Not a blood-curdling scream, but a kind of high-pitched one such as the type Lana Turner would utter.

I looked down at Michael. No knife. No gunshot wound. No nothing. I struggled to help him up.

"Are you all right, Michael?"

"Yeah, I'm fine. I just didn't see that log there. . . . It's so dark."

The truth was that Michael had tripped over something, but it wasn't a log. He flashed the light down at the sand only to find it was a man. A dead man. A dead man with a sheer glove twisted around his neck. In fact, it looked as if the dead man had struggled to get the glove off, but died before he could succeed. A terrible feeling came over both of us. We both knew who it was, but we had to be sure.

"Michael, I think we better turn him over and be certain."

"No way, Robert. I'm not touching a dead body."

"Michael, we need to be sure before we tell the police."

As I reached down to inspect Max more closely, Michael yelled, "Don't touch him!"

"Why?" I said, trembling.

"You'll disturb the evidence. We shouldn't touch a thing. We better leave him alone." Michael stared at the body for a moment, then a look of recognition flooded across his face. "This guy's wearing a ring just like Max's. *Exactly* like the one Max wore. Too bad he's wearing a long-sleeve shirt, otherwise we could see his tattoo."

Michael reached down as if he were going to turn the body over.

"Michael, what are you doing? What about the evidence?"

"Screw the evidence. I've got to know." He grabbed one of the man's arms and flipped him over violently.

Sure enough, it was Max. It's difficult to know what to say in moments like this, and neither of us could think of a word to utter. Michael, in fact, was so quiet that I thought he was going to burst into tears. His entire mood had shifted. In all candor, Michael wanted revenge and wanted

it bad, but seeing Max lying strangled in the sand was probably making him rethink his lust for Max's comeuppance.

"Robert?"

"Yes, Michael?"

"Would it bother you if I have an emotional outburst right now?"

"You go right ahead. I understand what you must be going through. It's pretty intense."

Michael was really struggling to control himself. "And you won't tell about it?"

"Michael, you're my best friend."

"I knew I could count on you." With that Michael pulled his foot back as far as it would go, and delivered a forceful kick to Max's groin. "Goddamned son of a bitch! Motherfucking prick!" Michael let out a loud breath, relieved at the release of pent-up emotions.

I was about to mutter something about respect for the dead, but decided that in light of Michael's highly emotional state, it would be better to hold my tongue. That is, until something caught my eye.

"Wait a minute, Michael. Shine the flashlight on the glove. I know that this may sound weird, but I could swear that the glove that's twisted around his neck is the exact one worn by Bette Davis in *All About Eve.*"

Michael, never one for old black-and-white movies, looked at me as if I were crazy. "How do you know?"

"I'm a homosexual, Michael. I just know. Those gloves are the same ones. Sheer, with a seam that runs down the outside of the arm. They're the same ones."

"So Bette Davis killed him, eh?"

"Michael, Bette Davis is dead. I don't think she came back from the grave to kill a homosexual-hustler-art thief."

Michael still didn't follow me, but then again, when did he? "So what are you saying?"

"I'm saying that this looks like the work of a drag queen."

Michael looked incredulous. "A drag queen! I'm telling

you, Robert, all this celibacy is doing strange things to your brain. Now what would Max be doing with a drag queen? And furthermore, what kind of drag queen would have the strength to finish off Max? He's not a small guy."

"Well, we have three possibilities. One, Max was partners with a drag queen who turned on him and killed him to avoid splitting the profits. Two, the glove is a red herring, left there to lead us off the trail."

"What's your third theory, Robert?"

"Well, maybe Max was into autoeroticism, and he pushed things too far this time."

Michael was silent for a moment, as if contemplating whether to hit me. "Robert, take a look at Max. Do you think that a guy with a chassis like that has to get off on his own? I don't think so."

"Okay, so theory number three is out."

Michael looked at me, then said, "Well, maybe Max was into drag in some way I never knew!"

Now it was time to roll my eyes. "Nice try, Michael, but you're completely off base."

Michael begged to differ. "You never know, Robert. I picked up this guy that was built like a linebacker. Smoked Marlboros. Had a tattoo of an eagle ripping a snake to pieces on his bicep. Pierced nipple, cock—you know, the whole macho works. The moment I get him home, I slip my hand down the front of his pants and I can feel this guy's got control-top panty hose on underneath. He said he wore it because it made him look better in jeans, but I wouldn't buy it. So I threw him out."

"Because he wore pantyhose?" I inquired.

"Oh, it wasn't the pantyhose that broke that camel's back. He wanted me to tie him up, piss on him, and force him to swallow dirty sweat socks that had been slathered in Vaseline."

"Michael?"

"Yes, Robert?"

"Don't ever tell me a story like that again."

"I swear to God, Robert. It's always the ones who act the most macho that you've got to watch."

"Michael, you're way off. The glove could be a red herring, but that seems like a lot of trouble to go to just to divert our attention. No, I really think that some drag queen killed him. I don't know how or who, but that's something we have to find out if we're going to solve this case. Now, let's go fetch the police."

"Couldn't I kick him one more time?" Michael begged.

Before I could say that it didn't seem ethical, Michael had planted a few more hard kicks in Max's crown-jewel case. Suddenly, a pair of powerful flashlights suddenly clicked on, illuminating Michael venting his spleen on a corpse, and me standing there watching. I'm no Agatha Christie, but as the police approached us, I'm sure that things looked a tad incriminating.

The next morning, a bevy of powerful lawyers hired by Michael had bailed us out of jail. It was the first night I had ever spent in jail in my life, so I expected to come out hardboiled and with a lifelong grudge against society. But it was not to be. Our only neighbor in an adjacent cell was a drunken teenager who slept the entire night.

The lawyers were hired by Michael's mother, to be precise. Mrs. Stark, as I guessed, convinced Michael that it would be better if she remained in Newport. "There's no sense having two family members caught up in a scandal," she said to him over the phone. When we left the town's police station, we were mobbed by a handful of reporters; most of them were from local papers, judging from their shabby clothing. They snapped pictures unceasingly until Michael and I and his coterie of lawyers got into Michael's Rover and sped off toward the Plover. When we got to our destination, there were reporters there too. More pictures. More questions being fired at us from the mob that followed us to the door of the house like a gang of angry

Pomeranians nipping at our heels for another dog yummy. Once we were inside, the reporters hung around for some time, then slowly drifted off until only one doggedly remained.

Once we were inside, the trouble began.

There was a knock at the door. Michael's head lawyer, Mr. Tidings, a serious man dressed in an exquisitely tailored suit, answered the door to find a team of police and sheriff's deputies holding up an official piece of paper.

"My name is Officer Shiffin, and we have a court order to search the premises."

Mr. Tidings examined the document, huddled briefly with the other lawyers, told me to go to my room and Michael to go to his, then admitted the police to the house, showing them to our two bedrooms, with half the lawyers watching the police search my room and the other half in Michael's room.

Oh, this was going to be just great. They were going to go through my belongings with a fine-toothed comb. Not that I had anything to hide. Well, not much. I sat there speechless while the police tore through my room. From down the hall, I could hear that Michael was not so unprotesting.

"Goddamn fucking police Nazi storm troopers! That's my best pair of leather restraints. And my cock-and-ball harness. I had those specially made in Italy. Now how am I supposed to get dates, I ask you?"

Back in my room, I stood by helpless as one of the cops opened the top drawer of my dresser, held up a copy of *Blueballs* magazine, smirked, then put it back into the drawer. Next came a chrome cockring, lube, and a black jockstrap. Now that I stood there watching, I wondered why in the hell I even bothered to pack such things. I guess that I felt that if I brought the items in question, they would somehow magically present the opportunity to use them. Like good-luck charms. After what seemed an eternity, they finished with my room, then went down the hall to search the other unoccupied rooms. Michael was still shouting obscenities in his room while a policeman came forth from Michael's bedroom with boxes of confiscated items, one of them obviously Michael's infamous rifle. An hour and several more embarrassing revelations later, the police left, leaving us alone with Michael's lawyers. They conferred mostly among themselves, then instructed us in what to do and what not to do, but ranking highest was their admonition not to leave Provincetown.

When all had quieted down and everyone had left, Michael and I decided to have a drink on the deck, but thought better when a photographer standing on the beach aimed his camera at us the moment we stepped through the door leading outside. Maybe it was better if we sat indoors until the few straggling members of the fourth estate tired of the chase and left us alone. Michael and I sat down in the dining area and looked at each other like two tired octogenarians.

A thought came into my head. In all the commotion, I remembered Max's note, which I had left on the hall table. I jumped up to retrieve it, only to find it gone.

"Michael? Did you take or move the note that I left here last night?" I said, trying not to let the fear in my voice come through.

"No," he answered, instantly deducing what I was up to.

"Well, did the cops take it?" I asked.

"I don't know. I don't think so. When they came in, it seemed that they came right to our bedrooms."

"Then WHERE IS THE FUCKING NOTE?" I screamed hysterically. "That note is the only proof so far that lets us off the hook, and now it's gone. This is just fucking great." I sat down and buried my head in my hands, not knowing what else to do.

Michael broke the uncomfortable silence. "Listen, Robert. We've got to get serious about this entire affair. We can't go running around to the gym and the bars all the time. We've got to get our shit together and find out who killed Max."

I looked up at Michael, stunned. I decided not to answer him since it would lead to all sorts of denials on his part. So I sighed and admitted that yes, it was I who was treating our time here like one big testosterone festival.

I decided to take charge. "Okay, so far we know that Max was killed by someone most likely in drag. Bette Davis drag."

Michael's face burst into a big smile. "Then all we have to do is go find a show with a Bette Davis impersonator and we've got our man—woman."

"Michael, it's summer in Provincetown. You and I are the only men in town who aren't dressed like Bette Davis. It's not so simple. So far, the only shred of evidence in our favor was the note written by Max, and that seems to have disappeared."

We decided we needed the mastermind of crime on our team, so we called Monette and put her on the speaker phone.

"Michael, I'm so sorry about Max," came Monette's voice over the speaker. "I don't know what to say."

"You could say that he was a rotten shit."

"Yes, absolutely. A rotten shit."

"And that he deserved to die."

". . . deserved to die," Monette repeated.

". . . and he . . ."

I decided to butt in and get things back on track. "So, Monette, we've told you the basics: the note, the body, the glove. There isn't much more to tell. So who do you think is behind all this?"

"The Kremlin," Monette answered.

Michael looked puzzled. "The Kremlin. Who's he?"

"It's a joke, Michael. A joke. Never mind. Go ahead, Monette."

"Well, obviously someone bumped him off."

"Obviously," Michael responded.

"Well, Max could've set up the first part: the marriage and stealing the painting and all that. But he's either been joined by someone along the way, or . . . he's been working with someone from the very beginning." Monette was on a roll, so neither Michael nor I felt it wise to disturb her. "Let's say that Max was working with a mysterious Mr. X from the beginning. The two searched for a target like Michael: a gay, bubbleheaded, vacuous, amoral slut who goes down more often than a cheap Navy submarine."

"Monette, darling?"

"What, Michael?" Monette asked, clearing her throat.

"I know people who could have you killed."

"Sorry, Michael, I was just reciting the facts of the case."

"Are you working for the prosecution or for me, Monette?"

"You're absolutely right, Michael. I'll continue. Now where was I?"

"Amoral slut," I reminded Monette.

"Oh yes! Amoral slut with a buttload of money and a painting that was worth even more." I could almost see Monette smiling on the other end of the phone. She continued. "Max and Mr. X make their plan. Max coincidentally runs into you, falls in love with you, gets you to marry him, then takes off with your Matisse while you're at the church. Max heads to P-Town with Mr. X, not only because the two of them want to have a gay old time, but they want to let the heat die down before they plan their next move. Well, Mr. X starts thinking that if he kills Max, he won't have to split the proceeds of the painting fifty-fifty anymore. Classic double-cross. After all, fifty percent, even on a Matisse, isn't that much. One hundred percent is much better. So he writes a note in Max's handwriting asking you two to meet Max on the beach at nine; he takes Max out there on some other pretext at, let's say eight-forty, then murders him. He makes his getaway, then calls the police and acts like some concerned citizen reporting a bunch of rowdy teens or something on the beach. The police show up and find the two of you standing over Max's body. The end."

I spoke up. "The only thing that's never made sense to me, Monette, is why Max went to the whole charade of the big wedding just so he could get his hands on Michael's painting. I'm sure he must've had ample opportunity to rip off the Matisse long before that?"

"Good point," Monette conceded. "Maybe to have Michael occupied at the wedding, which would give our thief a good head start to P-Town."

"That makes sense," I said. "So I guess that what we have to do is find Mr. X—who's probably long gone now. What kind of hope do we have now, Monette? We're never going to find Mr. X or the painting."

Michael snapped his fingers. "The painting. The painting. Robert, remember Mitchell on the beach? He was staying with an art dealer who handles some pretty fancy stuff. His party is tonight. This is perfect. Maybe we'll learn something."

"Did you hear that, Monette?" I asked, leaning toward the speakerphone.

"Yes, yes, I did. That sounds like an excellent suggestion. Maybe the two of you could say you're going to the bathroom and you just so happen to get lost on the way back. You do a little snooping. Tomorrow night, however, I suggest that the two of you go to a drag show."

Michael, who seemed to be lost in thought, spoke up. "Monette, you seem to know a lot about this crime stuff. Why don't you come up to Provincetown and lend us your mind?"

"Why thank you for the flattery, Michael, but I have to be honest that I don't think I can affor—"

Michael cut Monette short. "I'll pay all your expenses."

"And?"

"And I'll introduce you to kd lang."

"And?"

"And Melissa Etheridge."

"And?"

"And I'll pay *all* your expenses."

"Well, when you twist my arm like that . . ." Monette replied like a Southern belle.

What does one wear to an orgy? This is one of those questions most Americans never have to ask themselves, but it was one that was staring me right in the face. It wasn't as if I could turn to Miss Manners for help.

Dear Miss Manners,
I will be attending an orgy in Provincetown, and I was wonder-ing what to wear. I was thinking of rubber chastity shorts with a built-in catheter and enema valve. I've never been to an orgy before, so I want to know if this is appropriate.
                                                                Signed,
                                                                Clueless.

Dear Clueless,
Anything that makes you feel comfortable in a social situation is fine. Although, in my opinion, a head-to-toe latex bondage suit with D-rings would probably be a better choice, since a spilled drink or errant semen would wipe off with just a wet sponge. Plus, the D-rings give partygoers a convenient place to tie their ropes. Practicality is a consideration in situations like this. Have fun!
                                                                —Miss Manners

So I opted for the shortest shorts and a T-shirt with the sleeves rolled up. Michael came dressed like a Native American. A fur-covered loincloth and a headdress with feathers that went all the way down to the floor. Oh yes, and several war paint stripes on his face and chest.

"You're not going to wear that, are you?" I asked.

"Of course. Why not?"

"Well, for one, it's insulting to Native Americans," I added, trying to take the moral high road.

"Insulting? I would think they'd be proud to see someone keeping their traditions alive!"

"Michael, going to an orgy is not a sacred Native American tradition."

"Robert, instead of knocking things you haven't tried, just keep your mouth shut and watch the men all over town ogle me. While I think the men of Fire Island are a lot better, there are a lot of good-looking men here. You've got to stand out if you want to get dates."

"Michael, the reason men are going to look at you is because you have a killer—strike that—a humpy body. You could walk around in a shit-filled diaper and gay men will still be falling all over you."

"You think so?" Michael asked in wonderment.

"Fine. Let's go, Pocahontas, and you can show off your papoose to your heart's content."

I felt like a fool walking down the street next to Michael, but he had long ago reached that point where he ceased to care about what people thought of him. True to his prediction, men whistled and turned their heads all the way to the art dealer's house.

The fact that most of the houses in Provincetown were originally small homes belonging to fishermen of modest means made the art dealer's house look all the larger. Its hulking facade loomed over the street, intimidating all who dared to peek over the tall hedges that surrounded it. If the hedges didn't do the trick, the dogs would. There were at least a dozen Dobermans that constantly patrolled the grounds, flinging themselves at the chain-link fence every time a tourist lingered too long at the gate. We stood at a gate set into the hedges a good forty feet from the front door. We pressed the buzzer on the intercom and waited. Nothing. Michael pressed the buzzer again. There was a roar of noise from the speaker, no doubt the background sounds of a party in full swing.

"Yes!?" came a voice like the squeal of tires on a rain-slicked roadway.

Michael stepped up the to speaker. "Michael Stark. I'm a friend of Mitchell."

"I'll be right out," answered the voice, punctuated by smacks of chewing gum. "I've got tah help you through the dawgs. Stay put."

One of the large double doors on the front of the house swung open and out popped a curmudgeon of a man wearing a dog collar and draped with huge chains. Around his neck hung a sign that said "PISS PIG." I was definitely not going to like this. Piss Pig walked fearlessly though the menacing dogs, his gait restrained by the ankle chains that hobbled his feet. Eventually, he reached the front gate, unlocked it, and waved us toward the front door of the house.

Piss Pig stared at me first, then ran his eyes up and down Michael's costume. He smirked, then made a brief utterance.

"And how! C'mon. Nathan's anxious to meet you."

"How's Mitchell?" Michael asked.

"He's going to do a duct tape mummification scene with Nathan later this evening. It promises to be quite interesting. Right now, Nathan is still receiving guests."

"Mitchell was always good with tape. A real pro," Michael said, truly envious of Mitchell's talents.

We entered the house and followed Piss Pig into a large room where a man was bound and gagged with so much leather, you could hardly tell that there was a person inside if it weren't for a pair of eyes staring out from two eyeholes in a black leather hood. Piss Pig led us up to the bound form. I didn't know what to do, but I felt compelled to say something.

"Impressive."

Michael gave me a look that said "just don't say anything to embarrass me, even though that ship has already sailed."

Piss Pig motioned to the leather cocoon. "Nathan, I'd like you to meet Michael Stark. And this," he said motioning to me, "is Robert Somethingorother."

A muffled sound came from deep inside the mass of leather, followed by an almost imperceptible nod from the tightly bound head.

"Nice to meet you, Nathan," I added, automatically extending my hand to shake, not thinking that Nathan was in no position to shake hands. It was times like this that made me realize just how much I was out of my league.

"C'mon, Robert," Michael said, leading me by the hand before I could make myself into any more of a fool than I already had.

We walked into an adjoining room that was filled from floor to ceiling with art that I had seen in expensive coffee table books. A Rauschenberg here, a Pollock there. But no Matisse. The room was also filled with men in various costumes and stages of dress. There was an open bar attended by a naked hunk of a bartender, so naturally we stopped to pick up a drink. Or two. Or however many we needed to get a good eyeful. We had no sooner taken a sip of our wines when I heard Mitchell's baritone voice from across the room.

"Michael! I knew that you'd come," Mitchell announced as he pushed his way between us. "So what's this I hear about you making a snuff movie?"

"I'm not making a snuff movie. I just got framed in the murder of my ex."

"Whatever. Let's go take a walk around and see what we can find. There's some interesting things going on in one of the back rooms. This topman from Cincinnati is doing a monster dildo demonstration with this pig from New York." Mitchell put his arm through Michael's and led him off, trying to leave me behind. Michael, though dim-witted, could sense that Mitchell had it in for me for whatever reason.

"Mitch, we're forgetting Robert!" Michael reminded Mitchell.

"And that's bad?"

"Now, now, Mitch. I know Robert is not as experienced as we're used to, but he's a great guy. Robert! C'mon!" Michael called to me. "Let's go have a little fun."

A little voice inside my head told me to go ahead. Have some fun. Live life a little wildly for a change. Break out of my shell and just plain let go. But just then, an even bigger voice told me that I should just tell Michael and Mitchell to go ahead. "I'll just stay here out of trouble. In fact, maybe I'll play a little billiards," I said, heading for a nearby pool table. "You two go ahead and have some fun," I called, pulling the balls from below and racking them up on the table.

Mitchell's face turned bright red and he let out a burst of laughter and continued to laugh, pointing at me.

"What's wrong?" I asked.

Mitchell continued to laugh until he was doubled over. At this point, many of the rooms occupants were looking at me. I stood there holding one of the balls, not knowing whether to proceed.

"Those balls spent the entire night up Nathan's ass. I know—I shoved 'em up there!"

Mitchell, along with Michael and the rest of the room, roared with laughter as I put the billiard ball down carefully and muttered something about wanting to play Parcheesi instead. As the merriment died down and everyone went back to their sexcapades, I asked the bartender for another drink as well as the directions to the toilet.

It was a mystery. Was Nathan mixed up in this mess? And why would anyone want billiard balls up their ass? I mean, think of the germs.

I made my way along a corridor, catching glimpses of

various orgies through completely open doorways. A sling here. Naked men wearing gas masks and encased in rubber suits in another. Being a close friend of Michael could turn your view of the world completely upside down. You start out a nice gay boy from Michigan, and before you know it, it seems completely normal to have to some guy shoving dildos the size of the Hindenburg up your bum.

I reached the end of the hall and saw no hint of Michael's Matisse. I decided to go upstairs and take a look around. An occasional sex room here and there, but one door at the end of the hall was ajar and led to a large library and art gallery. I pushed the door closed behind me and turned on the light for a better look. Paintings were hung everywhere on the four walls. A Schnabel, Lichtenstein, Matisse. A Matisse? It looked like Michael's painting. It had to be. I moved closer for a better look. Oh my God, it *was* Michael's painting! I reached up to touch the painting—as if I could determine the authenticity of artwork. It was a move that I would sorely regret.

A shrieking alarm that must've been designed in hell tore through the air with such intensity, I thought my head was going to explode. Since I was already out on bail, I did what any red-blooded criminal would have done: I ran. Apparently, I wasn't the only one with the idea of hightailing it out of the house. Men came streaming out of various rooms naked, wrapped in leather, and one, encased in Saran wrap, was being carried out by two men who dragged their helpless subject as fast as they could, dropping him several times on the sidewalk. Men were yelling "Fire!" and "Everybody out!" I knew there was no fire, but I wasn't about to tell them. When I reached the front door, Piss Pig was trying to tell the terrified guests that it was just a false alarm, but to no avail. He stood at the front door restraining the few Dobermans that hadn't disappeared in terror of the alarm—which incidentally, sounded practically as loud outside as it had inside. Apparently, the Dobermans weren't as fierce as they looked.

Nathan's guests stood in the street staring at the house, expecting it to burst into flames as in the final moments of *Rebecca*. The real sight was the men themselves. They had been so terrified by the shrieking alarm, few of them gave much thought to the fact that they could have been arrested for standing in the street dressed (or undressed) as they were had it not been for the fact that this was Provincetown. Passersby stopped to get a look at these men, then, unimpressed, stared at the house expecting it to do heavens-knows-what. Presently, I saw Michael and Mitchell come out of the house and walk nonchalantly down the path to the street.

"Michael!" I called out with as much concern in my voice as I could muster. "Thank God you're safe!"

Michael pulled me aside, out of earshot from Mitchell. "I appreciate your help in looking for my painting, but it wasn't mine."

I protested. "But it looked exactly like yours!"

"It's not mine, Robert. It's similar, but not the same. I don't know much about my Warhol—"

"Matisse, Michael!"

"That's right, Matisse. As I was saying, I don't know too much about my painting, but I know what it looks like. Anyway, Robert, I appreciate your help, but stealing a painting is only going to get us into more trouble."

"I didn't take it. I just touched the frame to get a closer look and all hell broke loose."

"Well, thanks anyway. It looks like Nathan is pretty clean. I don't think he's mixed up in this mess. Well," Michael continued, "I'm going back inside. Care to join me?"

I looked at him. "I thought you said the place was clean."

"It is. It's just that there's a hot little number waiting for me in the basement."

"How do you know that he's still there? Most of the guys left."

"Oh, believe me, he's not going anywhere—until I let him, that is."

"Oh," I replied.

Mitchell, who had been hanging back from our conversation, looked at me and licked his lips.

"What about Nathan?" I inquired.

Mitchell volunteered an answer. "The little worthless whimpering whaleshit. I'll just let him hang there for a couple of hours while Michael and I have a little fun in the basement. If I weren't staying here free and getting paid for my services, I wouldn't give worms like Nathan the time of day. The things you have to do when you're career oriented!"

I woke up the next morning to find that the guy that Michael had brought home for me from the orgy ("procured for me," he said) had disappeared. So had my new wallet and new watch. Of course, the guy didn't touch a thing of Michael's. Just my stuff.

"Sorry about your things, but I just thought you could use a little help," Michael triumphed over me. "And let me guess. You didn't even get laid for all your trouble, did you?"

"No!" I replied indignantly.

"Got you drunk, did he?"

"No, Michael. He didn't get me drunk. But I did get drunk. After."

"Then how did he make off with your stuff?" Michael pried.

"We had been getting heavy in the bed and he asked me to go get a towel because things were going to get messy, he said. Well, when I found a towel that looked like it could be tossed after sex, I came back to the bedroom and he was gone. And so was my wallet and watch and whatever else he managed to get his cheap little hands on."

"The old would-you-get-a-towel ruse, eh? Robert, that's the oldest trick in the book, no pun intended."

"So I fall for any guy that falls on me. So sue me!"

"Robert, you've got to be more selective about who you sleep with," Michael said, pointing a finger at me for extra emphasis.

"*You* brought him home for *me*, Michael!"

"Oh, yeah, sorry," Michael said, apologizing slightly.

"Did you hear what you just said, Michael? I think the vase just got called Ming by the plate."

"I *am* selective. You don't see me going home with scags, do you? I have standards."

I wasn't about to let this one rest. "Michael, your only criteria about whom you sleep with are that they have a nine-inch penis and that they're breathing. Anything beyond that is gravy to you."

Just then, there was a knock at the door. Or, to be more correct, a thundering banging.

"Monette's here!" I yelled and bolted toward the door. I was never so happy to see anyone in all my life. As I opened the door, she dropped her bags and gave me a hug that I swear cracked a few ribs.

"Robert! My God, I'm happy to see you. How's everything?"

"Well, besides being under suspicion as an accomplice to murder, everything's fine."

"Always the Pollyanna, Robert. Well, show me to my room. I'll unpack and we can all get started trying to untangle this whole mess."

Monette settled in quickly and before we knew it, we were all gathered around the table on the deck to plot our first move.

"The first thing we—er—you need to do," Monette said, scribbling on a piece of paper, "is to find out all you can in the way of clues found at the murder scene."

"Monette, I don't think that the police are going to just hand us all the evidence until a grand jury has seen it."

"Yes, but there are ways of getting that information," Monette said, pointing at Michael's crotch.

I was shocked. "Monette, are you suggesting that we use

Michael as sexual bait to illegally get our hands on information that could help our cause?"

Both Monette and I turned to stare at Michael, who looked like a deer caught in the headlights of a speeding semi.

"Michael, darling," I said slyly. "Don't you think those shorts cover up a little too much of those legs of yours?"

Michael and I went to Town Hall to see Mr. Sandsome, the detective assigned to our case. We told him our theory about Mr. X. The detective listened intently, jotting down notes now and then. We asked to see any of the evidence found at the scene of the crime, but the detective turned down our request, saying it was confidential. Since Michael was never used to being denied anything in his life, this refusal made him all the more determined to find out what the cops had in their possession.

As the detective was walking us out to the lobby, Lady Luck decided to come over to our side in this mess. As Michael was finishing up his conversation with the detective, I noticed a rookie cop eyeing Michael a little too much. He made the pretense of filling out reports, but his eyes kept darting over to Michael. No doubt about it. He was gay. Even better, the cruisey rookie was just that: a rookie. Michael's sexual prowess would run rings around the inexperienced cop. Plus, our friend was exceedingly plain. As such, I figured that he didn't often get dates like Michael. As Michael said goodbye to the detective, I pulled Michael aside and told him what I had seen. He immediately swung into action like a gay Mata Hari, not merely returning the rookie's gaze, but staring with the hypnotic intensity of Count Dracula hankering after a Red Cross blood bank. Michael had a knack for this. Guys would look into his eyes and Michael would just stare them down until they were helpless sex slaves. I don't know how he did this, but it really worked. Before he knew what hit him, the rookie had told Michael his name (Tom Robinson), and Michael had invited him over to the Plover tonight for a drink or two, to which the rookie agreed.

We were supposed to go to a drag show that evening, but Tom took precedence. I made myself scarce as Michael awaited his prey. Promptly at nine o'clock, Tom showed up, raging with hormones. Michael proceeded to get the cop drunk and convinced him to let go and get wild—which he did. Much to the rookie's chagrin, I popped out of the closet that I had been waiting in and snapped a round of career-damaging pictures. Even though what we did was an obvious setup, the rookie cop was the last person on earth who wanted pictures of himself with a large latex ear of corn sticking out of his butt circulating around town. Note to myself: never eat corn on the cob again. We had been prepared to find a wealth of information, but were surprised when very little turned up. But as we reported our find to Monette the next morning, it was a good start.

"Listen up, Monette, there isn't a lot, but there are a few good tidbits. First of all, the police found photos of Max in Michael's room."

"I didn't bring any!" Michael protested.

"Well, they were there nonetheless," I said. "Oh, and one small detail. All the photos had Max's head cut out of them."

"Uh-oh!" Monette commented. "That looks kinda bad."

"There's more," I continued. "The coroner said that whoever finished off Max tried to strangle him with their hands first, but resorted to using the glove, which did the trick."

"It suggests a drag queen, but that doesn't support our theory totally," Monette replied.

"True. But this piece of evidence does," I continued. "There were a lot of high-heel tracks in the sand around the murder site."

"But this whole drag queen thing just doesn't make sense. What would Max be doing with a drag queen?" Michael asked. "Believe me, he wasn't into it. I could tell."

Monette's super-sleuth mind ground to a halt. "I don't know. Maybe he was into that sort of thing on the side. Or maybe his companion just happened to be a drag queen. Or there's the possibility that the gloves and the high heels could be a red herring—to make us think that it was a drag queen. But I don't know what's the purpose in that. Back to the gloves. It's not the gloves, per se, that made me think that Max's murderer is a drag queen, Robert. It just confirms it. Just think for a moment. Max was pumped. No woman could choke him to death. But a man who was equally built could do the job. Well, guys, I think it's about time that we took in some drag shows. In fact, every one of them in town. Starting tonight."

Just as I had convinced myself that life couldn't get any weirder, it did. That night, we found ourselves sitting in the Smuggler's Lounge on Commercial Street.

6

Is That Your Nose or Are You Eating a Banana?

I never would have believed it, but there we were: Michael, Monette, and me at the Smuggler's Lounge, waiting for the drag show to begin. If ever there was a quintessentially gay piano bar in the world, this was it. The decor was tacky beyond compare. And over in the corner, was the obligatory grand piano, in white no less. Seated around the piano were Broadway show-tune queens singing away. But most important was the presence of the one item necessary for a successful gay piano bar: a loud, obnoxious person whose sole purpose was to lead, in song, the drunken cadres that flocked around his piano. This particular obnoxious person was known locally as Large Larry. Despite his happy-go-lucky and outgoing public image, Large Larry was a bitter person. Bitter about his weight. Bitter about his clothes. But most of all, bitter that he should be sitting behind a large white piano night after night leading a drunken band of Broadway wanna-bes. It would have been all fine and dandy if Large Larry had kept his bitterness to himself like the rest of us, but this was not the case. Large Larry would constantly scan the crowds like some malevolent radar and attack unwitting victims with a barrage of tired old insults. This night, Larry had already made fun of a lady's red hair, one man's shirt, another tourist's shorts, and one of the bar-

boys—and we had been sitting in the Smuggler's Lounge
for only five minutes. Larry's gaze floated over in our direction, then swept over us and passed on without spotting us.
We were safe for now.

I looked for our drag queen performer, but the closed
curtain off to the side of the piano gave no hint that the
show was ready to begin. If I weren't a suspect in a murder
case, I wouldn't be here. Believe me, I was in no mood to
pay five dollars to see "It's a Drag," starring Naughty Pine.
The very title caused my bowels to tighten up so much, I
thought I was going to have a bout of acute colitis. I could
picture the whole show before it even began. Music, sup-
plied by Large Larry, would usher our star from behind a
chintzy curtain while a cheap floodlight commandeered by
the bartender would follow our entertainer to her spot on a
bar stool that had been hurriedly stolen from the bar just
minutes before the show. Our star would launch into a
lineup of tried-and-true Broadway show tunes, the lyrics
naughtily changed to evoke guffaws from an audience com-
posed mostly of queens from small towns in backward areas
of the country, notably New Hampshire. Our star would
probably have a couple of duet numbers with Large Larry,
then would presumably open up the floor for the customary
audience-bashing. As I soon found out, I was painfully on
target.

The lights in the bar went down and Large Larry pounded
out a thundering entrance number as a spotlight appeared
on the curtain, which parted to reveal one of the most pa-
thetically dressed female impersonators I have ever had the
misfortune to see. The guys from New Hampshire roared
and whistled, as if this were the only drag show they had
ever seen, which was probably not far from the truth. Naughty
Pine was nothing less than an insult to professional drag
queens the world over and should rightly have had every sequin ripped from every dress in her tawdry wardrobe. Bald
patches of cheesecloth peered out from her ratty wig, while

her dress looked like some castoff refused even by the Salvation Army. ("Even *we* have our standards, Miss Pine!") Her shoes were Jackie Kennedy needle-nose pumps—in pink, no less. At least this fashion misery had the sense to make sure her purse matched her shoes. Naughty introduced herself and launched into a spiel of her history. She told the audience that she used to do drag in upstate New York and went by the name Ada Rondack. Ha, ha. She then burst into song, gleefully mangling the words to so many cherished American classics that I could almost hear George and Ira Gershwin rolling over in their graves and puking copiously. For over an hour and fifteen minutes, we were brutalized by Naughty Pine's screeching voice and terrifically unfunny jokes. Naughty announced that we were near the end of the show, but that she wanted to take a few minutes to get to know, and pummel (ha, ha), a few members of the audience. The house lights went up, revealing an audience that had split into two factions. One side wanted nothing to do with this show and wished that they'd made a beeline out of the bar while the lights were down. The rest wanted Naughty to pick on them, thus giving them something to tell the folks back in Des Moines: that not only had they been to see a real drag performer, but that they had purposely been humiliated. Judging from the clothing this faction wore, Naughty would have an easy time. Like shooting ducks in a barrel.

Naughty walked into the audience with her microphone at her mouth, like some shabby Oprah, looking for a victim. She found one in a heterosexual couple that grew red with embarrassment as Naughty hovered over them, nodding her head as the audience egged her on to viciously attack the twosome.

"SO! Where are you two fashion victims from, eh?" Naughty asked, pushing the microphone into their faces. Talk about the pot calling the kettle black.

I kid you not, this was their answer:

"Iowa!" the woman answered proudly.

"Iowa, huh?" Naughty pondered. "What street do you live on?"

It may have been one of the oldest and tiredest jokes in the world, but the audience roared with laughter, especially when Naughty's remark was punctuated by a rim shot off a snare drum that Larry conveniently kept at the side of his piano for just such occasions. Naughty, no mere amateur performer, reacted to the rim shot as if she had been goosed, resulting in more laughter from the audience. I felt like a trapped animal. I wanted to go, but we had to stay so Monette could find whatever she was looking for. A more sensible animal would have chewed its leg off and made a bloody but quick getaway.

Naughty drifted across to the far side of the room, devouring an elderly gay couple from Ft. Lauderdale. When she had finished them off, she began scanning the room, trying to make eye contact with her next victim. At that moment, I unfortunately forgot the cardinal rule of being a New Yorker: never, ever maintain eye contact with anyone. Naughty caught my glance and homed in on the signal like a sequin-covered buzzard swooping down on possum road-kill.

"And who do we have over here? Where are you from?" Naughty asked as she shoved the microphone into my face. "Now don't tell me. Let me see. Three New Yorkers. All here on vacation. Now who's with whom? No, no, no, let me guess. The plain one is with Glamor Boy here. You did pretty well for yourself. How much does Glamor Boy charge by the hour?"

Michael, like the rest of us, tried not to reply to Naughty, hoping she'd give up the chase and move on. That Naughty had basically called Michael a hooker didn't seem to effect him much. He got called a whore all the time. But the fact that he was publicly being paired with "the plain one" was more than Michael could bear.

"No. He's not my boyfriend."

Naughty closed in for the kill. "Oh, thank God. He's not your type at all. He looks like he hasn't put out since the Reagan years."

More laughter.

Naughty continued. "Now don't tell me you're with this woman here," she said, pointing the microphone at Monette. "You *are* a woman, aren't you?"

Monette rolled her eyes and smirked a little but said nothing. I was so proud of her—proud that she didn't pick up Naughty and rip Naughty's heart out of her chest and show it to her while it was still beating.

Naughty turned back to Michael, figuring that with his good looks and expensive clothing, he would make an easier target than a six-foot-four-inch lesbian.

"So what's your name, pretty boy?"

Michael had no choice but to answer. "Michael."

"Michael, eh? And what do you do for a living, Michael?"

"Nothing."

"Nothing?!" Naughty exclaimed. "No job?"

"No. Not really."

Naughty's eyes lit up. "Okay, folks . . . let me get this straight . . . or at least gayly correct. Pretty Boy here is handsome. Great clothes—hey, you two from Iowa, look over here and learn a lesson. And you probably have a nice car, don't you?"

"A Range Rover," Michael imprudently replied. I could tell that he thought that his choice of vehicles would impress Naughty and tell her to back off, but the comment only provided fodder for Naughty to step up the intensity of her attacks.

"A Range Rover! And how did you afford a big, expensive car like that, I wonder?"

Large Larry, who had been hanging back until he wanted to explode, joined the fray. "I'm sure that he paid—but not in cash."

"Why, what*ever* do you mean, Larry?" Naughty teased.

"Well, I would think Michael has a job . . ."

". . . but it's outlawed in forty-nine states," Naughty finished Larry's thought with her heavy, male smoker's cackle.

Michael who had up until now smiled good-naturedly along with Naughty's jokes, was unable to contain himself any longer. Being insulted just didn't happen to a person of Michael's wealth. He burst from his chair and began throttling Naughty with his two hands. The most surprising thing was that no one, save Large Larry, came to Naughty's rescue, owing to the fact that Naughty's vicious ribbing had alienated everyone who worked at the bar. Large Larry, while a sissy of the highest degree, was still large and a figure to contend with.

The show that ensued was probably far more entertaining than anything Naughty could ever pull off on her own: me trying to pull Large Larry off Michael, who was strangling Naughty. Monette, who had evidently made up her mind to have no part of this, sauntered over to the bar, ordered a drink, and laughed with the employees. After several minutes of scuffling, a stalemate was reached, with the three of us being ordered to leave the bar by Large Larry.

"Gladly!" Michael screamed at Larry as the three of us walked out the door and into the street, but not without Michael making a quick sprint back into the bar to throw a bowlfull of maraschino cherries in Larry's face.

As we walked down the street, a strange thought occurred to me.

"Monette?" I asked. "Why did we have to sit through all that?"

"I don't know."

I was just a tad incensed. "What do you mean you don't know?"

"Just what I said. I don't know."

"Monette, sweety-darling, honey-snookums. You mean to tell me that we paid good money . . ."

"Five dollars," Monette said to set the record straight.

"Okay, a pitiful sum to sit there and listen to bad singing and get insulted for nothing?"

"Robert, we had to start somewhere."

"But why there?"

"It was the cheapest drag show in town. I'm looking for something, but I don't know what. But I'll know when I see it. So as long as we're looking, we might as well do it cheaply. But we didn't come out empty-handed," Monette replied.

"What do you mean?" Michael spoke up. "I'll tell you what I got! I got a cigarette burn in my shirt from that fucking queen! I'm gonna sue that fucking bastard and make her eat every sequin from that crummy dress of hers!"

Monette stopped walking and held up two fingers in front of us. "One, I chatted with the bartenders and found out that there are several other acts in town with Bette Davis skits in them."

I was amazed. "And what were the other things you discovered?"

"The woman bartender who looked like a cross between Lea DeLaria and Martina Navratilova asked me out on a date this weekend."

Monette looked through the town's paper, bypassing Michael's picture on the front page with the headline: NEWPORT HEIR DRAGGED INTO CROSS-DRESSER MURDER. There were vicious quotation marks around the word *dragged*. Since it was only 9:30, Monette reasoned that we had time to take in another drag show.

"Oh, my God! I don't believe it!" Monette moaned as she stared at the paper in horror.

"What is it?" Michael and I asked together.

"I don't believe it! This can't be true!"

"WHAT IS IT, MONETTE?" Michael and I practically screamed in unison.

"Listen to this," Monette said, reading verbatim a column from the newspaper. " 'Glut of Bette Davis shows hits Provincetown. Due to a freak coincidence, Provincetown theaters are hosting not just the usual one or two Bette Davis drag shows, but eight this summer season. The glut has caught theater producers by surprise, forcing a flurry of last-minute changes in an attempt to distinguish the various shows from their competition. At last count, the shows now open are *Who Gives a Fuck Whatever Happened to Baby Jane; Bette Get Your Gun: A Musical Spoof to the Letter; I'm Just Wild About Bette; You Bette Your Ass; Attack of the Forty-Foot Bette; It's My Party and I'll Smoke if I Want To;* and *Bette vs. Godzilla.* Adding to the glut is another show due to open next weekend, entitled *I Could Just Kick You To Death.* The show was slated to open this weekend, but was delayed by the recent injury of two drag queens.' "

Monette put the paper down and stood looking at us with her jaw wide open.

"Monette, if you don't close your mouth soon, something is going to fly into it. And in this town, that could mean anything," I said.

The newspaper article provided us with twenty-twenty hindsight. A quick glance around us revealed that we had indeed landed in a twisted episode of *The Twilight Zone.* Suddenly, we were aware of Bette Davises everywhere. They were beckoning people to come off the streets into dark bars for Bette Davis drag shows. They proffered plates of fudge in front of the confectionery shops. And one, dressed as the elderly Baby Jane Hudson, blew balloons and twisted them into animal shapes for passing children, only to pop the multicolored dachshunds with a hat pin just as the kids reached out to claim their prize.

"We can see *Speedway: The Judy Garland Story* at the Town Hall, or we could take in *I Fall to Pieces.* The ad says its 'a farcical psycho-drama comedic romp involving three chainsaw-juggling drag queens. I laughed. I cried. I vomited.' "

Michael crinkled his nose. "Who said that?"

"Let me see here. 'Provincetown's reigning queen of drag queens, Beyonda Sea'—whoever that is." Monette continued. "Hey, don't look at me. I didn't write it! I don't know about you two, but I think this one has potential. And besides, I'm a dyke. I just don't get the Judy Garland thing. I'd rather see a play about Ellen DeGeneres."

"Dear, delusional Monette," I interjected. "No one wants to see a show about women like that. I mean, look at Ellen. She's not a ruthlessly ambitious, bitchy, alcoholic, pill-popping, rapacious harpy bent on self-destruction. There's no theater."

"Well, I say that we go see *Fall to Pieces*."

"Fine, Monette. You win."

Monette looked at me with a mischievous twinkle in her eyes. "I always do."

The three of us made our way through the crowds to the Whaler Theater, a makeshift place to see a show if ever there was one, but it had to be better than Naughty Pine.

Thankfully, it was. A whole lot better. *I Fall to Pieces* seemed perfectly luxurious compared to that abortion of a drag show with Naughty Pine. This show had a real stage, albeit a hollow-sounding plywood concoction. The lighting was actually real theater lighting instead of two workman's lights clamped onto suspended ceiling tiles. And in stark contrast to Naughty Pine's show, someone had actually taken the time to write the lines for this play and even block the movements of the performers. Best of all, it was funny. Of course, how could it be anything but when the bulk of the action involved a group of free-spirited drag queens hacking prepubescent teenagers to bits with chainsaws? The real surprise came when the performers took a bow and the lead drag queen took the microphone to address the adoring audience.

"Thank you; thank you very much," Patricia said triumphantly. "Thank you for coming to see us. This is the first time we've done anything like this. A few months ago, we were just three out-of-work gay actors in New York City when we got this idea to do *Pieces*. But none of us had ever done drag before. So we thought, where else in the world could we go to learn the do's and don'ts of drag? Before you knew it, we were on our way to Provincetown. So to make a long story short, I'd like to thank Beyonda Sea, Provincetown's reigning queen of drag queens for giving us the moral support, technical support, and eyeliner tips that helped us become what we are today: underpaid alcoholics. Stand up, Beyonda."

From the front row, there arose one of the oldest drag queens I have ever seen. She must have been in her late seventies—a relic from the Cenozoic period. Carbon dating wouldn't help. Now I knew what theater critics meant when they stated that someone was "timeless." They were kindly saying that the person in question was just too old to tell. I say "drag queen" because Beyonda fell squarely into that territory, yet she seemed to gingerly straddle the line that separated the men from the women, being neither completely male nor female. You know, like Rose Marie. Smartly turned out in a white linen suit, Beyonda rose, tossed a few royal waves at her adoring audience, then sat down.

The crowd continued applauding, probably more from the fact that this ageless creature could even stand up at all. Eventually, the three drag queens made their last bow and the crowd began making their way toward the exits. Monette remained in her chair, thinking.

"Let's go, Monette," Michael said hurriedly. "The gorgeous hunk who was sitting in the third row is getting away."

Monette looked first at Michael and then me and said, "I want you two to get into a drag act in town. C'mon," she said, grabbing us by our T-shirts and pulling us toward Beyonda, who was taking her time gathering her possessions from the seat next to her.

"Miss Sea?" Monette asked, shoving Michael and me in

front of her like two serfs being submitted for the czar's approval.

"Why, yes, child, what can I do for you?" Beyonda said in a crackly Southern drawl.

"My two friends would like to get into the business and they'd like to learn from a pro like yourself."

"The business?" Beyonda asked. "Honey, this ain't prostitution—God knows it doesn't pay like it!" Beyonda chuckled and looked both Michael and me up and down. "Is this some kind of joke?"

Monette acted hurt, although Michael and I were bearing the brunt of the embarrassment. "Why, what's wrong with them?"

"Honey, you've got ta have a certain air about you to be a drag queen. Not everyone can pull it off. I mean, look at Wesley Snipes in *To Wong Foo.*"

Monette pleaded, "But you took on the three guys in tonight's play. They didn't know a thing when they started. Pleeeeeeease?" I had never heard Monette whine before, but it seemed to work on me and I wasn't even the one making the decision.

"I don't know. . . ." Beyonda contemplated tutoring Michael and me, then relented under the obnoxious whining of Monette. "All right, you two can stop by my place tomorrow and we'll talk. But not too early. And I'm not promising anything. Three-fifteen Landfill Road. Back behind Shank Painter Pond."

"What time?" Monette inquired.

"How about two o'clock?"

"Fine! Thank you very much, Miss Sea."

The three of us waited behind while Beyonda left the theater. After all, Michael and I didn't want a lot of witnesses catching us kicking Monette to death.

Michael was the first to break the silence. "Monette, i you weren't bigger than me, I'd kick your butt from here t Boston. Do you have any idea of what something like thi could do to my reputation?"

"If you go to prison," Monette shot back, "your reputation will make you one of the most popular girls in the joint. Get my drift?"

"Yes, Michael, I think that this is one time you have to swallow your pride and do the right thing."

Michael turned on me in an instant. "I'm not going on stage without your little butt at my side. Right, Candy Corn?"

"There's no way I'm doing drag. No way." I dug in my heels.

"You've got to," Michael pleaded with real concern in his voice.

"Why? *I* didn't kill Max. You did."

"I didn't kill him," Michael shot back testily.

"Well, the police think you did. I'm only an accessory!"

Monette, sensing correctly that Michael and I were going to fight like two prison inmates over a cigarette, intervened.

"All right, the two of you. Michael, shut up. Robert, shut up. There! Okay, let's not gang up on each other. We need to stick together. So if you two cats are done fighting, we can talk this over peacefully." Monette paused a moment to take a deep breath. "Okay, now, Robert, why won't you put on a dress?"

"It's . . . icky!"

Monette remained as calm as a psychiatrist. "I see. It's icky . . . but not icky-poo?"

"Monette," I said calmly, "you're patronizing me."

"Of course I am. You're behaving like a two-year-old. So what's the real problem, Robert?"

"Just what I told you. I'm not used to it. It feels so . . . strange."

"I'm sure that the first time you had another man's dick up your butt it felt strange, too. But you adapted."

"Well, when you paint it in such glowing terms as that, Monette, how can I refuse?"

"Robert, the two of you are in real trouble. The grand jury is going to be gathering evidence real soon, and what they have to go on looks pretty incriminating. You've got to do this. I have a real hunch that this is going to get us somewhere. We need some inside information and we're never going to get the stuff we need if we're standing outside with our noses pressed up against the glass. Now, c'mon. Chin up, boobies out."

I still had one reservation that had to be soothed. "Monette?"

"Yes, Robert?"

"You won't tell any of our friends that Michael and I did this, will you?"

Monette smiled at me with a smile that belonged more appropriately on a crocodile. "Cross my heart and hope to die."

"Let's hope it doesn't come to that," I replied.

After an uneventful morning spent at the beach, we prepared ourselves for what could be our drag debut. I had to admit it, whenever I hung around Michael, there was never a dull moment.

Beyonda Sea wasn't kidding about her address. There really was a Landfill Road in Provincetown, and I'll give you three guesses as to what could be found at the end of it. Fortunately, Beyonda's house lay a respectable distance from the aforementioned dumping ground. But really!

As we approached the house, I had to admit that it didn't look like a drag queen's residence. There was no marquee over the house spelling out Beyonda's name in lights. Nor was there any giant high-heeled shoe planter in the front yard. Not even a huge wig perched on the roof. No, Beyonda's house was a simple Cape Cod painted a sickening shade of sea-foam green, probably picked up at Sears's Autumn Paint Sale for Monetarily Deprived Drag Queens.

(Hurry! Three days only!) Even the yard was tidy, with bunches of flowers scattered here and there, but nothing out of the ordinary.

The first hint of what we were letting ourselves in for came when Michael rang the lighted doorbell. The tune that played when the button was pushed was "I Enjoy Being a Girl."

Just seconds later, the door flew open to reveal Beyonda in one of the tackiest muumuus I have ever seen.

"Ah, two handsome gentlemen callers come to see little ol' me. Why, come right in. I just got out of bed."

From the outside, you would never know that a drag queen lived there. Inside was another story. If you looked in the dictionary under *foofy*, there would be a picture of Beyonda's living room. Every possible inch was crammed with ostrich plumes, ceramic Russian wolfhounds, Erté sculptures, and lots and lots of red everywhere. Red furniture, red walls, red shag carpeting, red lightbulbs. There was no denying it. Michael and I had passed through a portal in the space-time continuum and ended up in some kind of drag-queen dimension.

"Come right in you two. Sit down and make yourselves comfortable. You are?" she asked, staring at me.

"Robert. Robert Willsop."

"And you?" she said, looking at Michael.

"Tim Mayhew."

"You're so fulla shit, Mr. Stark, that I could smell you back in my hometown of Biloxi." Michael was taken aback by Beyonda's comment and it showed on his face. Beyonda continued. "I saw your picture in the paper, Michael. Nothing goes on in this town without me knowing about it. Martini, anyone?"

Beyonda sauntered over to a drinks tray that was loaded to the point of being dangerously top-heavy. Michael's glance darted over to me, indicating that we had both better imbibe with Beyonda or risk offending her.

"We'll join you, Miss Sea," Michael offered.

"Good, good for you. I never trust a man who doesn't drink." Beyonda handed Michael and me two martinis in glasses decorated with black-and-white Pierrots, then threw her ample frame on a red sofa (or should I say divan) facing the two of us. "So what can I do for you two?"

Michael leaped into the abyss. "We want you to teach us how to do drag so we can get into a show in town."

"May I ask you a question, Mr. Stark?" Beyonda ventured.

"Yes?"

"Now, why in the world would someone like you want to get into drag? You certainly don't look the part. Your friend here is another story," she said, clearly pointing to me. "Mr. Willsop looks like he might make a good drag queen. He's got the face and a great feminine walk."

I didn't know whether to thank Beyonda for the compliment or to issue a contract to have her kneecaps broken.

"Well," Michael continued, "the truth is that I'm looking to invest some of my money in a series of drag shows, and I want to get a behind-the-scenes look at the shows before I sink all those dollars into a project."

Beyonda looked at Michael in disbelief, then exploded into gales of laughter, spilling some of her martini in the process. "Mr. Stark, let me tell you two things. One, you'll never make a dime investing in drag shows, no matter who's in them. I mean, look at this palace I live in. Fabulous, isn't it? And two, I don't believe one fucking word of what you said."

Michael remained defiant. "Does it really matter why Robert and I want to get into a show here in town?"

"Not really, Mr. Stark. As long as you don't murder any of my girls."

"I didn't kill that guy, Miss Sea."

"I know you didn't, honey. You don't have what it takes to be a murderer. You wouldn't want to mess your hair."

"Thank you Miss Sea—I think. Anyway, it's clear that we understand each other."

"Enough to trust you for now," Beyonda responded slyly. "Now," she continued, spilling a little more of her drink, "why don't we get to know each other a little better? I always like to know the girls I propose to work with."

"Then you'll take us on?!" Michael blurted out.

Beyonda was remaining coy. "I didn't say that. We'll see. Now tell me about yourselves."

Michael proceeded to give Beyonda an abridged version of his life and background, which consisted mostly of boyfriends gained and lost—all, of course, with names that regularly appeared in *The New York Times* or *Vanity Fair*. Beyonda seemed unimpressed. I was about to tell Beyonda my story when she jumped in front of me, champing at the bit to tell hers. It was when Beyonda began to recount her life story that things began to get interesting.

Beyonda Sea's name in real life was Bubba Walker.

"Weird, huh? Born on a farm in Louisiana. Now look at me. You'd never expect that I spent years behind the wheel of a tractor, would you? Now I'm Bette Davis, Bea Arthur, and Phyllis Diller, among others. Or at least I am until Labor Day, when I pack my things up and go on to Vegas. I'm booked there through the whole winter."

Beyonda rose from her divan and sauntered over to a shelf crowded with trophies. Every one of them, we soon found out, was for winning drag tournaments. I'd heard of trophies for bowling and baseball, but drag shows? I would have thought that a platinum sequin mounted on a plaque would be more appropriate. Beyonda picked up the tallest trophy with all the tender care reserved for a newborn infant.

"I got this one at the Miss Universe Drag Pageant in Atlantic City. Some of the stiffest competition I've ever seen. Absolutely cutthroat. One of the girls was putting itching powder in the wigs. Outfits were slashed to pieces. I had to put everything under lock and key."

"Wow, I never knew drag queens could be so brutal," Michael remarked.

"Honey, some of these girls would put Hitler to shame. And it's gotten worse as the years go by. Just too many drag queens chasing too few jobs. Even with the recent upsurge in our popularity, there still aren't enough places to make a living. But there you are. We're suddenly chic, according to the media. We're in fashion shows, TV series, talk shows, documentaries; we've even got hit songs out. Ten years ago, people didn't think that we existed. Even gays. They forget that we led the charge against the police at the Stonewall riots back in sixty-seven. Gay rights might not have come so far if it weren't for us. I got hit by a broken bottle that night. See?" Beyonda rolled up her sleeve to show us a scar that she wore proudly like a badge of courage.

I felt as if I were looking at a holy relic. "Some cop hit you with a bottle?" I asked in amazement.

"No, actually, it was rival drag queen called Anna Conda. She was getting back at me for winning the title of Miss Greenwich Village that year, and in all the commotion of the riot, she threw a bottle at me, figuring I'd never know who did it. But I found out. She said she was aiming at a cop who roughed her up in the Stonewall Bar just before the riot, but I knew better. I got her back, though."

"How?" I asked. I'm sorry, but I just had to know. Bitchiness always intrigued me.

"Divine wasn't the first drag queen to eat dog shit off a sidewalk," Beyonda replied proudly.

Beyonda was tougher than her muumuu suggested.

"You know, I just wish that we got more respect within the gay community. They tolerate us because they like our shows. They come, they laugh, and they even mimic us. But the moment we step foot in a gay rights march, everyone cringes because they're afraid we're going to embarrass them. They're afraid that we're going to become fodder for some wacko fundamentalist Christian group who's going to take videotapes of us and use it against gays. They're right, but so what? So what! Don't those guys wearing combat boots, tight shorts, and muscle T-shirts embarrass gays?"

Beyonda, oblivious that she had just described Michael's present outfit to a T, continued.

"That's the ironic thing. We practically started the gay rights movement, but our progress in the area of job protection, housing, protection from hate crimes is ten, maybe even fifteen years behind the mainstream gay rights movement."

"I know just what you're saying, Beyonda," I said. "Some people are so small-minded."

"Thank you, Miss Hypocrisy," retorted Michael.

I decided to change the subject, pointing to an overly large plaque on Beyonda's lifetime achievement shelf. "What's that award for?"

"That was given to me by the charity that I started, SFA."

"Saks Fifth Avenue?" I ventured.

"No, no, no, honey. Sequins For All. We collect dresses and makeup here in the U.S. and ship the stuff to needy drag queens in poorer countries."

I had to admit, it was a novel idea.

Beyonda could see right through me. "Now, I know just what you're thinking: a sequined gown doesn't quite rate up there next to food and medicine. But look at me! Do I look like the Peace Corps type?"

Beyonda had a point.

"My mama always told me to stick with what you know. So I did. Anyway, that's a brief overview of my life. About as exciting as watching paint dry, isn't it?"

"You should hear a recap of Robert's life here," Michael said, gesturing in my direction. "After a story like his, you'd be excited to watch a documentary on zinc mining. So what do you think, Miss Sea? Would you teach us the tricks of the trade?"

"For the last time, this isn't prostitution. It's an artform that . . ."

"Yeah, whatever," Michael said, finishing her off. "How about it, Miss Sea?"

"Mr. Stark, I make it a point of taking on new recruits only if they really want to learn the art of drag more than life itself. I mean, there are too many unprofessional drag queens out there. Look at Naughty Pine. I feel it's my duty to train people who have fire in their belly to learn drag. Men who want to put on a frock, stand up on stage, and take an audience in their arms and make them laugh and cry more than anything else in the world. And, when it's all over, to stand there on a pedestal and receive the adoration of the audience for a job done to the highest possible standards. I'm afraid that I can't be sure that you want to be a drag queen that badly, Mr. Stark. I'm sorry."

Michael stared at Beyonda with all the intensity of Liz Taylor chancing upon an unguarded family-size box of Hostess Twinkies. "Miss Sea, would a nice little check for five thousand dollars to SFA help change your mind a bit?"

"We can start right away," came Beyonda's immediate reply. "And I'll do even better than just teach you two the ropes. I'll get you into a show that's opening next weekend. It's called *I Could Just Kick You To Death* and it's headed by one of the best Bette Davis impersonators in the business. Perhaps you've heard of her? His name used to be Ellis Bachman before he changed it to Bette Davis."

The next sounds to be heard were those of Michael and me choking on our cocktails.

For the next few days, we hardly saw Monette as we seemed to work nonstop learning the do's and don'ts of drag. Actually, that was part of the bargain. Monette was forbidden to see either of us practicing, since it would give her ammo to last a lifetime. We'd never hear the end of it. Meanwhile, Beyonda put us through a crash course in everything we had to know, including the all-important dancing in platform heels and the application of excessive amounts of makeup without appearing to have on tons of makeup. Beyonda had secured a stage in town for us to practice on, and she drove us like two sequined pack mules. Never mind that the two parts in Bette Davis's show were merely in the chorus line; Beyonda was training us for the performance of a lifetime. Plus, her reputation was at stake. When Beyonda was finished with a student, she could be nothing less than professional—whatever that was.

The whole training thing was the most uncomfortable thing I'd ever done. I tried to tell myself that it was only a dress. And I was only putting on enough makeup to make Joan Collins look pasty. But it was so out of character for me. Maybe I was too Midwestern, but the first time I slithered into a dress for one of Beyonda's lessons, I had my first out-of-body experience. Like some toothless redneck recounting for *Reader's Digest* how his "body floated above the operating table after a near-fatal accident with a wheat combine," I saw this other person putting a dress on a body that just happened to be mine. As if that weren't weird enough, my fingers sported blood-red press-on nails an inch long, and my entire forehead was pulled up and back by a stocking cap hidden under the blond wig I was wearing, in order to give me, in the words of Beyonda, "more eyelid area to work with." It was a trick Beyonda taught us. It worked. I now had so much eyelid area, my parents back in Michigan could probably tell if I was surprised without ever stepping off their front porch.

Michael accepted his "emasculation" as he put it, with all the vim and vigor of a condemned man taking that last walk to the gallows. Beyonda was constantly telling Michael to smile bigger, kick higher, and use his arms more freely. In time, he made enough of an effort to seem as if he were enjoying the whole ordeal, but I knew otherwise. Fine. As long as he made a good show of it, I didn't care. The only thing that constantly nagged at me was the fact that Michael looked much better in a dress than I did. But then again, he always looked great.

It wasn't long, however, before all the training that Beyonda had been putting us through started to creep into our mannerisms. Michael refused to believe that he was ever anything but masculine, and he even got testy when I brought attention to a serious lapse. We were browsing through an antique store in town one afternoon when Michael pointed out an item that he had his eye on.

"Michael," I said, amused at the overly extravagant gesture he made toward an art deco lamp. "Did you see what you just did?" It was so funny, I began to laugh. Michael was completely unaware of his actions—as usual.

"What? I just pointed to a lamp. What's so unusual about that?"

"It wasn't *what* you did, but *how* you did it."

"What?" Michael shot back nervously.

"Only a drag queen would point at a lamp like that," I added.

Michael stared at his hand in horror, as if it had somehow been taken over by an alien force straight out of a 1950s sci-fi horror flick. I could see the tiny little gears turning in his head. Before he knew it, his hand would be demanding full-length red-sequined gloves and rings blazing with mammoth precious stones. The hand, of course, wouldn't be content with being the only fabulous part of the body. It had to have admirers. The hand would join in a conspiracy with the rest of Michael's body and take over, driving every last vestige of masculinity out of Michael in a pitched battle involving high-velocity come-fuck-me pumps and jars of cold cream. As much as I wanted to jolt him back to reality, it was nice having him on the run for a change. Why not play with his mind just a little more?

"Darling," I said, "don't worry; your secret is safe with me."

He looked at me in horror, shook his head, and repeated to himself, "My name is Michael Stark and I'm dead butch. My name is Michael Stark and I'm dead butch. My name is Michael Stark and I'm dead butch."

I guess the incident that almost pushed Michael off the deep end happened that very evening. Monette was out at

Herring Cove beach banging on a drum with a bunch of other tribal sisters (she really didn't care anything about the sunset goddess ceremony; she just wanted to meet some women), leaving me the house all to myself. I had just put on a CD of Madonna's greatest hits and was in my room looking at the dress and wig that I wore while practicing with Beyonda. Drag wasn't *that* bad. If only I could stop being so tight-assed for a minute, maybe the whole ordeal wouldn't be so difficult to accept. I approached the wig as if it were an alien eggcase and put it on my head just to see. I cranked up the music and began to move a little to the music until I caught sight of myself in a mirror. I stopped, feeling embarrassed at the sight of myself. Then I laughed. Then I looked again. Who cares? It was so silly. No one would see me. I began to dance a little more, then more, and before I knew it I was kicking my legs as high as they could go. It was just at that minute that Michael came home unexpectedly and caught me right in the act. If he had come upon me fucking and dismembering a sixteen-year-old paraplegic at the same time, he probably wouldn't have batted an eyelash. He just stood there motionless, looking at me as I stood frozen in mid-kick. At times, it was hard to fathom what was going on in that shallow mind of Michael's, but the look on his face said it all. It said, "I'm next, aren't I?"

The next day at exactly ten A.M., Michael and I packed our dresses into gym bags (for camouflage) and headed over to the Tidal Flats Theater, where we would soon make the first and only drag performances of our lives in *I Could Just Kick You To Death*.

Beyonda had obviously built us up to Bette Davis, but had never mentioned our names. After all, Beyonda didn't know that we were acquainted with Bette. It was no wonder, then, that when we presented ourselves to Her Highness as her two new girls, she thought it was some kind of elaborate joke foisted upon her by her bitchy friends. She just stood there, looking at us in disbelief.

"I just don't believe it. If I hadn't gone clean and sober five years, two-hundred and forty days, sixteen hours and fifteen minutes ago, I would swear that I was drunk."

Michael spoke up for the two of us, putting his arm around my shoulder to show that we were sisters, too. I didn't know whether Bette Davis was going to believe us, but we had to try. We had no choice. We couldn't let Bette know we were using her show to infiltrate the drag scene. She'd tongue-lash us, then throw us out in a heartbeat. The real injury would come when word got out—which Bette would certainly see to. Adapting an old gay saying, the fastest way to get word around was to telephone, telegraph, and tell Bette Davis.

"We've always dressed up in drag around our apartments. Isn't that right, Robert?" Michael asked, elbowing me discreetly so I would corroborate his story.

"Yes, that's quite right, Bette. Earrings, panty hose, the whole bit."

Bette Davis was still shocked, but a bit of skepticism crept into her voice. "Not that I know you intimately, but I've never heard anything about this through the grapevine."

It was my time to cover again. "Miss Davis?"

"Yes?" she replied.

"Michael and I are the only ones who know about this. And now you. This is something we do in private and we'd like to keep it this way."

Bette Davis seemed concerned, but she was, in her mind, Bette Davis, so the comments were never filtered. "My dear delusional Michael, in a matter of a few days, you're going to be dancing and singing in front of hundreds of people. Each night. How do you propose keeping your little secret a secret?."

"Heavy makeup and big wigs," I replied.

Miss Davis still seemed skeptical. "You don't strike me as

the type, but I'd have trouble finding anyone else to work for such coolie wages, so consider yourselves in. You know, I'm always surprised by the ones that get into drag. It's not always the ones you suspect."

"Exactly my point, Miss Davis. Look at Michael. He has this image of being a gay stud. When he's in public, he is. But the moment he's behind closed doors, he becomes Valerie Veeta—Val Veeta for short. I never know what I'm going to find Michael dressed as whenever I go to his apartment. Sometimes it's Joan Rivers. Other times he's wearing a teddy with his hair done up in a Pippi Longstocking hairdo. . . ."

"I don't think we have to *bore* Bette with all these stories, do we, *Rotunda?*" Michael said through clenched teeth.

"If you two have been doing this for years in the privacy of your apartments, then why go to Beyonda for instruction?" Miss Davis challenged us.

"Robert and I aren't professionals, Bette Davis. We just prance around my apartment. . . ."

"Prance around?" Bette was intrigued.

"Well," Michael responded while trying gracefully to extract his foot from his mouth. "Sometimes we play cards."

Bette wasn't about to let this one go. "You play cards in drag?"

"Why, yes," Michael responded. "Doesn't everyone?"

"Not in my experience, but then again . . . Well, what you two do in private is none of my business, so let's get started. I want to take you backstage and introduce you to the rest of the girls, then go through a short rehearsal. I don't expect you to know all the lines, but you'll pick them up."

"How many lines do we have, Bette Davis?" I just had to know.

"Two. Why don't you follow me and I'll introduce you to the girls. They're my punishment for something bad that I've done in another life. But that's what I get for trying to throw together a show at the last moment. You get the crumbs. The good ones are already in the other shows. Oh, well. But they're a nice bunch. They try hard, and I've just had them defanged, so they won't hurt you too much. After I introduce you, we'll have to do something about the stage names you've chosen."

"What's wrong with them?" I asked.

Bette Davis looked me squarely in the eye. "If you have to ask that, you *do* need professional help."

7

What's That You're Hiding Under Your Skirt?

We followed Bette Davis backstage and into the dressing room.

"This is my room," she said, gesturing to a door decorated with a large cardboard star covered in aluminum foil. "I have sellout shows in Vegas; I pack 'em in at Atlantic City and the Poconos, but I come here and all I get is a cardboard star wrapped in aluminum foil. Provincetown, the great leveler. Anyway, there's a locker for your personal things, but you'll have to share the makeup and changing areas. . . . In case you're a little shy, there are two bathrooms down the hall on the right. Believe it or not, some of these guys are shy."

"Robert's a little pee-shy," Michael volunteered.

"I am not," I protested. "Well, maybe a little. At least I'm not like you in public restrooms. You have no problem looking at other guys when they're taking a whiz."

"Oh, Robert, you make it sound so *tawdry*. I just like to look at other guys' dicks. That sounds pretty healthy to me!"

Miss Davis cleared her throat and tried desperately to maintain her composure. "Follow me and I'll introduce you to the rest of the cast."

At the end of the hall were several tables set up in front

of a large mirror illuminated by bare electrical bulbs that hung from extension cords plugged into hazardously overloaded sockets. The members of the cast were jockeying for positions that gave them the best view in the mirror. This was just a rehearsal, but some of the members had partial costumes on.

"Girls, can I have your attention, please? I'd like to introduce you to the newest members of our illustrious troop. They're beginners, but considering the acting that I've seen out of you, they'll feel right at home," Bette Davis said with a smirk on her face.

"You're just saying that to make us feel good, aren't you Bette Davis?" one of the girls remarked.

"This," she said, gesturing to the two of us, "is Robert Willsop and this is Michael Stark."

"Glad to meet you," the girls replied in almost perfect synchronization.

Bette patted me on the shoulder. "I'll leave you and Michael to get to know the cast. I've got some business to attend to. We start rehearsing in half an hour."

Michael and I were on our own now. Since all this was rather new to us, we didn't know quite know how to start or even act.

One of the cast members seemed to sense our discomfort and extended a hand to shake.

"I'm Vince. And this is Harry, Clint, Mark, and Ralph."

The names just didn't fit the girls I saw before me. Neither did their bodies, which were in various stages of undress. They were some of the burliest men I had ever seen. Bette Davis was right: you wait till the last moment to assemble a show and this is what you get. These guys looked like they had answered a casting call for a movie about the Teamsters.

Michael and I nodded to each of the cast members as they were introduced. When we came to Ralph, a look of recognition came over Michael's face.

"You seem familiar," Michael said.

How he could tell, I wouldn't know. Ralph had on a wig, false eyelashes, and a lime green body stocking.

"Maybe you saw me in *The Spanish Inquisition: A Musical* in San Francisco last fall."

"Nope," Michael answered.

Ralph racked his brain. "I know! I was in *Three-Panty Opera* in New York. That's probably where you saw me."

"Yes, I think I remember that."

Vince got up and took Michael and me by the hand, leading us through the "girls" to our lockers. While Clint, Harry, Mark, and Ralph had the swarthy looks of Hungarian longshoremen, Vince was different. His light brown hair and fair complexion stood out among the others. There was also an intense look that never seemed to leave his face, even when he smiled.

"Here are your lockers, where you can put your dainty things while we rehearse," Vince said, pointing to lockers that looked as if they had been thrown out of a men's prison. "You won't need a lock—the girls are pretty trustworthy. The only thing they steal is eyeliner. You can change in the booths if you're shy; makeup is there by the mirrors; hangers there; and these," he said, pulling out two identical black dresses, "are your first dresses of the evening. There are several changes throughout the performance, and we all match what Bette Davis is wearing. Right now we're just rehearsing some of the blocking. We'll go through a few songs so you can learn the tunes, but the lyrics are so simple, you'll quickly pick them up. Okay, I'll see the two of you out on the floor."

"Vince?" I asked timidly.

"Yes?"

"This is still a little new to us, so thanks for helping Michael and me along."

Vince smiled. "Don't mention it. The first time on stage is always the hardest. I know; I've been there before."

And with that, Vince returned to look intensely into the mirror one last time, then joined the rest of the cast onstage. Michael and I got into our sweats. Michael, as usual, had to wear his sexiest workout outfit, which was heartily welcomed by the other members of our little troop. But since many of them weren't sure if Michael and I were lovers, they maintained a respectable distance.

The show was actually pretty good, with lots of good lines and lyrics that really were quite funny. *I Could Just Kick You To Death* starts with Bette Davis coming out onstage with angel wings attached to her costume. Obviously, she's in heaven. She recounts her life as told through reenactments of clips from her movies, with the cast providing the song-and-dance portion of the entertainment. Bette Davis does a number taken from *Beyond the Forest*, where she's made up to be a woman in her late fifties trying to pass as a character in her twenties. The song? "They're Either Too Young or Too Old." That's followed by a sketch taken from *The Little Foxes*. We dance around the stage dressed as medicine bottles while Bette Davis sits on the couch, refusing to help her husband, who's having a heart attack. ("You want your medicine? Go get it yourself!") You had to be there. This number is followed by other enactments from throughout Bette's career. But my favorite is the part where Bette Davis, dressed as Baby Jane Hudson, kicks a Joan Crawford doll around the stage to the tune of "My Way." (Bette also remarks that she hasn't seen Joan Crawford since she got to heaven. And she's met *everyone* there.) Five more numbers follow, then the show turns back to the opening scene with Bette Davis standing onstage in a single spotlight, wings still sprouting from her shoulder blades. She pauses dramatically, looks around at her surroundings in heaven, then spouts the line that every queen has been waiting for throughout the entire play: "So this is heaven, huh? What a dump!"

The rehearsal went quite well, with Vince and the rest of the gang helping us through the routines. Bette Davis, who was known to be quite tyrannical at times, was actually quite sweet to us. Michael tried to buy her goodwill, and fortunately, she was selling.

We broke at noon and had to be back at the theater the next day for more practice. Since Michael and I were the new girls on the staff, we waited for the regulars to change their clothes and makeup. There wasn't enough room for all of us anyway, so we let them finish and leave. When Michael opened his locker, he froze.

"What's the matter?" I asked. "Find Jimmy Hoffa?"

"No. Someone's been in my stuff," Michael replied.

"How can you tell?" I asked.

"I distinctly remember putting my Homo sweatshirt on top. My Nikes are on top now."

"Is anything missing?"

"No, no. Everything is still here. Even my Rolex. Any faggot worth his weight in gold would've taken it."

"Obviously it wasn't a thief. Maybe it was one of the stagehands."

"Robert, this isn't Carnegie Hall. There probably aren't any stagehands until the day of the performance. They probably can't afford to pay them except on opening day."

"Well, then, who could it be? We left after all the guys were out onstage, and they were only a few steps ahead of us. That wouldn't be enough time."

"Someone went through my stuff. That I know."

"Let's see. The only person who was out of our sight for any period of time was Bette Davis. You don't think it was her, do you, Michael? Unless she's trying to find out a little more about us. I mean, she's suspicious as to why we're in her show."

"Not anymore," Michael said proudly.

"You wrote her a check, didn't you?"

"Let's just say that her suspicions have been allayed."

"Considering that someone just went through your things, Michael, I'd say that someone is curious about you." A strange, implausible thought went through my head.

"Michael, there is one other explanation," I said slowly, trying to form the logic in my head.

"And that is?" Michael probed.

"It doesn't seem possible, but Bette Davis could be Max's murderer."

Michael laughed out loud. "You've got to be joking!"

"Shhh. Keep your voice down. Someone might still be around. Think about it, Michael. Bette Davis was there at your announcement party. She was also at your wedding—the perfect place to be, since she could keep an eye on you and phone Max at your apartment to warn him on the chance that you left the church early. She just blew into town unexpectedly only a short time ago. She could've been up here in P-Town waiting for Max to arrive with your painting. And the glove found around Max's neck could be from the show. You remember how Bette Davis made some comment about how she was missing a glove from a costume before we started rehearsing? There is a scene from *All About Eve* that involves that exact same glove."

"Okay, it's possible," Michael conceded.

"And," I said, adding one more piece of evidence, "Bette Davis is probably pretty sick of doing drag shows on tight budgets just to make ends meet. But steal a painting, and she can retire."

Suddenly, there was a loud crash around the corner. The two of us leaped up and ran down the hall to see if anyone was there, but we saw no one—just a mop lying on the floor next to an overturned bucket.

"Well," I said, "that was an extraordinary coincidence. Michael?"

"What?"

"Am I paranoid or is everyone out to get us?"

"I think we're getting close . . . to what, I don't know."

We changed back into our street clothes and were about to leave the theater when Bette Davis approached us.

"I forgot to tell you two that me and the girls are going to hand out flyers to people at Herring Cove Beach this afternoon, and I was wondering if you two would help out. I have to tell you in advance, however, that I can't pay you for this—the show just can't afford it. It would mean a lot to the show because we can't afford to advertise," Bette Davis pleaded with us.

I could see Michael's hesitation, but I spoke up for both of us. Michael could wear dark glasses and no one would notice him. Plus, we needed to spend time with the girls in order to find out more about Bette Davis.

"We'll do it, Bette Davis. You can count on us," I offered proudly. "So what time do we meet the girls at the beach?"

"Two-thirty, at MacMillan's Wharf. Slip number seventeen."

"We're going by boat?"

"It'll get more attention," Bette said confidently. "Madonna isn't the only one who can practice shameless self-promotion. It doesn't take much to pack 'em in around here, but you've got to be inventive."

"Fine, we'll be there," I said, picking up my gym bag and preparing to go.

"Aren't you going to take your outfits?" Bette Davis asked. "I want all of us marching down the beach together, handing out flyers as we go. If that doesn't draw people in, nothing will."

"We're going in drag? On the beach?" I said, never thinking that this could even be a possibility.

"What did you expect us to go in? Diapers?"

I made one last stab at trying to get out of this. "But won't our heels sink down in the sand?"

"Of course they would. That's why I wear flats," Bette Davis replied. "See you at the wharf."

Michael looked at me with daggers in his eyes. No, make that AK-47s. Michael didn't like the idea of drag one bit, but now I had unknowingly committed both of us to walking around the beach in drag, handing out flyers to homosexuals parked out on blankets all over Herring Cove beach. Oops! Silly me.

"I want you two to wear the outfits that go with the 'My Way' number," Bette Davis instructed us.

Lovely. The "My Way" number outfit was by far the most flamboyant—a psychotic concoction of bows covering a dowdy housedress. Michael didn't say a word to me as we left the theater and headed back to the Plover. As we were walking down Commercial Street, I noticed a familiar face.

"Michael, that guy that was cruising me in Newport . . ."

"Cruising *me*," Michael sternly corrected me, his anger still apparent.

"Whomever. He's here and he's following us."

"Me."

"Okay, you. Don't you find that odd?"

"Robert, men have been known to chase me halfway across the world to get into my pants. It's not odd; it's natural. If I were someone else, *I'd* want to get into my pants."

"Now you know why I'm always telling you to go fuck yourself all the time, Michael. It's natural." I tried to get Michael's mind back on the subject at hand. "This guy isn't cruising you. There is a chance that he's wrapped up in this whole mess somehow and I want to know why. Why don't we both duck into this shop, and when the guy follows us inside, we'll be waiting there to confront him?"

"Fine, let's go," Michael agreed as we steered into the shop, discovering too late that this particular establishment specialized in lesbian sex aids and pornography. We went to the back of the shop and waited at the end of an aisle for our friend to run into us, which he shortly did. He came barreling around the end of the aisle, only to be confronted by Michael and me, standing with our arms crossed like two homosexual Terminators.

"Looking for someone?" Michael asked.

"No, just browsing," the sniveling little rat said unconvincingly.

I felt that we had the upper hand, so I grabbed a large strap-on dildo and shook it in the guy's face. "I suppose you're in the market for this, are you? Don't you have one of your own?"

"No, I was just looking for something for my wife," he said, stumbling for an explanation of why he was in this store. "She's a size-queen."

"Listen, pal," Michael said, grabbing the guy by the lapels. "You've been following us since Newport and I want to know why. I want to see some identification."

"Following you around? I'm just shopping around. . . . I don't have to show you anything," Mr. Rat shot back defensively.

Michael took the strap-on dildo from me and held it inches from Mr. Rat's face. "Listen, bub, either you tell us what you're doing here, or you're going to take this thing down your throat to the very end."

Right then, the owner of the store confronted the three of us, wanting to know what the commotion was all about.

"What the hell is going on here?" she demanded.

"I was just showing our friend here how to properly swallow a dildo without gagging," Michael explained. "You see, it's all in the breathing. You have to inhale while taking the entire shaft down the throat. Don't hold your breath. It also helps to form a mental picture in your mind of your throat expanding—like a snake. Do it right, and you can take twelve, thirteen inches with no problem," Michael boasted proudly.

"Do you three know where the hell you are?" the store owner asked incredulously. "Now don't get me wrong. I'm not a lesbian separatist. I'm actually for equal rights for all people. Gay, straight, black, white, whatever. But guys, this is a *lesbian* store. L-E-S-B-I-A-N! And this," she said, wrenching the strap-on dildo from Michael's hand, "is for lesbians. Not gay men. You can't wear this unless you've suffered some freak accident. Half the things in this store aren't going to do you any good."

Michael hated, more than anything, to be told he was

wrong. "I can so use a lot of the things in this store. I've used this before," Michael exclaimed, picking up a particularly veiny looking dildo and shaking it as if it were a live rattlesnake. He then lurched toward a pile of surgical-looking contraptions, picking one up in triumph. "Speculums! I've used these before, boy have I! And these . . ." Michael said, quickly grabbing a pair of oversized fake breasts so quickly that he didn't have time to consider their usage, ". . . I haven't used. All right, two out of three."

"You two have to leave right now, or I'm calling the police."

"The two of us? What about . . . ?" Michael trailed off.

In all the bickering and confusion, Mr. Rat had managed to slip away unnoticed.

I grabbed Michael by the arm, pulling him along like a dotty aunt being taken back to the asylum. "Forgive us," I said to the owner of the store. "He's Madonna's personal gynecologist and it just puts him under a lot of constant stress. I'm sorry for any inconvenience we've caused you."

I pulled Michael out of the store and into the street.

"Nice going. We can never go back into that store again! Worse, Mr. Rat's gotten away."

"I still say I could find some way to use fake breasts," he maintained.

"How?" I asked.

"We're about to debut in a drag show, aren't we?" Michael replied.

I hated to admit it, but Michael was right. All too right.

Since we only had a little time to kill before we had to head for the beach, we hurried back to the Plover, stuffed our outfits into our gym bags, then quickly filled Monette in on everything that we'd learned that morning. We told her about the girls in the show and of our sneaking suspicion about Bette Davis being Max's killer. She carefully wrote every fact down, and when we were finished, she said she wanted to check out a few things that afternoon.

"And what are you two up to this afternoon?" Monette

asked, eyeing the corner of a dress peeking out of my gym bag.

"Just to the gym. Michael and I want to get in a little workout before tonight. Monette?"

"Yes, Robert?"

"So you're going to check out a few things for us, are you?"

"Yes, I have a few things I'd like to look into."

"That's in town, isn't it?" I asked, trying not to give her any idea of where we were going.

"Yes . . . why?" she replied with the grin of the Cheshire cat.

"Oh, no reason. I was just wondering," I said. "Well, we're off."

"Later," Monette chuckled.

I'd swear that the moment I shut the door behind Michael and myself, I could hear Monette laughing at the top of her lungs.

Michael and I took our bags to the wharf, where we figured we'd be able to change. At slip seventeen, we saw a large cabin cruiser with Bette Davis and the rest of the cast on board, some in makeup and some in the process of putting it on.

"Come on board, we'll be shoving off soon. Myles is just testing the sound," Bette said matter-of-factly as a piercing blast of sound split the air.

"TESTING, ONE, TWO, THREE!"

Myles, whose boat I assumed we were on, handed a microphone to Bette Davis, who raised it to her lips and spoke:

"NOW HEAR THIS, CONTRARY TO POPULAR OPINION, I AM NOT DEAD. IN FACT, I AM VERY MUCH ALIVE, WHICH YOU CAN SEE FOR YOURSELF IF YOU COME TO SEE OUR SHOW, *I COULD JUST KICK YOU TO DEATH*, AT THE TIDAL FLATS THEATER, STARTING THIS FRIDAY NIGHT." She finished as wave after wave of echoes bounced around the harbor. "Yes, I think that will do just fine," she said as she daintily handed the microphone back to Myles.

"Myles has been good enough to lend us the services of his boat to promote our show. We're going to head around the point and cruise back and forth while Clint says something over the loudspeaker. Oh, and there will be some smoke grenades and some kind of pyrotechnics. You'll have to ask Myles about that stuff. I could never understand all that crap about which way the shrapnel would blow. Then, Myles is going to head right into the shore and we'll disembark and pass out the flyers for the show. They'll be beating down the doors to get in. Oh, yes, I mustn't forget this," she said, unrolling a large flag sporting Bette Davis's harpy-like visage captured in a four-foot caricature. She placed the flag in one of the boat's flag holders at the rear. "Sewed it myself."

"I suppose that the sedan chair is for you," I asked, pointing to the purple velvet sedan chair trimmed in gold braids.

"You are correct. I ride on the chair and hand out the flyers. You girls will carry me. If this doesn't pack 'em in, nothing will."

Myles started the boat's engine and Michael and I went below to put on our faces and outfits. As far as solving this murder case went, we still didn't have that much to go on, but I just felt that we were on the right track. Maybe it was just plain desperation making us feel that we were getting warmer.

"So, girls," I said to the rest of the cast across the boat, "how long have you all been doing drag?"

Clint, who seemed to be the natural leader of the cast by virtue of his take-charge personality and bear-like frame, took the initiative. "I've done a little drag here and there, but this is the first time that I've worked in a real show with a pro like Bette Davis. Harry," he said, putting his arm around Harry, "is my ex-lover. He's done a little more than I have. He's even understudied with Lypsinka."

"Well, not understudied, really. But I did read lines with him."

"Wonderful," I responded. "Pathetic," I thought. These guys are just too damn big to be in drag. Harry was almost as large as Clint and had the same five o'clock shadow by nine A.M. The innocent blue eyes that sparkled next to his dark skin were the only part of him that remotely suggested that he was capable of drag. Otherwise, I would have guessed that he tore trees out of the ground with his bare hands for a lumber company in Oregon. "And how about the rest of you? Mark? Ralph?" I plowed on.

"This is my first time," replied Mark. "But I've always wanted to. . . . I just didn't feel comfortable about the whole thing. But my therapist is helping me confront my drag thing and accept it," he uttered uncertainly.

The rest of the cast burst into the kind of rapid, approving applause associated with AA meetings and Twelve-step programs.

If I thought the other cast members were particularly ill-suited for drag, Mark won that category hands down. Older than everyone else, he had a gruff exterior that suggested years spent on some windswept plain in the Old West riding his trusty horse Trigger to cattle roundups. His windblasted complexion and six-foot-three-inch lanky frame would have looked better in a pair of skintight Wranglers than in a crinoline-lined hoop skirt.

"And how about you, Ralph?" I asked, trying to keep the ball rolling.

"Little ol' me? I'm a little more experienced than the others," he replied.

Clint, however, wasn't about to let that one go by. "Not from what I've seen at rehearsals."

Ralph tried to regain his dignity. He raised his nose in the air and said, "Can I help it if I was trained in classical drag? All these feathered boas and platform shoes are for amateurs! But as I told you, I'm from San Francisco and I've done several performances, and people are saying good things about them," he said, raising both arms to capture the adoration that wasn't forthcoming.

Ralph, despite the fact that he was a consummate queen, had a decent body underneath the drag that he constantly wore. I could tell from the size of his forearms. Plus, he really was quite handsome. His jet-black hair, intense brown eyes and square face suggested that he could have been a male model had he tried. But I guess the lure of the stage was just too great.

There was so much more that I wanted to find out, but just as I was about to probe further, we reached the beginning of the gay beach. Clint picked up the microphone to begin his spiel: "Bette Davis isn't really dead! Actually, she lives at the Tidal Flats Theater starting Friday and every night—except Tuesday! After all, a girl's gotta rest!"

After this had gone on for almost fifteen minutes, the boat headed for shore, where we waded through the shallows, carrying Bette Davis on the sedan chair and headed up into the crowds of gay men and women that populated this stretch of beach. Bette thought it would be a good idea if she smoked and ate grapes while she rode on her chair, and her instincts were right. For the most part, people eagerly stood up to snatch a flyer from Bette Davis's hand, but when Miss Davis came upon the occasional reticent sun worshipper who wouldn't stand up, she would humiliate him or her with such a barrage of witty insults, her victim would usually comply.

Since we stayed on the gay side of the beach, most of the people laughed and took the flyers Bette Davis handed out. Others snapped pictures. In fact, when we came upon one lesbian wearing a large floppy hat, she snapped several pictures of me. In fact, the constant whirring of her camera's motor told me that she was taking an entire roll of film.

"MONETTE!" I screamed.

I couldn't believe it. Monette had just gotten enough close-up pictures of me in drag to give her ammo for a lifetime. I tried to grab the camera from her, but two things stopped me. One, she was stronger than me. And two, it wouldn't look good for the show if I got into a scuffle with a potential attendee. There was nothing to do but move on—and knock over Monette's beer, wetting her towel in the process.

Bette Davis and the rest of us worked the beach, making our way down toward the gay men's nude section—as Bette Davis explained, "The show isn't the only thing on my mind." As we came upon a loud group of nude revelers, one of them got up from his blanket and wanted his picture taken with Bette Davis. It was Mitchell, who didn't recognize Michael and me. Mitchell was nude, naturally.

"I've always wanted to get my picture taken with Bette Davis," Mitchell gleefully pronounced. Bette motioned for us to put the chair down so she could oblige an adoring fan.

Mitchell pleaded for the rest of us to get in the picture, and Bette Davis motioned for us to fall in behind her, acting as a sort of backdrop for her and Mitchell.

"Lenny, get in closer," Mitchell shouted to the man from his party holding the camera. "I want a real close-up of all of us."

"You better get in close, Lenny. If you get Mitchell's dick in the picture, most film developing places won't develop it, you know," someone on a towel yelled.

"I've got a photolab in Manhattan that will print any-thing—and I mean anything!" Mitchell added. "Okay, Bette, you stand here and I'll . . . God, you look familiar," he said, looking at Michael.

Michael tried to shield his eyes with his hand, even though he was wearing dark sunglasses and full makeup.

"Now, now, Bette. Look straight into the camera so we can see your pretty face."

Lenny snapped the picture after what seemed like eons. We picked Bette Davis back up and, after another half hour or so, finished working the beach. We waded back toward the boat and were soon speeding back to MacMillan's wharf. We removed our makeup in the boat, vowing never to go in drag again.

When we arrived back at the Plover, Michael went right to his room and slammed the door. I went into the living room and found Monette sitting in a swivel chair, stroking a furry white cat.

"Excellent, Mr. Bond, you've found me. Do sit down," Monette said, motioning to a chair.

I was licked and I knew it. "I suppose the film is already on it's way back to your apartment in Brooklyn, via Lear jet?"

"Mystic Color Lab, actually, via the U.S. Postal Service. Just mailed them half an hour ago."

"And what, may I ask, are you going to do with them?"

"That's for me to know and for you to find out, Mr. Bond."

"Where'd you get the cat?" I asked.

"He was lying in the driveway when I came home," Monette responded. "I thought he lent a nice touch, now that my fiendish plan is complete. Speaking of fiendish plans, I've had one of my own."

"Spill it!"

Monette held up a Boston newspaper, pointing to a front-page article headlined: "POLICE SEEK NEW SUSPECT IN TRANSVESTITE MURDER." I was ecstatic.

I jumped up and grabbed the paper gleefully from Monette's hands. "This is wonderful! MICHAEL! GET OUT HERE THIS INSTANT!"

Michael came running, looked at the headline, then got down on his knees. "Thank God. I promised that if I beat this rap, I'd behave from now on."

Monette grabbed the newspaper back. "Don't get too excited, guys. You two are still prime suspects, but I've been talking to Detective Sandsome—the one assigned to your case—and he's seeing things my way. In fact, this headline is my doing. Well, with a little help from him."

Michael's face fell about as quickly as mine. "I don't get it," he said. "The headline clearly says—"

"Nothing more than Detective Sandsome wanted it to say," Monette cut in. "You see, he has his suspicions, too. We fed that line to reporters to see if the killer-at-large would allow some more evidence to mysteriously turn up. If some does, then we've got proof that someone's trying to frame you."

"If you weren't a lesbian, I'd give you a big kiss," Michael replied.

"Coming from you, Michael, that means a lot," Monette said. "But remember, you two, this doesn't mean that your drag days are over. You've got to do your show until we nab the killer."

"Why?" Michael whined.

"Because we need an in to the drag community. No one's going to give us the time of day if you're not one of them. Plus, you need to keep up your normal activities so who-ever's trying to frame you doesn't suspect anything's wrong."

"Donning women's clothing and dancing and singing isn't *normal* activity for me," Michael clarified to Monette. "In fact, I'm so sick of acting like a goddamn woman, I'm going to go out and do something manly tonight."

"Such as?" I inquired snottily.

"I don't know right now. All I can think of is going to the *Mommie Dearest* night at the revival movie house."

Thursday morning, there was a rain of toads. Or there should've been. It was one of those days that needed a big yellow banner across it proclaiming "Police line. Do not cross."

The evil karma started even before I was awake. Michael had gone to the door—nude, of course—to pick up the paper that was regularly delivered to our house. It was part of his daily routine, because he wanted to see what the papers were saying about him. Only this time, when he greeted the paper, he was also met with hundreds of flashes of light and the whirring of dozens of cameras. The reporters, who had abated somewhat lately, were once again on our tails for some reason. That reason became apparent the moment Michael looked at the paper, screaming loudly enough to wake both Monette and me along with half the pilgrims buried on Cape Cod.

"What? What's going on?" Monette asked at the top of her lungs.

"Look!" Michael screamed, pointing to a picture on the front page of the newspaper.

Monette and I grabbed the paper from Michael and huddled around it, unprepared for the photo that greeted our eyes.

It was Michael in drag. No doubt about it. Michael in full, glorious, delicious drag. To the left of the picture was another of Michael, but this visage was merely one someone had filched from many of the New York publications Michael's picture often sprang up in. Before and after photos. The three of us devoured the news story like a bulimic fashion model at a caterer's convention. The story, if it can be imagined, was more damaging than the photos. It went into lurid depth about how Michael's recent bout of transvestitism was connected with the promotion of a drag show in Provincetown—opening this Friday. Michael was a member of the cast.

Michael turned redder than a cartoon character. I half expected gushes of steam to start issuing from his ears at any moment. "I'M GOING TO KILL THAT BACKSTABBING MITCHELL LITTLE BITCH!" he screamed.

"How do you know he had anything to do with it?" I inquired.

"Because he's standing in the picture, that's how," Michael said. "It's that picture that he posed for on the beach yesterday. The one that he had taken with me—although he didn't know it was me."

I could see the gears turning in Monette's head. "So if he didn't know it was you, why would he turn it over to the paper for use in a story about you? Obviously, he didn't know what he had."

"One of his friends must've known. Little pricks!"

"It's possible, but it just doesn't make any sense," Monette continued. "If Mitchell couldn't tell it was you, how would his friends know?"

Monette had a point, but a point that Michael wanted no part of. He stamped down the hall to his bedroom, then returned with a pile of clothes, sorting through it and throwing on bits and pieces so that he'd be presentable to the reporters.

"Well, someone did it! Someone sold my picture to the papers just to make a buck. That much is clear! And I'm going to find out who. Fucking ruining my reputation! I'll find out who did this to me and that person is going to pay," Michael sternly warned, flinging the front door open and walking out into the crush of reporters. Monette and I ran to the window to see his Range Rover roar to life then peel out, sending a phalanx of reporters who barred its way scrambling for dear life as Cruella De Vil roared off on her mission of skinning a Dalmatian whose name was Mitchell.

"Want some breakfast?" Monette asked, obviously aware that Michael was wrongheaded as usual.

"You know that Mitchell is innocent, don't you?" I said.

"Yes."

"And you know that Michael will be back in a matter of thirty minutes, knowing no more than he knew when he left—which isn't much, if you know him like I do."

"Mitchell didn't do it. It's too obvious. As for his friends, it could be one of them. But I don't want to be too premature. Let's wait for Michael to get back. As usual, he'll tell more than he realizes he knows."

Sure enough, no more than a half hour later, Michael returned, his head bowed somewhat in remorse. *Somewhat*, I said. People of Michael's station in life never really apologize. They could destroy someone's life with a well-placed comment, then issue a faint-hearted apology that threw additional blame back at the victim.

Monette fixed him with her gaze the moment he walked in the door. While Michael and Monette never really saw eye to eye, you could tell by the look on Michael's face that he knew Monette had already surmised the entire situation without budging from her bowl of Count Chocula.

"Mitchell didn't turn those pictures in to the newspaper, did he?" Monette asked like an all-seeing mother with eyes in the back of her head.

"He swears he didn't," Michael replied, despondent that he had been proven wrong.

Monette continued. "And Mitchell swears on a stack of Bibles that none of his friends would've done it, either."

"You know, Monette, you should be answering phones for the Psychic Hot Line."

"I thought this would happen," Monette answered authoritatively.

The blood rushed to Michael's face. "If you're so smart, then why didn't you stop me before I went over to Mitchell's place and made a complete fool of myself?" he said exasperatedly.

"You didn't hit him, did you, Michael?" Monette inquired.

"Absolutely not. Honestly, Monette. What do you take me for? Some sophomoric juvenile with a childish sense of vengeance?"

"How many years' subscription to *Ladies' Home Journal* did you order for Mitchell before you arrived at his house?" Monette asked.

"Five years, so what?!" Michael retorted defensively. "Why didn't you stop me if you knew so much?"

"Because I didn't know everything. Now I do," Monette replied, raising her voice dramatically. "I now know who the murderer is!"

Michael and I were beside ourselves. "YOU DO?"

"No, not really. I just always wanted to do that," Monette said gleeful at being the master of the situation. But being the soft-hearted person that she was and seeing the crestfallen look on Michael's face, she couldn't gloat for long. "Actually, I'm glad you did what you did, Michael. I wanted you to confirm a theory that I've had in the back of my mind for a few days," Monette replied.

"And that is?" Michael begged.

"I'll bet Mitchell said that someone broke into his place and took his camera."

"Not the camera. Just the film," Michael added. "How did you know?"

"And Mitchell swears that it wasn't any of his friends who were at the beach with him that day?" Monette continued with her line of unflagging logic.

"Even better. The three guys who were with Mitchell on the beach that day were all on a sailing orgy that night. Mitchell can confirm it."

"A sailing orgy?" Monette asked, then decided that it was better not to ask. "This is absolutely perfect. More perfect than I can imagine." The look on Monette's face said that the jig was about up.

Even though Michael and I weren't totally sure of what she was going to say, you could almost feel the hope rising in the room.

"Gentlemen," Monette began, "I think you two better sit down."

"Yes, yes?!" Michael and I echoed.

"I've narrowed it down. I can safely say that our mysterious Mr. X is a woman."

Michael and I were stunned. "A woman?! But who?" we both asked simultaneously.

"Just what I said. A woman. At least she is twice each night Fridays, Saturdays, and Sundays, at eight and ten o'clock at the Tidal Flats. Yes, my friends, the murderer is one of your cast members."

8

And the Murderer Is . . .

It was a long time before anyone spoke. Monette sat in a chair, grinning from ear to ear.

I was still in a fog, partly wondering how Monette could have deduced this, and partly from the horrifying realization that I had been dancing and singing next to a cold-blooded murderer. "So . . ." I started slowly, not wanting to move too quickly for fear of another shock. "Tell us how you've reached this conclusion," I asked meekly.

Monette was on top of the world. "The photo in the paper was the shred of evidence that made everything come together. This whole mess makes sense now. You see, everyone's been looking at this whole affair from the wrong perspective. Michael's painting has nothing to do with anything!"

Michael got suddenly testy. "So the fact that someone made off with my multimillion-dollar Warhol—"

"Matisse," I corrected.

"Whatever." Michael continued, "It means nothing?"

"Actually, the stolen painting means nothing . . . and everything."

"Monette, you're being totally cryptic," I chimed in.

"Great detectives are supposed to do this. Haven't you ever watched *Masterpiece Theater?*"

"No argument there," I added. "All I know is that Colonel Plum did it in the library with the candelabra."

"The painting is the key to the whole thing—precisely because it means nothing. That's the beauty of this whole plot. Everyone's been assuming that Max stole the painting—which he did—and made off with it only to be done in by his accomplice who wanted to sell it and keep the money all for himself. Well, that's all wrong. The accomplice wanted the painting not for the value, but as a lure. A lure to get Michael up here to P-Town."

"But what's the point in that?" Michael asked.

"To punish you. Embarrass you. Destroy you. And it all revolved around framing you for the murder of Max."

"Well, I'd say that whoever it is has done a real good job. My reputation is practically ruined," Michael added dejectedly.

"Precisely. Whoever wanted you up here planned to do this all along. And framing you for Max's death was only the beginning. Even since the murder, the punishments haven't stopped. If they had, you would've been in real hot water. Because that would've meant that the killer had left town, taking clues with him and leaving you holding the bag. But thank God, he didn't. And that is the best, most wonderful thing of all. Some member of your little group has an obsession with destroying you completely for something you've done to him in the past."

Michael was baffled, which was normal for him. "But I don't know any of them. Except Bette Davis." He hesitated. "You don't think she'd do all this just because I wouldn't let her be maid of honor in my wedding, do you?"

"I don't know," Monette said. "We have to assume that everyone's a suspect for the time being."

Monette's explanation was good, but it didn't answer everything. "So I assume you're going to tell us why Michael's picture in drag is so important?" I asked, holding up the newspaper once again. Michael averted his eyes, trying not to see the photo of himself on the front page.

"Because it means two things. When the detective down at the police station and I leaked that story to the papers that Michael was no longer considered a prime suspect, this picture turns up. Obviously, the murderer got scared that all his work was for nothing. Our mysterious Mr. X had to step up the embarrassments even further. And I say embarrassments because framing Michael for Max's murder isn't enough for this person. This guy will stop at nothing to destroy you completely. Even breaking and entering."

"Breaking and entering?" I asked.

"Yup. Remember the note that Max sent asking you two to rendezvous with him on the beach? Well, remember how no one could find the note the next morning when the police were combing through the house?"

"Yeah?" Michael replied.

"Well, neither of you misplaced that note. Mr. X broke into this house and took it while you two were at the beach waiting to meet Max. Or while you were in police custody. It doesn't matter."

All of a sudden, everything was falling into place in my mind. Goddess bless Monette!

Monette continued. "Mr. X also broke into Mitchell's house and took the film from Mitchell's camera. Not the camera, mind you, like a thief would. Just the most important part: the film."

"So how do you know, assuming Mitchell's innocence, that one of his friends isn't Mr. X? Can we rely on their sailing orgy alibi?"

"We don't have to," Monette added triumphantly, like a poker player laying down a royal flush.

"Not one of them knew it was Michael under the makeup when Mitchell posed with you. I could hardly tell myself. If I hadn't had an inkling of what you two were up to when you left that morning with your gym bags, I wouldn't have followed you down to the wharf, then taken a taxi to the beach when I saw what your little crew was up to."

"Just as an aside, what gave you your inkling?" I asked.

"I caught a glimpse of a sequin sticking out of your gym bag," Monette said. "But I digress. Mr. X was obviously one of the cast members because he saw Mitchell's friends snap the picture with Mitchell's camera. So Mr. X finds out where Mitchell is staying and breaks into the house, steals the film, and sends it anonymously to the papers with just enough information about the show for the reporters to follow up on."

Not that I wanted to poke holes in Monette's story, but I thought I had discovered one. A big one. "All right, Agatha Christie; if Mr. X broke into the art dealer's house where Mitchell was staying in order to get at the incriminating film, then there would've been trouble. The house has an alarm system."

Monette smiled. "I'm so out in front of you Robert, I'd need binoculars to spot you. I checked with the police and the alarm *did* go off. But since nothing turned up missing, it was considered a false alarm."

"What about the dogs? You can't get into the place without going past them."

"Probably threw them some food. Dogs get distracted easily when their stomachs are involved. Or maybe he put sleeping pills in something he fed them."

"But Mitchell said the film was missing. Why didn't he report that?" I continued my line of questioning.

"I think I can answer that question," Michael chimed up. "He didn't know it at the time. When I confronted Mitchell about the pictures, he denied it, then got his camera and found that the film was gone. He was really surprised. I know him."

"See, Robert, the pictures helped Mr. X advance his vengeance on Michael two important ways. One, getting Michael's picture in the paper in drag is probably the most devastating thing Mr. X could do short of framing Michael for Max's murder. Think of it: Michael will no longer be one of the hottest men in New York. Or the world, for that matter. Gone are all the circuit parties. The leather parties . . ."

"Er, hold it right there, Monette," Michael interrupted with a look of horror on his face.

"From now on, no one will look at Michael Stark as the Man with the Golden Pecs. He'll now be known as the Girl from Ipanema."

"That's enough, Monette," Michael said, clearly frightened by the mental images Monette was spinning out from her vengeful mind.

"No more rollerblading with Barry Dillard in L.A."

"Monette!"

"No more weekend parties at David Geffen's house on Fire Island."

"NO!" Michael screamed, holding his hands over his ears.

"I just wanted to rub it in a little," Monette said. "Anyway, where were we?"

"No more rubber truncheon demonstrations at the LURE bar . . ." Michael added.

"I didn't say that!" Monette responded.

"Oh . . . never mind," Michael said, slinking away. "Anyway, continue."

"Oh, yes. Reason number two about the pictures. An added injury inflicted by the picture in the newspaper was that it would cause a rift between you and Mitchell, as well as throw suspicion on Mitchell and away from Mr. X. To keep us chasing yet another red herring. Oh yes, yes, yes! I just thought of another fact that proves Mr. X is one of the cast members. Every one of them, with the exception of Bette Davis, is enormous. Max was no ninety-eight-pound weakling. It would've taken a pretty strong guy to finish Max off."

Michael had a look on his face that indicated he was going to say something brilliant. As usual, he was dead wrong. "Max could've been drugged, then anyone could've finished him off easily."

"And who would've done that?" I asked.

"Bette Davis! She could've had a poison pill hidden in one of her rings. You know, the ones where the jewel hides a secret compartment."

Both Monette and I looked at each other, always stunned by the things that came out of Michael's mouth. It was a good thing Michael was gorgeous.

"Michael?" I said.

"Yes, Robert?"

"Why don't you let Monette handle the detective work?"

Michael fell silent for a moment. Then this face lit up again, indicating that he was going to issue another doozy, but he apparently reconsidered. He chose to say nothing. Thank Christ.

"Go on, Monette," I offered, trying to keep things on track. "Now that we're sure that Mr. X is one of the cast, I suppose you're going to suggest some fiendish way to trap him."

"You've read my mind, Robert. Actually, I am."

"How?" I asked.

"I've got it!"

"Yes?"

"You're going to invite the entire cast out to dinner and we're going to ask a lot of questions in order to expose Mr. X. And Michael's going to pay."

"We?" I asked.

"Yes, *we*," Monette clarified. "To a very nice restaurant. The best in town. One with actual tablecloths on the tables. And no plastic lobster bibs. And real silverware. Or at least really nice aluminum."

"We?" I asked again. "Why you?"

"Two reasons," Monette said. "One, I can ask the right questions."

"And the other?" I continued.

"I'm flat broke. I could use a decent meal."

9

Waiter, There's a Gun in my Soup!

Michael and I spent the rest of the morning tracking down the rest of our little troupe in order to invite them to a cast party dinner. Luckily, all of the members were heavy partiers, so when we rang them all up at noon, they were still in bed. They all accepted greedily, mostly due to the fact that the budget for our little production was so tight, the alternative to turning down Michael's invitation would have meant a plate of Fig Newtons and one bottle of sparking cider served in Dixie cups an hour before curtain time the night of the show.

We made a reservation at Cafe Remora, arguably the best restaurant in town. Naturally, I had a lot of hesitation about getting a half dozen hooch-hound drag queen wannabes in a respectable restaurant around one table. I'd hate to be the waiter. If it weren't for Michael's kind offer of picking up the tab, the waiter would undoubtedly have gone untipped.

That night, just as we were preparing to go to dinner, I expressed my reservations about the whole thing.

"Monette," I said, adjusting the waistline on my best pair of shorts. "I know that we need to zero in on Mr. X and quickly, but do you think it's a good idea for Michael to pick up the tab? After all, some of these guys are party machines, and with what amounts to an open bar, they're bound to get drunk. These guys are partiers."

"And that's bad because?" Monette trailed off.

"They're going to get drunk and smash up the place."

"They're drag queens, Robert."

"Okay, they'll verbally tear some of the patrons to shreds because of their criminal dress sense. Get a few drinks in this bunch and they're liable to say . . . just about . . . anything," I finished, finally understanding Monette's plan. I smiled mischievously. "Monette, you really are brilliant. You're hoping that they *do* get drunk so you can trip one of them up into exposing himself as Mr. X. Monette, I take my hat off to you."

"Robert, I'm not one hundred percent sure that Mr. X is part of the cast, but I feel my intuition is correct. Don't get your hopes up too much."

"I'm ready," Michael said, walking into the living room, stuffing his polo shirt deep into his jeans in order to pull the shirt tight and show off his ample chest.

I took one last look at what I was wearing and felt it was okay. In retrospect, I should have worn a wet suit to dinner.

We arrived at the restaurant before the others so that Monette could set the stage for what she planned to do.

"Now listen up," she intoned as we settled into our places at the table. "We'll spread out so we can ask more questions. Try to ask questions about each person's past. And remember what you hear, because we're going to call around and check up on our girls tomorrow. We need to find the one person whose stories don't match reality. I'll play referee and ask the big questions. Michael, could you give me a twenty?"

"Monette, you've already seen to the fact that I'll be picking up the tab. You need more?" Michael asked, perturbed, not about the money aspect of the evening, but the way that Monette, and not he, was in control of a social situation.

"You'll see," was all that Monette said before she disappeared into the kitchen with our waiter. In a matter of a few moments she returned, followed by the waiter bearing a bottle of Dom Perignon and a handful of champagne flutes. The waiter poured the delicious bubbly, then left with the bottle. Monette raised her glass to propose a toast.

"To tonight and to the exposure of Mr. X!"

We all drank.

"Either it's been a long time since I had a good bottle of champagne, or the waiter's trying to palm sparkling cider off as Dom Perignon."

Monette took another sip from her glass. "Actually, it's ginger ale. For the rest of the evening, the waiter will be serving us ginger ale poured from a Dom Perignon bottle. The cast can—and should—get as drunk as we can get them, but I don't want any of us to get even the slightest bit tipsy this evening. We just have to make sure that our three glasses need filling at a different time than the rest of the cast, otherwise the girls will get ginger ale and the jig will be up."

"Good thinking, Monette," I said, amazed at the cleverness of her mind.

True to nature, the girls were all on gay time and showed up at least forty minutes late. Bette Davis, Clint, and Ralph showed up in full drag, with Mark and Harry pretty much in street clothes but wearing a glove or scarf just to let people know whom they were dealing with. There was a lot of jockeying for places at the table, but as soon as the cast saw the champagne flutes and the waiter open a bottle of Dom Perignon, nobody seemed to care where they sat. Monette, however, had seen to it that the three of us were positioned around the table so that we could chat up different members of the cast.

"Now be careful, girls," Bette Davis said, releasing a

great cloud of smoke that she promptly French-inhaled through her nostrils and into her brain. "I let you borrow your costumes from the play on one condition: that you don't get any food on them. We can't afford to get anything dry-cleaned."

"We'll be careful, Bette," they all chorused in unison, then downed the contents of their glasses at a speed that would have put Ernest Hemmingway to shame.

"So, Bette Davis!" Monette spoke up. "Do we have a hit on our hands?"

Bette Davis carefully thought this one over for a nano-second, then replied, "What we have on our hands is something that is best handled with latex gloves."

The cast, used to Miss Davis's constant barrage of insults, chuckled on cue. On cue because Bette Davis *did* sign the paychecks, small as they promised to be.

"Oh, c'mon, it can't be all that bad," said Monette. "Your crew seems pretty professional. At least they're a damned sight better than Naughty Pine."

"Naughty Pine?" Bette Davis remarked with a look of such disgust on her face that I thought she was going to vomit. "You mean *Shoddy* Pine. I'm still thinking that if some of you girls don't improve, I'm trading you to her show."

Everyone cackled at her threat.

Before long, the three of us had split up and began chatting with various cast members in an attempt to find out something that would point to the murderer. I talked mainly to Ralph and Clint, while Monette plied Bette Davis and Vince. Harry and Mark were left to Michael.

For all my efforts, I found out very little. Clint was a bartender at The Wrinkle Room, a gay bar in New York. He lived in an apartment so appalling, even socialite-philanthropist Brooke Astor refused to enter it while touring the degrading conditions of Lower East Side apartments. Bored of his job as a bartender, Clint tried to get into acting. He had landed bit parts in several plays off-off-off-off-

Broadway, his favorite role being that of Tevye in an all-mime production of *Fiddler On the Roof*. But as a whole, the big parts just didn't materialize, so he started leaning toward drag. Clint had a sneaking suspicion that his enormous build and deep voice were probably a detriment to his career. I informed him that in fact, he had everything he needed to play leading ladies like Bea Arthur. Clint usually came to Provincetown each summer, getting a job as a waiter and renting out his apartment in New York to people who needed to change their address frequently. Then, a miracle happened: Bette Davis came to town. Clint's worries were over. Despite her deserved reputation as the Dragon Lady of Drag, transvestites would give their right dancing leg to work with the great Bette Davis. And luckily, by the time Bette Davis came to town, all the other drag queens in town were committed to other shows. Clint, in a tryout for the show, got the last open part, beating out a queen who was so drunk, she fell down no less than fifteen times during her two minutes on stage. But despite the dubious circumstances of Clint's big win, he was a happy man. I decided it was best not to shatter his bubble.

Ralph had been doing drag on and off for years. Of course, this statement was completely at odds with the performances he constipatedly squeezed out during rehearsals, but I felt that his unflappable belief in his performance—good or bad—in itself proved that he was indeed a drag queen. Not a good one, but an optimistic one nonetheless. Ralph had gotten several parts, including the Queen of the Night in a ribald version of Mozart's *The Magic Flute*. Ralph was especially proud of the fact that they had almost secured Jeff Stryker for the leading role, but "Mr. Big" (as he is sometimes called) canceled at the last minute due to an unfortunate accident involving his "talent" and a carelessly slammed car door. Anyway, Ralph spent most of his time in San Francisco, even acting as a replacement in the Ballet Trocadero troop. Ralph moved to New York a few months ago and was looking for a part when he heard about tryouts for Bette Davis's show. On a wing and a prayer, he secured a ride to Provincetown that cost him a mere fifteen minutes and a loss of his pride. But it was worth it, he said proudly. Ralph, as I have noted before, was a rather large man, but since he was always in drag, it was hard to tell how much was muscle and how much was fat. As with most of the cast, I didn't want to know.

After everyone had wolfed down enough appetizers to feed the TV cast of *Roseanne*, Monette broke off from probing her two subjects and made a signal that Michael and I do the same. At just that point, our entrees had arrived, and not a moment too soon. Even with all the conversation that kept mouths in a constant state of bitching and cattiness, the cast had managed to polish off eleven bottles of Dom and showed no sign of abating. Monette's plan was working beautifully, with one big exception: Bette Davis. She was still sipping at her first glass of champagne. Monette had noticed this fact and motioned to me with a nod of her head in Bette's direction. The look on Monette's face was worried. It said, "I think she's purposely staying sober."

Vince, normally a very in-control kind of guy, broke through the conversation with a loud laugh in response to something Harry had said.

"I'd be the lass to argue wif you. You *dooo* have beautiful legs. Isss jus too bad God put 'em on upsie-down!" For a drag queen, insults directed at the legs of another are tantamount to spitting on Judy Garland's mausoleum. If that weren't bad enough, Vince punctuated his insult by flipping a small morsel of food from his spoon, which landed on Harry's frock, sticking there momentarily before sliding down into his lap. There was a moment of silence not unlike that of a group of people standing around a nuclear warhead, watching the detonation counter ticking down the remaining seconds to zero. Harry took a slow, deep breath and let it out. The blood began to rush into his face with such intensity, I thought his head would pop off, leaving his stumplike neck spurting blood timed to his pulse. Harry politely put his fork into a crab-stuffed ravioli, broke out in a mischievous grin, and catapulted a ravioli with drunken aim directly into Mark's face by mistake. Mark retaliated by flinging a piece of tuna with the same drunken aim and hitting, not Harry, but Clint. In a flash, food was flying in every direction. Within seconds, even Michael, Monette, and I—who had stayed as neutral as Switzerland—found ourselves covered with food. Oddly enough, not a single morsel managed to hit Bette Davis. The girls, after all, knew what side their bread was buttered on.

Waiters scattered, patrons ran, and tables were flipped over as the cast drunkenly stumbled over food that was smeared over every uncovered surface in the place. Because of the rate at which food was tossed, it didn't take long before all the available ammo was spent, causing our drag warriors to collapse into chairs or onto the floor, pointing at each other and laughing hysterically.

Slowly, the cast began to get up, picking up chairs and setting tables upright again. Just as I began to scrape some flounder in a mango-lemon sauce off my shirt, Clint exclaimed, "Oh, my God, look at that!" in a scream so high that I didn't think it was possible in a man that big.

There, lying on the ground next to Bette Davis's purse, was a gun. Even more startling was the fact that the gun couldn't have come from anywhere else except Bette Davis's purse. And if that wasn't coincidental enough, right next to the gun was the glove missing from the *All About Eve* musical number. The glove's twin, of course, had been wrapped tightly around Max's neck the night we found his body on the beach.

You could have knocked Michael and me over with an ostrich feather. Bette Davis was acting as cool as a paper-thin cucumber. She stuffed the glove into her purse without a word, then looked up at the stunned faces around her.

"As much as you girls should be shot for your performances, I would never do the job myself. The critics will certainly finish you off. Anyway, I don't even own a gun. I don't have to. I can vanquish an enemy with one blow from my tongue."

"I'm sure it's not your gun," Monette said, carefully picking up the object in question with a dinner napkin.

I caught up to Monette, explaining that the glove was *the* glove.

"I suspected that," Monette sighed. "First the gun, then the glove. It's all too easy."

"You mean that Bette Davis is not the murderer?" I asked.

"Well, there is the possibility that Bette Davis is making it look like someone else is clumsily trying to pin the rap on her, thereby shifting the suspicion away from her. I've seen it done before in mystery novels. Point the blame at the most obvious, but make it so obvious that people begin thinking that it's *too* obvious—that the murderer is trying desperately to frame this poor innocent person."

Since every morsel of edible food was now indistinguishable from the carpet and wallpaper, the cast began leaving.

I pulled Monette and Michael aside. "Monette, I'm getting more confused as time goes by. I hope you're not in the same boat."

"Yup. And I feel that it's got a leak in it."

"Oh, Monette, how can you say that!" I pleaded. "You were supposed to clear this whole mess up."

"Who do I look like? Agatha Christie? I said I've read a lot of mystery novels. Thousands of them. But this is real life; it's harder. We've got to go home now and write down everything we've heard tonight while it's still fresh in our minds. Tomorrow, we'll start seeing who's a lady and who's not."

The three of us looked at each other as if there was no hope, then decided to make for the door, only to be stopped by the maître d'.

"One of you three is going to pay for this," he said with just a hint of sarcasm in his trembling voice.

"I don't see why we should!" Michael retorted. "Your

restaurant is a mess—food all over the floor, rickety furniture that falls over at a touch—a dump."

Nevertheless, Michael ended up paying the bill, which was sent to the Plover, hand-delivered the next day. I must say in all good conscience that although the tab was $5,980.57, the food wasn't really that good.

10

It Felt Like the Last Day on Earth

I thought it was fitting that the day of our drag debut was also the very same day that Provincetown held its annual Drag Race. The festival, like so many in Provincetown, was basically just another excuse for men who shouldn't ever put on a dress to do so, but this particular festival had one big difference: instead of sashaying down the main street of town in dresses and high heels, this event required participants to sprint thirty-one blocks in full drag.

Despite the fact that the Drag Race Festival had the appearance of a lively and carefree event, it was taken seriously, as evidenced by the strict rules governing heel height, dress length, and the minimum number of accessories a participant must wear. The Drag Race, adapted from similar events around the country, had grown into a huge event in P-Town and was attended by drag queens from around the world. Part of the reason was because just being in the Drag Race brought instant status to those who ran the fashionable but ankle-turning course. The main reason, however, was the purse given to the winner. The "purse," as you might already have guessed, was a pink vinyl pillbox number carried by the winner of the first annual Drag Race in Provincetown years ago. The hallowed purse also happened to be filled with five thousand dollars in prize money, most of which usually went to charity. *Most*, I said.

Of all the days to appear for the first time in drag, fate had to pick this day for the opening of *I Could Just Kick You To Death*. Thank you very much. The town was packed, the beaches were packed, and worst of all, the opening night of our little play was sold out. As if that weren't strange enough, Bette Davis called us that morning to crow about the fact that people were approaching the playhouse box office and offering upward of two hundred dollars for any ticket that could be scared up.

"Wow," I said, speechless at the level of interest in a last-minute, poorly acted, poorly advertised song-and-dance review.

"I told you that our little publicity stunt at the beach would work wonders," Bette said on the other end of the phone, her declarations punctuated by the clink-clink of ice cubes in what was probably a highball glass. "Too many of these other productions don't know how to stir up publicity. Amateurs! I've set queens on fire, shot them out of a cannon, and had them wrestle alligators, and I've had standing-room-only shows night after night. And I'm proud to say that very few of my girls have ever gotten seriously hurt."

As much as I felt that being in *I Could Just Kick You To Death* would scar my psyche for life, I felt fortunate that at least I wouldn't be limping through it. "You know your stuff, Bette Davis," I agreed.

"You bet your pumps I do. This afternoon, I'm paying these four highly muscular studs to carry me through the crowds in town. You can't rest on the laurels of a good opening night."

I could almost picture Michael and me traipsing along the beach again in drag.

"Well, I've got to get going. I've got a sedan chair to catch. See you at the playhouse at four," she reminded me, then hung up abruptly.

"Who was that?" Monette asked as she cornered me.

"Bette Davis."

"What's she want?"

"She's all puffed up like a Romanian farm woman with a water-retention problem. She said the play's sold out already and—get this—people are offering to pay hundreds of dollars just to get a ticket to tonight's show. I don't get it."

"I don't either. From what I saw at your last rehearsal, your play sucks; you and Michael couldn't act your way out of a paper bag; and I've seen elementary school plays with better production values."

I wiped the spit out of my eye and looked directly at Monette. "I hope the next time you get a yeast infection, you reach for a tube of Ben Gay instead of Vagisil."

Just then, Michael came down the hall completely nude with his "overnight guest." He didn't bother to introduce him to Monette and me but gave him an insincere kiss on the right cheek, told the guest that he'd call him, and shoved him out the door and into the waiting arms of the small band of photographers who still dogged Michael.

Instead of spending the day dodging photographers and having fun, Monette thought we should spend the day checking up on the backgrounds of the cast members.

Thankfully, the Plover was owned by homosexuals, so it had four separate phone lines. Michael, Monette, and I stationed ourselves in separate rooms, each taking a cast member and calling to corroborate each cast member's story. We called theaters, acting troops, the Screen Actors Guild (big waste of time there, since apparently none of our girls had ever been in front of anything as impressive as a camera)— anything that would help us spot the phony. After calling for almost four hours, we compared notes and found what we should have known all along: our girls were all consummate liars. The entire cast had lied so extensively about their careers in drag, that most of them were completely unheard of. They hadn't played certain theaters, hadn't been in certain plays, hadn't even lived in certain cities. In short, we were back where we started.

Monette kept up her calls to no avail, while Michael and I decided to spend what little remained of the day inside, playing whatever board games we found in the closet. Michael, true to his nature of always wanting to come out on top, looked at other people's cards during euchre, gave himself secret bonuses during Monopoly, and, committed the ultimate homosexual sacrilege of cheating at Mystery Date.

It was bad enough that we decided to spend the entire day indoors when it was gorgeous outside, but what really ruined our day the most was the fact that about every two minutes, Michael and I would look up at the clock, dreading the moment that the little hand would be on the four and the big hand on the twelve. With each passing second it seemed to tick louder, even though it had an excruciatingly quiet operation.

Michael was the one to break the deafening silence.

"Am I just imagining it, or are we getting nowhere?"

Monette, who was off the phone in another room, boomed in reply, "On the contrary, Michael, we're not even getting that far. In a few weeks and with a little luck, we'll be all the way up to nowhere."

I could hear Monette getting up and coming down the hall. "Okay, let's not be so glum. I'm ninety-five percent sure that the killer is part of the cast. We just need a break in this case. Just one clue could split the whole thing wide open. This person is after you big-time. It's only a matter of time before he slips up."

I raised my hand. "Monette, you don't think that the killer is waiting for tonight to make his big move, do you? Like pull out a gun and shoot Michael in front of every-one?"

Michael's gaze riveted on Monette.

"Well, anything's a possibility, but I think Mr. X doesn't want to expose himself. If I'm right, he just wants to tor-ment Michael as long as he can. I guess the crowning achievement would be to have Michael get convicted for

Max's murder. Guys, I can feel it in my bones that tonight you're going to get the clue we need. And believe me, I have big bones. You've got to be on the lookout for anything suspicious. No detail is too small to be overlooked. Tonight's the night."

Michael looked down at his watch, then gazed up at the two of us with a look of complete dread.

"Don't worry, Michael," I said earnestly, "I'll be there to protect you. I've saved your life once before and I'll do it again."

"It's not an ambush that I'm worried about. It's three forty-five. Time to go ruin my reputation for all time in front of thousands of people."

I tried to be supportive but had to be realistic too. "Michael, the seating capacity of the Tidal Flats Theater is eighty-five people. And besides, not one person in the audience is going to know who you are."

"You promise me?" Michael asked like a seven-year-old boy. "What about the story in the newspaper that said I'd be in the play?"

"No one will know. I promise."

And I really did mean what I said to Michael just then. It was just that someone else had other plans.

11

Which Way Did She Go?

Michael and I arrived at the theater promptly at four o'clock. It was a beehive of activity, with tattered folding chairs being set up for the audience, the sound man watching his reel-to-reel tape machine refusing to function at the eleventh hour, and the lighting woman testing out her ragtag spotlights that Underwriter's Laboratories would have condemned outright had they laid eyes on them.

We went through a full-dress rehearsal, where everything went remarkably well; then we changed out of our outfits and sat around eating mediocre takeout. The whole time, Michael and I were scanning the others, looking for anything suspicious: shifty eyes, purses held too closely, and bras that were overly padded. Michael did what he did best: he looked for bulges in clothing.

"Did you see the way Mark was scratching at his crotch?" Michael whispered in my ear. "He's probably got a forty-five caliber down there."

"I've seen him naked, Michael. He's got more of a three-fifty-seven magnum."

"No, no, Robert. A gun. I think he's got a gun down there. I mean, if you put a gun down inside your underwear, it would itch, wouldn't it?"

Michael was completely serious. I looked at him, dumbfounded that he had gotten this far in life. "Michael, Mark doesn't have a gun down inside his underwear. It's probably inside his dick. You see, he went to Libya to have a special penis-gun installed in his cock. Terrorists use it all the time. All he has to do is get an erection, aim, and shoot."

Michael looked at me with daggers. "Well, let's see what you've come up with. What have you spotted that's out of the ordinary?"

"Well, let's see. In a matter of minutes we're about to burst into song and dance in drag, being led by a guy who thinks he shares his body with the spirit of Bette Davis. The audience is packed with people paying upwards of two-hundred dollars for tickets to a drag show. And ten minutes ago I saw Vince fall to his knees and burst into tears because he had a run in his panty hose. No, Michael, I haven't spotted anything out of the ordinary!" I said in a hysterical whisper. "I'm sorry, Michael. It's just the stress—it's really getting to me. It just seems so hopeless."

"That's okay. Don't worry, Robert. I feel lucky tonight. I think we're going to see whatever we're supposed to see that will solve this whole mess."

"Do you really think so, Michael?"

"No, but it sounded good."

I tried to remain optimistic, but as a recovering Catholic, any sense of self-esteem and positive energy had already been slapped out of me years ago by vicious nuns deprived of other sexual outlets. The most I could do was smile back at Michael.

"Okay, everybody," the stage manager interrupted. "Thirty minutes to showtime. Let's see some action."

We went to our lockers, then to the clothes rack to pick out our first costume of the evening. Michael and I joined Mark, Harry, and Vince at the makeup mirrors while modesty sent Clint and Ralph to the bathroom to dress. Bette Davis went into her dressing room, then called out to the two of us.

"Oh, would you two give these earrings to Ralph? He

lost one the other day and I just got the replacement. The drugstore just got some more in."

Michael and I took the earring down to Ralph, asking each other what we were going to do. Michael, never one to consider other people's feelings or privacy, barged right in on Clint and Ralph without so much as a knock. Clint was almost dressed, but Ralph was naked and bending over, putting on his nylons. There, on the left cheek of Ralph's muscular butt, was a tattoo of Rocky, the Flying Squirrel from the *Rocky and Bullwinkle* cartoons.

Ralph hurriedly covered his butt from our view.

"Sorry, Ralph," Michael said, trying to conceal a smile, "but Bette Davis said you were one earring short. Here," he said, throwing the earring to him.

"Thanks," Ralph said, probably not knowing what to say.

Michael and I closed the door behind us, then snickered to each other.

"You said you were looking for anything out of the ordinary. Well, you got it," I commented.

"Yeah, it's . . ."

"It's what?"

"Nothing. I can't figure out why a guy with a nice ass like that would ruin it with a stupid tattoo," Michael said.

"You have a tattoo on your arm. You and Max got one together, remember?" I reminded him, holding his arm up for him to see.

"Yeah, but it's not stupid. It's an eagle."

"That's not stupid?"

"It's butch. Marines wear eagle tattoos."

"So do toothless guys who live in trailer parks."

"Good point. I gotta have it taken off as soon as I get back to New York," Michael replied.

"Michael?"

"What, Robert?"

"Do you think we're going to ever get out of this mess?"

"Oh, yes. Absolutely."

"When, Michael?"

"Tonight."

"You seem awfully sure of that. What makes you think so?"

"I just have a feeling."

"Are you sure it isn't indigestion? I question the idea of Mexican takeout just before a show. It's a small theater with poor ventilation."

"Don't worry, Robert. I think the air isn't the only thing that's going to stink after tonight's performance. This play reeks enough as it is—oh hi there, sweetie, kiss, kiss, break a leg," Michael said in an insincere show of support to Mark as he sauntered by.

"Twenty minutes, girls," the stage manager called, reminding us of our date with destiny.

Michael and I finished dressing, keeping our eyes on Mark, Harry, and Vince as they dressed. Harry was putting the final touches on his face, the mascara wand vibrating as he nervously applied it to his long eyelashes. Was he hiding something? Vince was ready to go and stood smoking a cigarette, dragging each puff deep into his lungs. He finished dressing, then looked around to see if anyone else was looking at him. He reached into a small makeup bag and pulled out a large shiny object that I couldn't make out because he was still hiding it in his hands; then he put the still-hidden object to his lips and kissed it. It had to be a gun that Vince was kissing for good luck. One shot for Michael, then one for me. Somewhere up in my head, a little brain cell hit the panic button, sending my body into action.

"Hey, what's that?" I demanded, my mouth running way ahead of my brain. "I wanna see that."

Vince looked plainly horrified, as if I had spoiled his diabolical plot. "What?" he replied, clearly trying to hide the object in his hands. Michael and Harry came closer to see what was happening.

"What's in your hand? You got a gun there, Vince? The jig is up. Hand it over," I said, emboldened by the presence of Michael and Harry as my backups. "C'mon."

to all these people who yearned for it. Before I knew it, I was actually enjoying it.

Michael was another story. I was able to glance at his face from time to time, and what I saw really worried me. He was in another world. Stage fright? It seemed impossible that a man who had skydived, bungee jumped, gone underwater cave diving, and often had his fist up other men's butts would let a bunch of strangers spook him, but it was possible.

Since Bette Davis had structured the play to eliminate difficult dance steps and split-second timing that would've tripped up the amateur cast, Michael seemed capable of remembering his lines and steps while his brain was on autopilot. What happened next was even more frightening. He began to get a crazed, demonic look with a smile that oscillated and contorted with conflicting emotions as they struggled to take control of his face. Michael, I feared, was finally cracking under the strain of being the prime suspect in Max's murder.

I couldn't watch over Michael anymore, since my only line was coming up. We were bunny-hopping in a circle around Bette Davis, and as I reached the front of the stage, the bunny-conga line would stop and I would say, "What, Bette?"

The truth is, I never got the chance to utter my line. Michael pulled down Ralph's dress, exposing his butt, and screamed with every ounce of air in his lungs, "I KNEW I RECOGNIZED THAT TATTOO! SANTOS! MURDERER!"

Well, almost no one in the entire theater knew what to do, except Michael. "YOU'RE TRYING TO FRAME ME FOR MAX'S MURDER!" Michael continued hysterically.

At that very second, close to a dozen men in the front rows of the theater jumped to their feet with cameras in hand and unleashed a torrent of flashes.

Ralph—er—Santos took advantage of the temporary diversion created by the photographers and bolted down the aisle of the theater, trying to make his escape. Michael followed in hot pursuit, followed by me, the remaining cast members, Bette Davis, Monette, and to be honest, over a dozen members of the audience.

I have never been a believer in coincidences, but this moment was it if ever there was one. As our party raced out of the theater, past the barricades, and into the street, we were immediately engulfed by a tidal wave of drag queens sporting large numbers on their dresses. We had inadvertently entered the Annual Drag Race. Santos was just yards ahead of Michael, staying in the road since the edges of the street were lined with police, barricades, and elbow-to-elbow people. As I chanced to look back, there were Bette Davises everywhere, followed by a phalanx of Joan Crawfords wielding wire hangers, a few Tina Turners, and an assortment of other outrageous drag queens. Michael and I were running so fast, none of us dared to kick off our shoes in mid-gallop for fear of twisting an ankle and losing our pace, so we kept our breakneck speed. Thankfully, I had insisted on buying sensible shoes for both Michael and me, so we were able to keep up with our prey. Before long, Santos broke through the finish line tape and turned north up a side street, heading away from the Drag Race crowds. We dodged strollers, cats, sidewalk signs, and even cars as we crossed Bradford Street—our huge party all in pursuit of Santos. Santos turned up High Pole Hill Road. This meant that he had a good chance of being cornered, since it was a dead-end street that led to the Pilgrim Monument, a 255-foot tower of granite complete with a winding stairway that led to an observation deck at the top.

Lady Luck must have been a lesbian, since Santos made a right turn, taking him into the high-fenced parking lot that would force him into the museum, where there was no escape. He ran past the ticket window without paying for admission, then jumped the turnstile. Michael and I did the same, not wanting to lose him when we were so close. After all, we still had to extract a confession out of him somehow.

Instead of going into the museum, Santos made straight for the tower, knocking over people right and left. He flew up the wide, winding stairs while unbelieving tourists looked on, probably thinking that the Drag Race finish line lay at the top of the tower. Up and up we climbed, my lungs heaving in and out in a desperate attempt to keep up with Michael and Santos. As I slowed near the last flight up, I could tell by the loudness of the shouts coming from the members of our chase party that most of them were only a few flights behind us.

As I reached the observation deck, I stopped. Michael was standing just thirty feet away from Santos, who just happened to be standing on the edge of a window ledge of the observation deck, threatening to jump. What a tired cliché, I thought.

"DON'T GET ANYWHERE NEAR ME, ANYONE, OR I'LL JUMP! I SWEAR IT!" Santos yelled, shaking visibly, makeup running down his face. He looked like a drag Alice Cooper.

"Michael," I advised like a seasoned psychologist, "be careful or he might jump. He means business."

"But I want him to jump," Michael replied.

I thought it wise to counsel Michael that this would not be a good idea, since we needed Santos as a prime suspect and that, as a rule, prime suspects were generally better kept alive.

"Oh, right. Good point. First we get him to confess in front of everyone, then he can jump."

"Michael, you may not like Santos, but it is a human life we're talking about."

"Robert, tell it to someone who cares."

Seeing that it was pointless to argue with Michael, I merely waited for the rest of the party to arrive. Clint was the first to arrive, followed by Harry, Vince, Mark, Bette Davis, Monette, a group of reporters with cameras in hand, and various people that I had never seen before. Surely, someone would know what to do.

After five minutes of muffled conversation, it was clear that no one knew what to do—except me. I shoved Monette forward enough for Santos to see. Monette looked back at us, afraid to rejoin us, then stared at Santos with foreboding.

"Okay, well . . ." she started nervously. "Here we are, yes sir."

This was followed by a long, uncomfortable silence. Monette once again struggled for words, opened her mouth, then shut it slowly again. Nervousness was no longer the driving emotion in Monette. Frustration was. In fact, I could see the struggle within her, coming out on her face.

"Oh for God's sake, come down, er . . ."

"Santos," I volunteered.

". . . Santos," she continued.

"I'm not coming down," was Santos's reply.

"Why kill yourself?"

"I jump or I face a murder rap. I'd rather die than spend the rest of my life behind bars."

"What so wrong with that?" Michael piped up. "Year after year with a bunch of rough, tattooed men who'd kill each other for your affections. What's not to like?"

"Michael," I said, butting in. "Why don't you let Monette handle this? She's doing fine without your help."

"Thank you, Robert. Now where was I?" Monette continued.

"Rough, tattooed—sorry, we were talking about why Santos shouldn't jump," I said.

"Oh yes, the not-jumping thing. Santa—"

"SANTOS!" Santos corrected.

"Yes, Santos. We know you killed Max. Why?" Monette asked, taking a gamble that he'd open up and sing like a canary.

Santos took a deep breath and looked down to the ground, then at Monette. "For revenge," he said slowly.

"Revenge?" she asked.

"Michael said he loved me. He dated me for two weeks—"

"I DID NOT!" Michael returned. "I never dated anyone for that long. Except Marcus, and you ended that. . . . I loved him."

"*Max*, you jerk," Santos countered. "His name was Max. See, you forgot him just like you forgot me."

"Michael?" Monette asked ever so politely. "Excuse me, but I'm about to have a bout of Tourette's syndrome. SHUT THE FUCK UP!" She waited for silence, then continued. "I have to admit, your plan was brilliant. Absolutely brilliant."

"Of course it was brilliant!" Santos snapped back, his ego showing signs of responding perfectly to the stroking Monette had just given it.

Monette recognized this immediately, then decided to lay the flattery on even thicker. "You really had me stumped from time to time. I could figure out bits and pieces, but never the whole story. Tell me about it. I mean, how did you manage to lure Max into the whole thing and get him to do your dirty work for you? You don't mind telling us, do you? Pretty please?" Monette whined ever so slightly.

"I might as well. I haven't got anything else to do," Santos replied. He had a point. "I was in love with Michael," he began slowly. "Really in love. And I thought he was in love with me." Santos paused, almost contrite—that is, until the anger rising in his face swept any repentance aside. "Then I found out he was cheating on me! When I questioned him about it, he said I was suffocating him and that I was clinging too tightly to him. Then he called me and dumped me. Just like that!"

Michael felt the need to clear his muddied name. "I couldn't take a shit without him asking me where I'd been! He followed me everywhere. And called me all hours of the day and night."

"Obviously, Santos wasn't completely without justification," Monette responded. "Please continue, Santos."

"So I decided to get revenge. I wanted to embarrass him, destroy him, then make him pay."

"But you needed an accomplice so Michael wouldn't know it was you behind everything," Monette surmised.

"I needed the right bait. And I found it in Max when I was out in Los Angeles. He was a porn star just starting out, and he was from L.A.—so no one would probably know him here in New York. He had everything Michael would fall for: stunning looks and an incredible body. Plus, Max had a little sophistication to him. So, I got him to fly out here on the promise that if he wanted to stop doing porn and never work another day in his life, all he had to do was become lovers with Michael, steal his painting, and drive it up to Provincetown, where a private art dealer would buy the painting with no questions asked. I told Max that a private collector wanted the painting for his collection and didn't care if it was stolen. In fact, that it was better that way because it would just disappear into his collection and never be seen again. We'd split the money fifty-fifty and part ways. Like all porn stars, he thought with his dick."

Monette (and just about everyone in the vicinity who knew of Michael's reputation) turned slowly toward Michael with accusing eyes. The silence, as they say, was deafening.

"Can I help it if my libido is a little more active than most people's?!" Michael said in his own defense.

"Michael, if they could find a way to hook up your sex drive to the U.S. power grid, this country could swear off fossil fuels for good," Monette remarked. "Now, where was I? . . . Oh, yeah, so Santos . . . you found Max and, I imagine, fed him a lot of information about Michael so that he'd be everything Michael was looking for in a man."

"Exactly. Before he even met Michael, Max knew even the tiniest details about him: what he liked to eat, what side of the bed he slept on, where he liked to go dancing, his favorite flower, even how he liked to play lumberjack when they made love."

There was a great roar of laughter from the crowd. Even Monette doubled over with laughter.

"Please, please," Monette pleaded, trying to get her breath back. *"This* I gotta hear!"

A smile appeared on Santos's face, knowing that he was again going to embarrass Michael. "One of Michael's favorite fantasies is that he likes his lovers to wear a special pair of lumberjack boots with heavy wool socks and a knitted stocking cap when they fuck. And," Santos continued, swooping in for the kill, "they have to say to him that they're going to tear into his timberline with their giant redwood."

The crowd positively howled on hearing this last bit. Some were on the verge of choking, they were laughing so hard. After a few minutes, however, Monette was able to continue—though not without some difficulty.

"Oh, boy! Whew! So . . . you, er . . . ah . . . trained Max to appeal to Michael. The two of them meet—not by sheer coincidence—and Michael falls for Max. At the wedding, Max steals the painting, then hightails it to Provincetown, where you are waiting.

"But what I want to know is how you got Michael to go to the porno theater to see Max up on screen."

"An anonymous call."

"Yes, I got a call a few days later," Michael said, confirming Santos's statement.

"Why didn't you tell me that, Michael?" Monette said, tearing imaginary hair from her head.

"I didn't think it was important."

"It wasn't important. IT WASN'T IMPORTANT?! Michael, why don't you get up on the ledge with Santos so I can push you both off!"

"Keep going," Santos encouraged.

"Michael's no rocket scientist, but you figured that he'd locate Max through his agent. But what if he didn't?"

"I'd give him a little push. A hint. A clue. An anonymous call. Whatever it took to get him up here."

"Because once you got him up here, you'd strangle Max, then pin it on Michael."

"Maybe," Santos replied with just a little hint of resistance.

"One question. How did the police just happen to find Michael and Robert standing over Max's body?"

"An anonymous call to the police. Timed exactly for nine o'clock."

"I see. And I imagine that while Michael and Robert spent the night in jail, you broke into the Plover, took the note that was supposedly from Max, and planted the photographs of Michael and Max minus Max's head in Michael's luggage so the police could find them."

"Max stole a few of them from Michael's apartment. I thought they would come in handy later on. Max didn't have a clue why I wanted them. Now I have a question for the three of you," Santos said unexpectedly.

Michael, Monette, and I looked at each other, wondering what Santos was going to ask.

"How did you land in the drag show I was in?"

"I think I can answer that," I answered triumphantly. "Sheer, astounding, remarkable coincidence. Plus, it was the only show in town that wasn't cast already. If the killer had just arrived in town from New York, it made sense that he would land in *Kick You to Death*. Also, Monette thought that the glove around Max's neck wasn't intentional."

"You're right; it wasn't. I twisted it so tight, I couldn't get it off his neck. He was drugged anyway. I did it during intermission at the drag show I was performing in," Santos confessed. "The glove was from the show."

"Which show was that?" Monette asked.

"*Shut Your Mouth, Sweet Charlotte*. It wasn't doing well, so I came over to *I Could Just Kick You to Death*."

"Was it any good?" Monette inquired.

Santos looked off into the distance, trying to collect his thoughts. "Well, some of the jokes were pretty good, but the overall direction seemed to be lacking. The play started strong, then it seemed like the characters were struggling with the material. Weak finish. And art direction—well, there wasn't any. Just cardboard. Overall, I'd give it a C."

"A C, huh? Well, I suppose this play gave you a perfect alibi, too, didn't it?"

"You are correct. I went into the backstage bathroom, locked the door, slipped out the window, met Max, strangled him, and slipped back through the bathroom window, and nobody ever knew that I had left the premises. There was only one flaw. Just after I finished Max off, someone was coming along the beach, so I had to leave the glove."

"So after you framed Michael for Max's murder, you didn't stop there, did you?" Monette persisted.

"No, I didn't," Santos replied. "Perhaps you tell me what I did next?"

"You thought your drag would give you the perfect disguise. You could walk around town and no one would recognize you under all that makeup—which, I may add, looks like you spread it on with a trowel."

"Well, at least I *wear* makeup," Santos replied cattily.

Monette was not to be outdone. "Well, at least I know that you're a winter and you're wearing spring makeup colors. But back to the story. When Michael and Robert landed in *I Could Just Kick You To Death*, you probably couldn't believe it."

"Of course I didn't want them right next to me, but as they say, keep your friends close, but your enemies even closer."

"Like when you broke into Mitchell's house that one night and took the film of Michael on the beach in drag. I assume you sent them to the press that night?"

"I didn't have to send it to them. I called them anonymously and they came arunnin'. I made good money with those photos, too."

Michael couldn't hold himself back anymore. "Lousy

prick! Why don't you just make everyone's life easier and jump?" Michael asked as he tried to rally the crowd into chanting "Jump, jump, jump."

"Michael, please," Monette asked with oh-so-much patience in her voice. "With Michael and Robert so close to you, you had to guard your backside, pun intended. You had to dress in a room by yourself, because you knew that as soon as Michael saw your tattoo, the jig was up. And that led to your downfall, didn't it?"

Santos took a deep breath. "I guess there's not much more to tell, is there?"

"So you agree that you did all this?" Monette asked, trying to draw a conclusive confession.

Santos closed his eyes, summoning up the reluctant words. "Yes, I did everything that you said, oh clever one. I want to come down now."

Santos's sudden change of heart made me feel uneasy. I don't know why, but I moved closer to Michael.

"I guess I have to face justice," Santos continued. "I have just one request."

"Yes, what is it?" Monette said, trying to keep Santos cooperative.

"I want Michael, the only man I've ever loved, to grab my hand and help me down. That's all I want."

Monette, Michael, and I were all standing together, so we could each see the look on others' faces. Monette and I gave Michael a "be careful" look and nodded our heads, giving our consent for him to help Santos. I was afraid that Santos was going to pull Michael off the edge of the tower with him, but that was pretty much impossible. Santos would have to pull him up onto the ledge and then pull him another five feet or so to the edge. Michael was pretty strong, and Monette and I could help if needed. Michael seemed relatively safe, but all the same, my muscles were coiled like a cat's.

Michael walked toward Santos, who smiled demonically at his approach. The moment Michael got within five feet,

Santos reached under his dress and drew out a gun and aimed it at Michael.

I don't know what got into me, but I leaped at Michael's legs, tackling him and sending him flying onto the cold stone floor. A shot rang out, missing its target. The look on Santos's face betrayed his disbelief that once again, his plans had been foiled. But his hatred of Michael prevailed. He raised his gun again, this time taking a second to aim carefully. I scrambled to shield Michael's body, completely stunned at my heroic maneuver, realizing that I was going to die. Shit! My life didn't even flash before my eyes. Killed by a drag queen! Just as he pulled the trigger, there was a snapping sound that came from below Santos's feet. His heel had given way, sending him wobbling back and forth like Jerry Lewis with a stack of just-washed dinner plates. The gun fired, sending a blaze of pain up my arm. Santos began waving his arms crazily, trying to regain his balance as Monette rushed up to grab him by the leg. Too late. Santos toppled backward off the ledge and disappeared. There was no scream of terror. Just a "Fuck you, Michael," yelled with a vengeance.

Monette, stunned by what had happened, turned slowly away from the window, holding on to the sole piece of Santos that remained: a shoe with a broken heel.

Michael and I staggered up, with Michael exclaiming that I had been hit, and indeed I had. Michael helped me off with my shirt, revealing a trickle of blood.

"SOMEBODY GET AN AMBULANCE, PLEASE. MY FRIEND IS HURT!" Michael yelled in unexpected terror.

"Uh, Michael . . ." I said.

"YES, WHAT IS IT, ROBERT?! DON'T DIE! CAN YOU HEAR ME?!"

"Michael," I said calmly, "I think the bleeding's stopped. It looks like the bullet just nicked me."

"I . . . I . . . uh . . ." Michael managed to say before he passed out. Since Michael was pretty muscular, I tried to break his fall a little, but my arm still throbbed, so I let him go, his head clunking on the floor with a surprisingly loud thunk. He'd be okay.

The rest of the party, dazed by what had happened, rushed to the ledge, as if somehow to recapture the action that had so irretrievably taken place.

Monette came up to me and hugged me, both of us bursting into a momentary display of tears.

"I guess all that evil that Santos caused was his undoing," I said, trying to say something profound in case any of the reporters present were listening.

"Evil! Hah!" Bette Davis suddenly spoke up, holding the shoe Santos had just vacated. "It was *Payless*. Cheap shoes are what did him in," she said, throwing the offending shoe to the floor. "I've always said that you end up paying for cheap shoes."

Words to live by.

The scene was quite chaotic for the next hour or so. Michael regained consciousness and expressed his sincere regret (over and over) that he didn't have a chance to, and I quote, "see the asshole prick bounce when he hit the ground." Shucks. My wound turned out to be superficial, nothing more. But there was much more to be explained.

As it turned out, a lot made sense once we talked to a few people. The reason the audience was full of reporters was because Santos had called them anonymously, promising them pictures of Michael in drag if they attended the show. Mr. Rat, the mysterious man who had followed us from New York to Newport to Provincetown, was a detective hired by the company that insured Michael's picture. He was keeping an eye on us to see if Michael had "stolen" the painting himself and was filing a claim so that he could get the money, then sell the painting to a secret collector. According to Mr. Rat, it happened all the time. The rest of the audience had apparently actually gone to see the show for the performance. When the cast and the reporters ran out of the theater, those remaining thought it was all part of the show, so they gave chase. Until Santos took his unexpected swan dive off the ledge, they were under the impression that it was all part of the act. And as for Michael's Matisse? It was found in the apartment Santos was renting and would be returned after the obligatory inquiry into Santos's death.

Oh, and it looked as if Michael, Monette, and I were all going to be famous. In addition to the newspaper reporters in attendance, there were also reporters from several magazines, including one from *Vanity Fair*. They all wanted our stories, but we begged off of their requests for information in the meantime. We weren't fools, though; we did give them our phone numbers so that they could contact us back in New York, which meant tomorrow. We had had enough of Provincetown for this summer. The remainder of the evening would be spent—just the three of us—at a very good restaurant, at which we would order the most wonderful dinner we could imagine along with several expensive bottles of champagne, and have Michael pick up the tab. After all, he owed me his life (again) and owed his freedom to Monette. This was a fact that we weren't going to let slide by. This was the ammo that the two of us had been looking for, and we were going to use it until it ran out, which we planned to be a long time from now. Ain't life grand?

12

Home Again, Home Again, Jiggity-jig

Monette and I woke up the next morning with hangovers. Michael had a hangover too, but having an extremely gorgeous man in bed with you more than compensated for a lousy headache.

Michael slowly kicked his guest out of bed, kissing him long and hard in front of Monette and me as we devoured our third bowl of Count Chocula. I was having enough trouble keeping my breakfast down as it was.

But all was good. The attorneys that Michael had hired for both of us assured us that we could return to New York and that we would soon be completely off the hook for Max's murder (thanks to the copious notes the reporters took at the top of the Pilgrim Monument).

"You know," Michael said wistfully, "I don't think I'm ready to go back yet. I want to stay here for a while."

"Could your wanting to stay here have anything to do with the bedbug you slept with last night? I mean, last night you said you couldn't wait to get out of P-Town," I reminded Michael.

"Oh, okay. I'll spill it. I'm in love with this guy," Michael said dreamily.

"What?!" Monette and I said simultaneously.

"I've really fallen for this guy," Michael said.

"That's nice," I said as Monette and I got up to put our arms around Michael and congratulate him.

He never knew what hit him.

Monette and I finally began to relax on the drive back to New York. After all, Michael's Range Rover had all the comforts of home.

"So, what are you going to do when you get home?" I asked Monette lazily.

"Well, I've got to get caught up on my softball and soccer practice. Oh, yes, and I've got some photographs of you in drag that I've got to take care of."

"Let me see," I said, musing at where my image would end up. "Leaflets dropped from a plane over New York City?"

"Not diabolical enough," she replied. "You know I'm much more fiendish than that."

"The 'Transvestite Seeking Transvestite' heading in the personals column in *Dragazine?*"

"Nope, think harder."

"Oh, Monette, you know that you're too smart for me. I'll just have to wait and see what you've got planned."

"Right you are! I'm just too smart for you, Robert."

Monette was *almost* right. If she were *that* smart, she would have spotted the Ziploc bag filled with honey that I slipped into her luggage just before she zipped it closed. Those tiny pin holes that I put in the bag should be doing their job just about now.

"I guess there's no point in asking Michael what he's going to do, is there? He doesn't seem to be able to talk very well with that gag in his mouth," I said.

A muffled torrent of words came from behind the back-seat of the Rover.

"Are you sure he's okay? Restraints not too tight, are they?" she inquired.

"He's fine. They're padded," I replied. "He'll get out of

them when we get back to the city. Which, according to my calculations, should be about an hour and fifteen minutes from now. Besides, I know for a fact that Michael's spent several days in those very restraints. Don't ask me for the details, because you don't want to hear them. Trust me."

"And what are *you* going to do when you get back?" Monette asked.

"I don't know," I said, hitting the ten-way power seat adjustment that tilted me back into a comfortable reclining position. Perfect for taking a nap. "But I do know what I'm going to do now. I'm taking off for a little island off the coast of Spain. Me and Rupert Everett have some unfinished business to take care of," I replied, drifting off to sleep.

Please turn the page for an exciting sneak peek of
David Stukas's newest novel
GOING DOWN FOR THE COUNT
coming from Kensington Publishing
in August 2002!

When Count Siegfreid von Schmidt, one of the richest, hand-somest, and mostly openly gay men in Germany, fell madly in love with me, my friends couldn't believe it—especially my dearest. Monette, my lesbian friend, was naturally very happy for me, but insanely jealous, also. This probably explains why she stated—and I quote her—that she "must have been sucked through a wormhole in the space-time continuum and come out in a wacky, parallel universe where nothing made sense." I made a mental note to get back at her in a completely childish manner at a later date.

My other best friend, the gorgeous, chronically untal-ented, and sex-crazed heir-to-a-herpes-ointment-fortune, Michael Stark, had a different reaction. He laughed. And laughed. And laughed. In fact, he laughed so hard he lost a cap from one of his meticulously polished teeth.

But in all sincerity, I was the most stunned. *Who, me?* I thought, looking around at everyone but myself. *Me?* I had a right to be skeptical, after all. In fact, not just a right, but a proven track record.

Rich, handsome, internationally traveled, and cultured are not the sort of terms normally used to describe my dates. Mine were mostly 3-D: drunk, drugged, or desperate. Did I mention psychotic or mentally crippled?

But it was true. The count and I were seen everywhere around New York, eating in trendy restaurants, dancing in cutting-edge clubs. Yes, my life had turned around from tear-inducing boredom to jet set in a matter of weeks. Everything was going my way.

If it weren't for his dead body lying with his head in a toilet, a knife in his back, and me being the last person to see him alive, I wouldn't have had a thing to complain about.

When I began to think how I got into this situation, I had to look back in a vain attempt to unravel the whole mess. It didn't take long, however, since the two largest crises in my life had one thing in common: my friend Michael Stark. The man could provoke disaster in my life from three states away. In fact, I can blame him with complete assurance for getting me into the largest fiascos of my existence. This particular one started when I was having dinner at a very nice restaurant with Michael in my adopted city of New York.

"... so this guy takes out this rubber chicken and starts beating this guy up with it. Whack! Whack! The guy's back was covered with big, purple bruises and he was loving every minute of it," Michael spouted breathlessly, recounting a scene at a sex party he'd recently attended. "It was so perverse. You wanted to laugh. The guy on the receiving end didn't do much laughing, though."

"Michael, please, I'm eating . . . a rubber chicken?" I asked, weirdly interested.

"Yes!" Michael said excitedly. "Pretty wild, huh?"

"Michael, I know your sexual tastes and mine are a little different," I started, but was cut off at the pass.

"You mean I get it on a regular basis?" Michael added cattily.

"If you mean *hourly*, Michael, then you're correct. By the way, what's keeping you from pillowing the waiter? After all, we've been here over an hour."

"He's not my type."

"I thought any carbon-based life-form with a large you-know-what was your type."

"Well, at least I *have* sex, Robert. I think the wives of Wall Street investment bankers get it more often than you do."

"That's because they're paying for it," I protested.

"Maybe you're on to something. Yeah . . . the solution to all your problems, Robert! Pay! If you did, you'd be guaranteed to have sex. I know some escorts who would be perfect for you. They could dress up like a Catholic bishop and have sex with you. Or they could watch you organize your apartment while they jerked off."

"Make fun all you want just because I'm not as kinky as you, Michael. I'm more of the romantic type. You know—soft music, champagne, candles."

"That reminds me. I saw the most fascinating hot-wax demonstration on this incredibly hunky guy at the Bound for Glory Bondage Club last Thursday night."

"Michael, I'm trying to be romantic and you're talking about dripping candle wax on some naked guy at some sleazy sex club where the term 'groin pull' takes on a whole new meaning!"

"Yeah, and?" Michael asked, incredulous that I thought there was something wrong with the scene he had just described. Michael was very muscular, gorgeous, rich, popular, vain, and unbelievably selfish. But above all, sex was what blew air up Michael's skirt. "The reason why you can't bed a guy—any guy—is that you're so sexually repressed. Guys don't want to date the Pope. You can talk all the romance shit you want, but you prove your worth in bed, believe me."

"Michael, you've been on more mattresses than the quality control guy at Sealy Posturpedic. Just you wait. As traditional as my values may be . . ." I started.

". . . prehistoric is more like it," Michael added.

I brushed Michael's comments aside and continued,

"... they'll help me snag some guy who believes love is very much alive. A guy who wants to spend afternoons walking along the beach, watching old black-and-white movies, or sharing a good book."

Michael began grimacing as if I had just asked him to picture Donald Trump naked.

"That's right, Michael, *r-o-m-a-n-c-e*. It's all about being with someone and looking up at the stars at night..." I tried to continue, but was cut off by a stunningly handsome man at the next table who seemed to be finishing my sentences for me.

"... and picnics in the woods on a warm spring day, poking through old junk stores on a Saturday afternoon, and a glass of wine while overlooking the Amalfi coast of Italy. Excuse me for eavesdropping on your conversation, but I couldn't help myself. I feel exactly the same way. My name is Count Siegfried von Schmidt. I didn't want to seem impertinent, but what you said touched something in my heart. I am looking for a man who feels old-fashioned love is not dead. That love is measured not by what you do in bed together, but by the time you spend with each other. How do you Americans say? The quality time. I feel there is more to be gained by spending an evening just staring into the embers crackling in a fireplace on a frosty autumn night with a lover than a thousand nights of sex."

Before I knew what was happening, Michael was circling his newfound prey.

"My name is Michael Stark, and I think what you said is completely wrong. I'll be happy to show you exactly how wrong you are," he said, almost peeling the clothing off the count with his words.

I don't know what got into me, but instead of abdicating my tenuous romance with this mystery man to Michael like so many before, I ran to my battle station.

"Michael, I think the count was talking to *me*. You see, he seems to be more interested in romance that leaves a person with a sense of personal and spiritual fulfillment, not some baffling urinary tract infection."

"We'll let the count decide, shall we?" Michael added, figuring his handsome face and muscular body would certainly steal the count's affections.

"Actually, I don't want to create discord among two who are obviously very great friends. But I would like to give my phone number to this marvelous gentleman here," the count said, gesturing toward me with his Rolex-clad arm.

"Are you sure you don't want me? Guys always prefer me. Always!" Michael replied, his voice suddenly reeking with desperation.

"You are very handsome and have the kind of body that definitely excites me. But it is your friend here I am most interested in."

Suddenly, my world didn't make sense anymore. This couldn't be happening. Then it dawned on me: this had to be one of the extremely elaborate practical jokes my lesbian friend Monette played on me—and vice versa. I decided to test the waters.

"Did Monette put you up to this?" I asked.

"Monette? I don't know what you mean."

He seemed genuinely baffled by my request. Of course, it was difficult to tell completely, since the count was wearing dark sunglasses. His signature, I suppose. Or a way of fending off the flashes of paparazzi cameras I imagined were a fact of life for a person with a title—if he was indeed a real count.

"Never mind," I said, feeling it was safe to proceed.

"Here is my card, and I will write my cellular phone number on it so you may contact me." He scribbled some numbers on a beautiful business card with a fountain pen that had obviously been owned by some countess or czarina. Yup, *Count Siegfreid von Schmidt* it said right on the card. And two German phone numbers: one in Berlin and the other in Hamburg.

"Now, I have shown you mine. Please show me yours," he said with complete innocence. Or did he?

Michael piped in, never losing a chance to vanquish a competitor. "You don't want to see *his*. It would take a particle accelerator just to get a glimpse of it."

"Thank you very much, Michael," I replied, not knowing if it was a good idea to hit Michael in the face with the empty wine bottle that sat on our table. Too many witnesses . . . plus, it wouldn't make the best impression on the count. "For your information, if the count wanted to see yours, he could just rent any porn video from Mammoth Films!"

"C'mon, Robert, you know for a fact I only made *one* porn film as a lark."

"Then why did *Battering Ram* have three sequels?" I queried Michael, not letting him off easily.

"I only starred in the first one, Robert. The other two were just cameo roles," Michael responded.

The count merely smiled. Although his English was almost perfect, I couldn't tell if he was being diplomatic and had decided not to get in the middle of our catfight, or if he didn't quite understand what was going on between Michael and me.

"I don't know what your plans are, but I would like to see you tomorrow," the count gently begged.

"Well, let me see . . ." I said, trying to create the impression of having a busy and demanding social schedule.

"He's probably going to a mesmerizing exhibit on book jacket covers at the New York Library," Michael interjected, managing to throw one more punch before the bell rang.

Actually, I was going to hear a lecture by Amanda Preistly, best-selling author of *Go Fuck Yourself—A Single Person's Guide to Having Sex with the Most Important Person in the World: You!* But in light of the fact that I had a live man interested in me, I decided to forego dragging the count to a book lecture about masturbation as the only orgasmic alternative to those who didn't have the six-figure income to pay for love. If I wasn't going to inform the count about my plans, I certainly wasn't about to let Michael know them.

"I can rearrange a few things," I finally relented. "Yes, I'd like to see you very much. It would be an honor."

"Good. I would like to take you to a lecture. Gordon Kuzuleekas is speaking about his latest novel. It's about a group of Lithuanian intelligencia fleeing czarist Russia and emigrating to America in the early 1900s. On their way to America, however, they enter a hole in the space-time continuum and find themselves in a futuristic world populated by robots. It promises to be quite engaging."

"I'd love to go," I gushed. I would go see a documentary on the love life of Supreme Court Justice Ruth Bader Ginsburg if the count asked me.

"I will call on you tomorrow. Ten o'clock. Yes?"

"That's perfect . . . Count," I stumbled, not knowing what to call him.

"Siegfreid, please."

"Siegfreid it is. Ten o'clock."

"Until then," he said. He got up from his table and left the restaurant, leaving an air of mystery and intrigue in his wake.